# WHEN HER HEAD HITS THE PILLOW

Elaine

Enjoy

## CHRIS DALE

# About this book

# WHEN HER HEAD HITS THE PILLOW

Every night when Marie deVille closes her eyes and goes to sleep, she slides into a parallel world where she meets her ancestors in a vivid, real-life dream. She steps back to the 17th century into a family life she never knew existed, that has eerie comparisons with the developments in her own life in 2017.

She works in advertising and marketing. Her job takes her on an assignment in the north-east of England … into a frightening place that brings her 17th-century dreams to life. Here she meets her modern-day family she never knew she had and many people she knows well but has never met.

This story slides between tales of life in the mid-1600s to modern-day 2017 life, and encompasses everything from romance to family feuds and murder.

The consequences are to change her life forever.

First published in Great Britain March 2018

Second Edition 14 06 2018

Copyright © 2018 Chris Dale

All rights reserved.

The moral right of Christopher Dale to be identified as the author of this work has been asserted in accordance with the Copyright, Designs and Patents Act 1988.

All rights reserved. No part of this publication may be reproduced or transmitted in any form or by any means, electronic or mechanical, including photocopy, recording or any information storage and retrieval system without the permission in writing of the author and from the publisher.

This book is a work of fiction. All the characters, names, businesses, organisations, some of the places and events in this story are fictitious and the product of the author's wild imagination. Any resemblance to actual persons, living or dead, or events is entirely coincidental!!

# DEDICATION

To my good friend and neighbour Lisa Pyle, for suggesting the subject of this book and giving me the inspiration to write it, although it has turned out to be a very different tale from the original idea.

I also dedicate this to all my close friends and to my supportive wife Gilly, who all put up with my continuous obsession to write books.

# ACKNOWLEDGMENTS

This is my ninth book. It was yet another challenge given to me by my friend and neighbour, Lisa Pyle, inspiring me to write something different. This work is total fiction and any references or comparisons are purely coincidental and a figment of the author's imagination.

My thanks also go to John Kain who tirelessly proofreads my books for me; to my team of 'beta' readers who make sense of my writings and help with the spelling and grammar flow of this book; to Janet Cook, who has read all my books so far. To AJ, my ex PA, who finds it hilarious that my spelling and grammar are unchanged from the 1990s when she used to correct all my business letters and presentations; to Gillian Powell who is studying to become a proofreader and has agreed to help me with this manuscripts. And to my sister Trisha Blatter who helped with some of the 'gynecological' elements of this book!

My additional thanks go to Pete Bowdler, Creative Director of Zoo Marketing & Advertising in Mottram-in-Longdendale, near Hyde, Manchester for the design of the front and back covers of this book.

Pete was the principal designer of all the label artwork and advertising during my time in retail and has a wonderfully-creative brain towards designing, and his help with this cover has been invaluable.

# 1
# MONDAY
# JULY 2017

She comes back to her empty house after a long, hard day at work.

It's late.

It ended with too many shots at the local bar down the road with her work colleagues.

Hungry, she looks into the fridge to see what's on her shelf ... nothing so she grabs a bag of crisps and a bar of chocolate, as this is all she has on her shelf.

*'Crisps and chocolate in a fridge?'* she says to herself in amazement, *'damn ... forgot to go food shopping again.'*

She dares not to take food from her housemate's shelf as it caused too much stress the last time.

They are all out, so she has the house to herself.

She switches the TV on and flicks through the channels. Nothing much of interest.

Her life has become mundane. No romance or even an office flirtation. All her friends have active love lives and are always out going places. She just spends boring weekends wandering around London's markets or going home to her parents in Shoreham -by-Sea.

Basically, her life is dull and uninspiring and the only thing keeping her interested in her job.

She gives a huge sigh.

She goes to bed, picking up her Kindle … falling asleep within 5 minutes.

… then it starts …

… she is transported into another era and what becomes a recurring dream …

… or is it a nightmare?

# 2

# 1648

The year is 1648. Charles the 1st is King of an unsettled country and living in self-inflicted exile on the Isle of Wight having escaped from Hampton Court Palace. England's Long Parliament passes the Vote of No Addresses, breaking off negotiations with the King and thereby setting the scene for the second phase of the English Civil War. To gain favour and support, the King of England gave huge tranches of land to his courtiers, and in turn became ruled by Baronets and Marquesses, who all became very wealthy and powerful men. Oliver Cromwell and Thomas Fairfax are the commanders of the parliamentary army and effectively are ruling the land. By December, the King is arrested for treason to stand trial in January.

Flintwell Hall in Lincolnshire is a 22-bedroom country house owned by Henry Fortiscue Bankes, the 1st Marquess of Flintwell. It is a long way from the civil war and all the troubles of the land, so its inhabitants are cocooned in a peaceful existence.

He is a man in his late 60s who is married to a

younger wife, Marie Celestine deVille, The Marchioness of Flintwell, his fourth wife. Marie is 25 years old, the daughter of the French Duc et Duchesse de Touraine, who live in the Loire valley … at the deVille family home. Marie is bored with the Marquess as he spends most of his time in Parliament, at court in London, or with his mistresses, and insists she stays up in Lincolnshire.

Born and raised in France, Marie studied English amongst her music and Latin lessons. Her father, Duc Louis Bernard de Ville, held an important role in the court of the Regent Queen Anne following the death of King Louis X111 and the accession of the Dauphin King Louis XIV, who was only ten.

As a child growing up on a vineyard, Marie was very much a 'tomboy'. She learnt to ride horses, fence and fight as well as her brothers and the other boys in the village outside their family estate. She was taught by one of her father's guards.

Her father wanted to get Marie out of France because he feared a revolution, so he organised an arranged marriage with Henry Bankes when she was only twenty. The fact that she was still childless accentuated the interest that Henry Bankes obviously showed her. He was so grossly fat and she, so petite at five feet two inches, that any intimacy was always very difficult.

Marie had a circle of close girlfriends, her best friend being Lisa Dashwood, and several male friends who were always available to keep her company with music, dance and reading. She also held fencing duals with most of her male friends and nearly always won.

Her father's architect had designed a building that he attached to the rear of their family home in the Loire Valley which was constructed of wood and glass and they called it an Orangery. Similar constructions were designed by the Dutch and they were becoming popular as venues for parties as well as being used as greenhouses to grow plants, exotic trees and fruit.

She persuaded her husband to build an Orangery on the south facing side of their great house, where she would be kept amused growing exotic products. He consented immediately as it gave him more reason to exclude her from his life in London. It took six months to construct and as soon as it was completed, Marie wasted no time at all with her friend Lisa in designing and furbishing the interior.

The girls would plan tea parties and musical events and hold discreet candlelit dinner at the Hall when her husband was at court in London, inviting all the local single and young married people to join them.

They formed a sort of secret society which would meet in the Orangery at the Hall. This secret society's main objective was to have "dalliances" with both men and women in the specially designed interior. They could have intimate meetings in the many secluded corners of the huge structure where specially-made seats carved out of marble would double as a 'chaise longue' where people could embrace in private!! The abundance of foliage from banana trees, firs and shrubs around them would shield them from prying eyes.

In this era, people dressed in heavy clothes to keep warm. Undergarments were not invented and a romantic coupling usually was made fully clothed, very rarely naked in a bed, although this did happen.

Marie was very popular with most of the servants in the Hall, as she treated them all with courtesy, and occasionally, with gifts. She always made a point of visiting the servants' dining hall once a week to eat with them. This brought her huge favours and a great loyalty.

But the Marquess had his spies, namely the gamekeeper, who was infatuated with both Marie and Lisa, having designs on both of them in his deluted mind. He spied on them having these secret meetings with men and women, and was torn between his loyalty to the Marquess or the chance to have a relationship with the women.

Marie knew that he spied on them. She found a secret door at the side of the new Orangery that led to a small spiral staircase used to set the watering system going. From the roof beams one could see into some of the secluded corners.

She caught him looking at her when she was with Lisa's brother, Charles in an intimate embrace. Her skirts were raised sufficiently for the gamekeeper to presume what was happening.

He was grinning. The dirty old fool. He stank of shite, had no teeth, and his breath could kill a deer at fifty paces. She didn't like him … no … she feared him. She knew he would sometimes peer in through the window at her weekly bath. He would stand on ladders outside her window. Her maids told her they caught him one day. He was pretending to fix the window pane.

She would somehow have to engineer a situation where proof could be given of his unsuitability for his job, to encourage her husband to dismiss him.

♦♦♦

Charles rode up to the Hall using the back path through the woods.

Marie was expecting him.

She had recently bathed in perfumed water, and wore clean skirts. Her anticipation of their forthcoming tryst made her tingle with excitement and she felt aroused at what she hoped would be a huge climax. She asked her personal maid to ensure the game-keeper was well away from the Orangery.

Charles secretly wanted to take Marie away from Henry Bankes and hoped that he would die from the pox or an other disease which London was famous for. Divorce from such a powerful man would be impossible even though his father, the Earl of Ashwood was of similar status to the Marquess.

He left his horse with the gardener and marched into the Orangery through the east entrance.


He was bold as he took her into his arms and they kissed, his face still wet from the light drizzle during his ride.

He could not wait for her.

They went into their favoured corner and removed his riding coat and under jacket.

He raised her skirts and petticoats before undoing his belt and removing his under garment.

He was hard and impatient …

She was wet and impatient ….

# 3

# Tuesday

# July 2017

Marie woke up suddenly with a gasp of breath.

She sat up in bed … confused … where am I?

She was hot and sweaty … and alone.

It was dark. Her T-shirt was soaked in sweat. Her sheets and duvet were a tangled mess, as if she had been thrashing around in bed during the dream … and they were damp, too.

It was a very explicit dream. Vivid to say the least.

She felt … turned on by the dream which unusually she still remembered in quite some detail.

Marie was indeed twenty-five, living in a rented house she shared with three other old university friends in Clapham Common, South London … it was July. And no, she was not a Duke's daughter, although her name was Marie deVille, and she was half-French, on her father's side. Her spoken English had a very slight trace of an accent, having been schooled in both France and the UK, she was also fluent in French.

Her bedroom door crashed open and in strode her best friend Lisa Dashwood, looking worried. In her pink silk PJ's and strawberry blonde hair gathered up in two pigtails, she slumped down on the bed and took Marie into her arms.

'Hey babes, are you alright?'

'Yes, thanks Lisa. Just another dream.'

'My God you are soaked, babes. You need a shower.'

'Oh … Lisa, stop fussing.'

'Must have been a good dream though. I could hear you groaning as if you were having an orgasm.'

Marie giggled.

'You sure you haven't got a dishy bloke stashed away in here? Sounded as if you had someone. If so we share OK? Uni rules, don't forget!'

'Ha-ha … god Lisa … it's the third time I've had the same dream. And it's so … umm … raunchy.'

'Let me get the kettle on and tell me all about it.'

'Lisa, it's three in the morning and we have work. Can we meet up tonight and I will tell you all about it. Please …?'

'Okay. Promise you will?'


Marie settled back into bed and tried to visualise what Henry Bankes looked like. He was tall but hugely rotund and couldn't ride in a saddle. She could see the gamekeeper alright. But, her last dream was of the handsome, dashing Charles, making out with her in the corner of the Orangery, fighting to keep her heavy cotton skirts and layers of satin petticoats up so that they could enjoy a glorious coupling, hidden by palms and exotic fruit trees.

What did all this mean?

She fell asleep until the alarm on her mobile shrilled at 7am. Time to get up and go to work.

Looking at herself in the bathroom mirror she looked awful. She washed her face and cleaned her teeth before jumping in the shower. What she saw reflecting back at her was a short, skinny, flat-chested girl, with long black hair. She had a very low opinion of herself and next to her friends and housemates she was a Plain Jane.

She wondered if she would ever meet anyone soon. Her sex life was non-existant. Charles, her dream partner, was engaged to the dreadful, horsey Leticia and at work, all the men were well above her pay grade and seemed to ignore her, chasing after the more glamorous girls in the office.

After a short tube ride, she walked into work looking drab and feeling exhausted. She dumped her shoulder bag on her desk and went straight to the coffee machine.

She worked as an Advertising Executive for an up and coming young marketing company based in the city. They had several prestige clients in both the luxury car market and in high-end boats or yachts. Her bosses were two whizz kids in their early thirties, who set up this agency four years ago and exploded onto the market with their radical and off-the-wall methods of advertising, which their clients loved.

Marie got to go on photographic and video shoots to places like Monte Carlo, Nice and Puerto Banús with either Randolph or James, the owners, and the film crews. Through these visits she met some very wealthy people.

At 3pm, her mobile pinged.

*'Hi babes. You promised to tell me about your dreams. 6pm at The 3 Keys Inn?'*

This was the local pub just around the corner from their house. It would be a relief to tell someone about her dreams and Lisa was still studying medicine at St Thomas' Hospital.

Lisa was unmistakable. On entering the pub most of the men at the bar looked around and gazed at her with grins on their faces. Some she knew … the regulars and would be cheeky to them. She was tall, elegant and had long blonde hair reaching her waist. She was Marie's very best friend. They had grown up together and had gone to school, then University together, before Lisa decided she wanted to study Psychiatric Medicine.

'So, deVille, you French tart. What's going on with you?' she greeted her friend in her usual manner.

'Bored, fed up, frustrated, and in love with your brother. Nothing changes Lisa.'

'How long have you been having these dreams babes?'

'For about a week now. Most dreams you forget as soon as you wake up, but these are vivid … you know, I am there in them. They are so real, I can smell, feel and see what's going on.'

'Okay. Let's start from the beginning,' she said sounding like a shrink already.

She shouted at the bar man, 'Harry … two large ones please with plenty of ice.'

He nodded and brought over two large vodka and slimline tonics. Lisa pinched his bum as he bent down with the tray of drinks and some peanuts.

'That's extra you know. I can charge by the hour if you want me,' he said smiling at her. He looked up at Marie and blushed, 'It's free for you, Marie.'

'Piss off Harry ... she is out of your league.'

Lisa took Marie's hands in hers and stared at her for a short while, searching her face.

'What are these dreams about, babes?'

Marie sat quite still, not knowing how much to say.

'I'm in the 17th century, in the North East of England. I'm married to a man much older who spends his time with the King of England. We own this huge house in the

Lincolnshire countryside and to amuse myself we have parties in the Orangery. But there are some unsavoury characters … I can smell the stench of the place, a mixture of extreme body odour, candlewax and farmyard manure. It sounds horrific and it's … only …' She stops, hesitating to go on.

'Only what?'

'You see, your brother Charles is my lover. But we are spied upon by the gamekeeper who is loyal to my husband and tells him what I get up to with my friends in the Orangery.'

'ORANGERY?', she exclaimed. Lisa's eyes were wide and the expression on her face was one of bewilderment.

'Yes, we had it built and I designed the interior so that we could have … you know … discreet …'

'Yes … go on.'

'You know… umm … dalliances.'

'Dalliances? Where did that come from? Am I in your dreams, too?'

'Yes, you are. You helped me design the interior of the Orangery.'

'Now I am getting worried about you, babes.'

'Oh, Lisa … the trouble is that it is sooo realistic. I mean the scenes. The tea parties, the dresses. We wash once a week. We don't wear any knickers or bras … in fact they hadn't been invented then. The hygiene is awful. People smell disgusting. I wear a lot of talc and perfume, but it's nothing like Joop or Dior.' She giggled at the recollection.

Lisa sat there with her drink halfway to her open mouth, transfixed like a statue, unbelieving of her best friend's state of mind.

'And, this morning when I came into your room, who were you having an orgasm with?'

She looked at Marie.

'No … Oh god NO! … Not my brother?'

Marie gave her a blushed face, embarrassed at the admission.

'Lisa. I'm transformed when I step over to the other side. I can feel, touch, smell and see everything as if I'm actually there. I'm scared stiff of going to sleep now.'

'I think you need professional help babes. I know of a few people I work with. Let me talk to them.'

'Are you sure?'

'Yes, don't worry babes. We will get you sorted. Now, to get plastered, okay?'

That night, Lisa and Clare, her other house mate, spent the evening in the 3 Keys Inn and they all stumbled home a little bit inebriated to say the least.

Marie declined offers of coffee and went straight into her room. She collapsed on the bed, just managing to remove her work clothes before snuggling into her duvet and straight to sleep …

… within minutes ...

… she stepped over again …

# 4

# 1649

With the trial and execution of the King on 30$^{th}$ January, and the political unrest in London, Henry Bankes voted for the Act to declare England to be a Commonwealth on 19$^{th}$ May, took a position in the Houses of Parliament, then decided to escape any possible retributions by going back to his house and lands.

Flintwell Hall, a four-day coach ride from London, sat in the southern cusp of the Lincolnshire Wolds surrounded by 100,000 acres of parkland and farmers' fields. The estate was managed by an Overseer or Steward, numbered 20 farmers, and derived its income from profits made on its produce and livestock.

The Hall itself was built in 1601 and was a three-storey rectangular edifice fronted by four enormous pillars that reached to the roof line. It was constructed of sandstone and flint with large leaded windows that let a lot of light into the high vaulted-ceilinged rooms. It had a slate roof and a multitude of ornate chimney stacks from the fires in every room.

The grand house was quiet. Marie was in her day room reading a book of poems by candlelight. It was mid-morning on a dark and overcast day and the servants were preparing luncheon. The Marquess was expected home at some time and Marie was not looking forward to his return. The note she received by messenger yesterday was curt and demeaning. He implied she was being unfaithful and wanted a full explanation.

There was a commotion out in the front of the house as a team of sweating black horses pulled into the walled courtyard at a gallop. The carriage rocked as a huge man pushed open the door before the coachman had time to open it and climbed unsteadily out of the carriage. He stood and looked up at his house with his ruddy complexion, before climbing the steps to the front door. The servants all gathered in a double line to greet their master home, lead by the head butler, James Howell.

Lord Henry Bankes used his stick to steady himself as he walked into the grand hall and removed his ostentatious feathered hat, handing it to a servant.

'Welcome home your lordship,' the head butler greeted him with a bow.

'Where's that French whore of a wife?' he shouted.

He was in a very bad mood. The jowls on his fat face trembled, resembling a blood hound without the spittle. His enormous bulk waddled through the inner chamber that led to the long gallery where he received most of his guests. A housemaid handed him a very large pewter mug of port, of which he took a huge mouthful of and swallowed in one gulp.

'Has she not been found yet?' he screamed in his high-pitched voice. 'Find the Frenchie now,' he demanded to no one in particular.

'Her Ladyship is in her private chamber, sire. She is being summoned as you commanded.' The head butler bowed again.

The far end door opened with a creak and John Beldan, the First Footman walked quickly into the room and whispered something into James Howell's ear. Servants were to be seen but not heard. The only one able to address his Lordship was the head butler.

'What is it man?' he demanded in his foul mood.

'Mr Thomas Tilley, the gamekeeper wishes to have an audience with you, sire.'

'Ask him to wait. I want to see the French wife first.'

He lowered himself into a chair, his bulging belly hanging over the edge, his riding boots splayed out in front of him, his breath coming in short spasms as he sipped his mug of port.

Marie walked uncertainly into the long gallery from a secret door that led from her reading room.

Her skirts rustled as she walked slowly towards her husband. She could smell him before she was even ten paces away. He could not have washed in a fortnight and the stench of stale sweat, alcohol and his body odour made her gag.

'So, you show yourself at last,' he bellowed.

'A votre service, mon Seigneur. Good day my lord, my husband.' She bowed very low in front of him showing off her small but perfectly pushed up breasts in the tight low-cut bodice of her gown.

'Account for yourself in my absence,' he demanded.

'Mon Seigneur, je ne comprende pas,' she said.

'In English, wife.'

'I am at a loss to understand your question my Lord. I have supervised the erection of the Orangery as you commanded and have had a few of our good neighbours over to view it in your absence.'

She looked directly into his little beady eyes, sunken deep into his fat, sweating, pink face.

'I am led to believe that there have been certain parties and gatherings galore in the last few months. Hey? That young upstart Dashwood has been a permanent fixture here at your beck and call. Hey? What do you say to that? Well wife?' he demanded.

All the servants were standing perfectly still in the room. They knew who had fed the master this information, and they all felt for their mistress, having to stand in front of him, being questioned with the servants present.

'My Lord, if you spent more time here at your home with your wife and less time with your whores at court, we would not be having this conversation,' she said defiantly regretting every word as she spoke it.

His face reddened. He raised himself off the chair with difficulty and roared at her, his breath the stench of a sewer.

'How dare you speak to me with such blatant disrespect, you French whore. Go to my bed chamber and await me. I shall deal with you in private.'

This was a complete nightmare for her as she knew what he intended. She curtsied, turned and walked away from him in tears.

'Thomas Tilley,' he shouted, 'come here at once.'

As Marie walked down the long gallery, she passed Thomas Tilley. He had a smirk on his grubby face and he grinned at her showing his rotten teeth with a knowing look of total disrespect.

Marie climbed the rear staircase to the upper floor of the grand house where the bedrooms were located for its principal owners. The second and third floor rooms were for house guests.

Henry Bankes' bedchamber was at the other end of the house to hers, and as she approached his room she shuddered at the recollection of the last time she was here. She hoped that he would pass out from an excess of port and weariness from his journey, would render him unable to function.

She sat in a chair in his outer chamber waiting for his arrival. She waited a full two hours although she knew not what the hour was.

She smelt him before he appeared, limping from his gout and out of breath. He barged past her into his room, removing his outer garments as he approached his enormous bed.

'Wench, come here,' he commanded in a loud voice.

She entered the dimly lit room. Only eight candles flickered in their holders around the room. He was down to his filthy outer britches and she knew what his intentions were.

'Come and lift your skirts that I may take the privileges of my wife.' His podgy hand grabbed her long silky hair and he pulled her to his bedside. He made her bend over the edge as he lifted her layers of petticoats to reveal her smooth round bottom.

He approached her from behind, his hand pushed on the small of her back as he forced her onto the bed. His other hand forced her legs apart …

Out of the corner of her eyes she saw him pulling at his breeches, searching for …

# 5

# Wednesday

# July 2017

3am.

She screamed out aloud and sat up suddenly in bed, shaking with fear.

She was covered in sweat, her forehead, her armpits and her back.

She realised that she was safe and alone in her bed, but once again her sheets were damp from sweat which meant she had to go to the laundrette on the way to work, again.

Her bedroom door burst open again and both Lisa and Clare barged in looking frightened at what they had heard. They stood by her bedside looking down at her.

'Another one babes?' asked Lisa.

She simply nodded, still shaking.

'Bad this time?'

She nodded again, tears streaming down her face.

'I wish I could get rid of this stupid dream. It's so frightening … so vivid. You know, like I'm there in the dream … living it, feeling it … oh god … smelling it, too. It stank in those days.'

'Okay babes. I am going to get you an appointment with Doctor Steph Granger. She is brilliant and will be able to help you.'

'Thanks Lisa. I need to get some sleep now as I have an important meeting with the partners tomorrow … no ... I mean later this morning with a new client. God, I feel drained.'

As her housemates turned to leave her, 'thank you both so much. I keep waking you up at stupid o'clock, don't I? Sorry girls. I'll sort this out. I can't go on like this.'

Marie knew that she had some skeletons in her cupboard. Her father had told her about her ancestors. They were French aristocracts in the 17$^{th}$-century and she recalled that her name was passed down the female line through the years. And her family – the deVille's were something to do with wine.

*'I must find out more about them,'* she said to herself.

She fell asleep peacefully, waking to her alarm clock at 7am.

As soon as she walked into her office, her assistant handed her a handwritten note.

'You are required in their office now, Marie. Good morning by the way.'

'Oh, thanks Rachel.' She was curious.

Randolph Fortescue and James Clifford, founding partners of the agency, are in the office they still share. Another man, she can't quite see, was also there.

'Ah, here she is. Charles, may I present Marie deVille who will be principal designer on your project.' Randolph did the introductions.

Marie walked into their office as the man with his back to the door stood up to greet her.

'Charles … gosh … how are you? Didn't expect to see you here.' She went up and put her arms around his neck and kissed him on both cheeks. 'How's Leticia?'

'Ugh … you two know each other?' James said in surprise.

'Yes, we do,' Charles replied. 'Marie and our family go way back and my sister Lisa is her bestie and housemate to boot.'

'Well I never!' exclaimed Randolph, 'this bodes very well.'

Marie was confused. What did Charles Dashwood have to do with their agency? Wasn't he into property development?

'Marie, please take a seat,' James started. 'Charles is the lead project manager for a new company that is turning an old hall into a boutique hotel. He has come to see if we wish to pitch for the advertising and marketing of the new business, once renovations are completed. There are two other agencies in the running.'

'You can thank Lisa for giving me your agency name last weekend when I saw her at home in Shoreham. She couldn't remember if this is what you did, but Randolph and James have assured me that you are their very best.' He smiled at her.

She suddenly remembered her dream the night before last and blushed. Charles looked at her as if she was blushing at him.

'So, what's the project then, where is it?' she asked.

'Flintwell Hall in Lincolnshire. It's been around since 1602 and needs a lot of internal renovation. My consortia bought a share in it from the Bankes family a year ago to pay for death duties when the 9th Marquess of Flintwell eventually dies. He is living on borrowed time and I am good friends with his eldest son who will inherit the title as the 10th Marquess. His family have slowly sold their land over the last two centuries, until the only thing left is the old hall in about 40 acres of parkland. It will make a brilliant boutique hotel, if we market it right.'

Marie had gone deathly white, her paleness and inability to speak caused the three men in the room to shout for help.

'Marie, are you okay?' Charles asked taking her hand. He felt her brow for temperature and found her perspiring despite the coolness of the air-conditioned room.

Rachel, her assistant, came into the room with some chilled water. Everyone just stood and looked at her ... helplessly.

Marie's mind was doing somersaults and all for the wrong reasons.

*'Did she hear right? Did Charles say it was Flintwell Hall?'*

Her vivid dreams crept back into her mind and she felt quite faint.

'I am sorry Charles. We are not sure what's wrong with Marie. She has been working too hard, burning the candle as they say. Perhaps we can assign someone else to the job,' James was saying.

'NO! ... PLEASE DON'T!.'

They all jumped at Marie's sudden explosion into the conversation.

'No, I want this job. It was just the name I recognised for some reason, that's all and I didn't sleep well last night either.'

'As long as you are sure Marie. We can move some of your work over to Steven and Molly and it's about time we stretched Rachel a bit, so she can take more responsibility working with you on this project.' Randolph was always very supportive.

'I think the best plan would be for Marie and Rachel to join me tomorrow at the Hall and we can show you what we are doing, then you can start to think about the launch and the marketing positioning. And, of course, to scope out your financial proposals for the work into a final offer.' Charles looked at them all for agreement.

'Does that give you enough time to hand work over to the others and be ready to go north tomorrow?' asked James.

'Yes, it does,' Marie answered. 'But can we go by train and get a ride to the Hall for say early evening?'

'If you catch the 4pm it gets you into Newark by 6pm and I will meet you at the station. We can discuss our plans over dinner on the way to the Hall. Suggest you pack for a few days as we can't show you it all in a day.' Charles was smiling at her.

Marie had recovered her complexion and was feeling better.

After the meeting, Charles took her hand and walked her out to the lifts.

'Marie ... aghh ... Lisa has obviously not told you that Leticia and I have split. She was too demanding and always pushing me to propose to her. I don't like that in a woman and it put me off.'

'Oh god, I'm sorry Charles. I didn't know. Lisa is on shift work at the hospital so we are a bit like ships that pass in the night.'

'Are you really ok?' he asked, searching her eyes.

'Yes, I am thanks, just very tired right now.'

'Lisa did mention that you have been having terrible nightmares.'

'Oh?' Marie bristled with anger at Lisa's broken trust.

'Don't get angry, my French beauty. She is very concerned for you and only mentioned it to me because I know Steph Granger very well and she wants me to get her to see you … you know … as a favour. These shrinks can be bloody expensive and you don't get them on the NHS.'

*"My French beauty, he called me. I fancy the pants off this guy … and now he is single again, and I am about to spend a few days with him … whoop, whoop!"*

'Thank you Charles, for everything. And I am really looking forward to working with you on this job. You know we will have it in the bag.'

She reached up on tip toes to give him a kiss on each cheek.

*"God, he smells divine."*

'Until tomorrow then Frenchie.' It was the nickname he called her when they were growing up. Charles was five years older than Marie, so now just 30.

The lift doors opened and he was gone.

She stood there for a few moments taking it all in. The love of her life, not only single again but soon to become a work partner, too. And the Hall from her dreams … what did it mean?

Marie hoped that Charles could get his friend Dr. Granger to see her soon.

She spent the rest of the day briefing the other teams on her current work commitments and preparing Rachel for the trip up north. She booked their train tickets, finally leaving the office after 8pm.

She was exhausted, with the broken sleep and the long day, all she wanted was to grab something to eat and then to sleep … but to sleep properly without any terrifying dreams.

She got home to an empty house, once again with her takeaway Chinese and a cheap bottle of Pinot Grigio from the local supermarket.

She was glad she was on her own as it gave her a chance to call her father to ask him about her family background. It was an enlightening phone call, her father worried about why she wanted to know. But it made her realise that her dreams were a message from her past.

Still … scary!

She left the girls a note:

*Hi Lisa & Clare,*

*I am going away for a few days up to Lincolnshire with Charles on a new project we are helping him with. Hopefully you will get a few nights undisturbed sleep!!*

*Catch up soon and tell you when I'm back!!*

*Love Marie*

Tomorrow would be a long day as she had clients coming in to meet the new team leaders before she left for the train.

She went to bed at 11pm dreading closing her eyes …

# 6

# 1649

It's a bright sunny day at last.

Her maidservant brought her breakfast of cold meats, Manchette bread, some cheeses and a draught of small beer for Marie to have in her bedchamber. Marie had decided to go riding with her best friend Lisa, and her riding clothes were removed from the garderobe and laid out on her bed.

Their horses are brought out to the front of the house by the grooms. Just as they are about to mount the side-saddled horses, James Howell, the head butler came running down the front staircase.

'Your Ladyship,' he is out of breath.

'Take your time Howell, get your breath back. I don't want you falling ill right now,' she said kindly.

He bowed. 'Your Ladyship. My Lord the Marquess has requested us to organise a masked ball in three weeks time and you are to draw up a list of intended guests from the local gentry. His Lordship asked me to give you this note.' He handed her a handwritten scrawl; unmistakably his as he could only just write.

She took the note, broke the wax seal and read it quickly, handing it over to Lisa.

'The impertinence of the man! He wishes to make a fool of me.' Marie was clearly upset.

'I don't quite understand,' Lisa reread the note which was difficult to decipher.

'Come on, let's get going and I will explain on the ride out of ear shot.' As she mounted her horse, her legs striding to the right. They left the courtyard at a gallop, and headed towards to the fields.

In the upper windows, Henry Bankes watched with interest as he saw his wife read his note, shaking her head and handing it to that awful bitch Lisa Dashwood.

'Oh, to be rid of the Dashwood's forever,' he said to himself. Lord Dashwood opposed him in everything he suggested in the house, especially in recognising Charles, Prince of Wales as the new King Charles II of England, Scotland and Ireland.

*'Interesting to see that Lisa is her confidant and that she showed her the note.'* It was meant to be insulting, demeaning with implied innuendo. In direct contradiction to his view of Lisa Dashwood, she was still an attractive

filly, and he had designs on having her as a mistress ... *'how about that then ... his wife's best friend as his mistress.'* He chuckled to himself in amusement at the thought.

As they reached the brook, they slowed their horses down to a walk.

'Marie, what is wrong?'

'Oh, god heaven help me. That fat, putrid, self-indulgent cad of a husband wants me to dress as a vestal virgin at the ball, intimating that we have not consummated our marriage. The fact that he is permanently drunk and has a little tail he cannot rise makes it my fault.'

Lisa held back a chortle and listened quietly.

'He stinks of faeces, hasn't probably washed in a month and his belly is so huge he can't even see his ... thing ... so he pisses inside his breeches. How on earth do the Royal family and the rest of Parliament accept him?'

'That is truly horrid.'

'I hate him and curse my father for arranging this marriage. If it wasn't for you I would live in total misery.'

'Have you consummated your marriage?'

'Yes, we did on the night we married, before he became so rotund. It was a quick and unexciting coupling to gratify himself. And he knows it.'

'What are you going to do?'

'Take another lover, and hope I don't become with child.'

'My brother I take it?'

Marie smiled at her best friend.

'You don't mind do you Lisa? I do love him you know. When my husband's tumours finally kill him, I will have wealth as well as my whole heart to give to your brother.' She threw her head and bodice backwards and laughed out aloud.

'We will then become true sisters.' She giggled and took Lisa's hand.

'I have a wicked thought.' Marie was riding close to Lisa still holding her hand.

'Go on … what are you thinking of?'

'How can we accelerate his departure from this earth?'

Lisa turned to look at her best friend … aghast at the suggestion.

'What … you mean … we … um … kill him?

'Well if we don't, we find someone who will for us. Make it look like an accident or an overdose of port. He can fall from his horse, or slip down the main central staircase, or fall from the rear balcony.' Her mind was racing with possibilities to use his drunken state to assist in ending his days and her misery.

'The masked ball,' Lisa suggested. 'We can think of something at the masked ball. There will be an abundance of people there to witness his demise.'

They rode on into the woods that led to the lake where they would water their horses.

♦♦♦

Leaning against a tree was Thomas Tilley the game keeper with Abel Jones the head groom. They were under orders from His Lordship to watch the women and report back if they had any illicit meeting on their ride out. He was hoping to catch her with Charles Dashwood red handed.

Thomas Tilley himself had designs on the Marchioness. He had seen her through the glass panes sat regally in her bath tub. Her marble white skin, her jet black hair and her small perfectly rounded breasts and hard pointed rosy nipples over her taut stomach made him feel alive and she featured in his dreams every night. He wanted her. He had seen her with that Dashwood character in the Orangery, but could not swear on the bible that he saw them coupling, which is what his master had asked him.

He was aware that his master was unhappy about the freedom she had when he was at court. He was also aware of how much the other servants in the household hated and despised him, including that ex-naval officer James Howell, who wheedled his way into the household as Head Butler. He even had suspicions over his own helper Abel Jones, who was a simple lad but easily led.

Where could he catch them out and win favours from His Lordship? ... at the masked ball he was told about this morning. He could dress up and no one would know and he could take her in the Orangery. He licked his lips with desire at the thought.

He followed them on his own horse through the woods, down the bridal path and into the next farm. She stopped to talk to the farmer and his wife and waved at the workers in the field. She was very popular with the manual workers. They never saw His Lordship; mind you he couldn't stride a horse if we found one strong enough to carry his bulk. He tittered at his own joke.

◆◆◆

On reaching the lake, they dismounted their horses using an old tree stump as a stepping stool, and led them to the edge to drink. Marie looked all around her and marvelled at how beautiful her house and lands were.

'What are you thinking about?' Lisa interrupted her thoughts.

'Only how beautiful this is. We are so lucky to be here. I know I curse my Father for sending me here, but without His Lordship I would have a happy life.'

'When is he due to return to London?'

'After the masked ball, me thinks. He has not said, and I fear his cowardice is keeping him up here. He fears for his own life with the current unrest in London. I wish he would return now and befall his fate under Cromwell or Fairfax.'

'I will speak with my brother on our discussions for the masked ball. Maybe he will have some suggestions to fulfil your wishes!'

'Oh Lisa, you are such a good friend. Please do

not get into any trouble though?'

'We need to be a bit careful around him,' Lisa said nodding towards the woods. 'He has been spying on us since we rode out, skulking in the woods, thinking we haven't noticed. He gives me the creeps.'

'I had no idea he was there. You are observant. Yes, he sometimes pretends to be fixing the window of my antichamber as I take a bath and peers in at me. I have caught him twice now.'

'Have you told anyone?'

'No, but my handmaidens have mentioned it to Howell, who will deal with him, so I am informed.'

'He is as repugnant as your husband.' Lisa shuddered at the thought.

'So, tell me dear friend, who has taken your fancy. You have not spoken about Mr. Wentworth for some time. Are you still receiving him?'

'Oh, the man is a total frustration. One minute he doesn't leave me alone, the next he disappears for months on end. I cannot have a relationship with such a man.'

'Is he at his father's disposition? Maybe he has to attend Parliament and is away like my husband?'

'Honestly, I have not asked him what he does. All I know is that his father Lord Wentworth has been a firm long-time friend with my father, which is why we are being encouraged to meet,'

'Have you kissed him yet?' Marie said with a mischievous smirk.

'Oh, Marie, you are blatant with your intrusion on my private affairs.' She gave a loud laugh.

They continued to walk around the edge of the lake taking in the sunshine, fresh air and views before re-mounting their horses.

They crossed the stream by the small dam that fed the lake, and galloped back to the stables.

Skulking at the back of one of the stables was Thomas Tilley, observing the women's return and hoping to catch what they were saying to report back to His Lordship. He had sent young Abel into the brew house to help with next week's fermentation of beer for the household. Flintwell Hall was very lucky to have its wines supplied by Marie's father's vineyards on his estate at her family château in the Loire Valley. His Lordship's favourite port also came as a gift from the Duc de Touraine.

All Thomas Tilley hears is tittle-tattle about society

gossip and the bloody masked ball. He thinks His Lordship is mad holding this elaborate party for the local gentry, all done with the sole intention of catching his wife 'in flagrante' with the Honourable Charles Dashwood. In fact, His Lordship had ordered him to have a bath in the lake and join the masked ball as a guest to be his eyes and ears, and to fetch him as soon as he sees the two culprits in a compromising position. Well, he has never been to a function like this before and he is going to enjoy himself, and bugger what His Lordship wants. He has his eyes set on Her Ladyship and if not, that self-important bitch Lisa Dashwood. He knows how they use the alcoves in the Orangery for secret trysts and if he makes sure the wine flows at the ball in certain directions he could entice them into the Oangery under false pretences.

Now to think up a suitable name so that it does not cause suspicions; although His Lordship did say he would come up with one as part of his masquerade. Sebastian Holliday Esquire. He likes that!

As Marie entered the Hall, Mrs Cribb the Housekeeper approached her and bowed.

'Your Ladyship. I am told that you will be organising the Masked Ball for His Lordship. I have some plans for your approval, and cook has also written a meal plan for the evening. When would it be convenient to go through this with you?'

'I am most impressed Mrs Cribb,' she said with a surprised tone, 'how about tea in the Orangery and ask Mrs Pottage to join us as well. James Howell and John Bedlan might as well be in the discussions as they will need to understand the details.'

'Very well, Your Ladyship. In an hour in the Orangery. I will organise tea for you both.' She curtsied at Marie and bowed towards Lisa.

Marie and Lisa made their way to the Orangery through the Great Hall. They saw a glimpse of Thomas Tilley and Randolph Blake, the Estate Steward in His Lordship's study, no doubt reporting back fabricated tales.

'How exciting … a masked ball, Marie. We should invite the ladies and men from our club. As they will be "incognito" His Lordship won't know who is there and who is not.' Lisa was showing a growing excitement at being involved with the planning.

'Henry still wants me to present the guest list to him for approval before the invites are sent out. I know he will ban our friends if we include them.'

'So, we produce two lists. One for his Lordship to approve and the real one for the doorman and footmen.'

'You are cunning as well as beautiful Lisa Dashwood. And whom in particular do you want there? … as if I didn't know.'

'Well, my parents and brother should be on His Lordship's list. He cannot ask for them to be removed as it would be political suicide for him, besides we are your nearest neighbours.' Lisa giggled behind her gloved hand.

By the time Mrs Cribb brought the tea with Mrs Pottage, Marie and Lisa had completed both the guest lists. One had forty more names on it than the other … a total of one hundred and fifty people would be invited.

'Now to discuss and agree menus, refreshments and quantities, which must not be discussed with His Lordship,' Marie said firmly to Lisa.

Once everyone was seated in the Orangery and tea had been poured for Marie and Lisa, Mrs.Cribb started to explain her ideas. The Hall would be opened on the ground floor to receive guests in the Long Room and the Library through into the Orangery and the courtyard garden outside. They would have musicians at one end of the Long Gallery and a quintet in the courtyard garden, if it was dry.

Additional help would be found from the farming families on the estate. The brewhouse had been ordered to make additional ales available for the evening and Marie had sent a despatch to her father requesting more wine and champagne.

Mrs Pottage had produced a very clever menu of small bite-sized morsels of food that could be eaten as one stood, from trays circulating around the room along with bottles or jugs to refill everyone's glasses. This had never been done before as far as Marie was aware and she loved the idea.

The musicians would be hired from Lincoln city and additional chairs would be sought as well. As for the Orangery, James Howell suggested the foliage and trees be removed to the greenhouses, but Marie and Lisa wanted to use the seclusion they provided to have some fun during the masked ball.

The meeting was nearly over when Henry Bankes waddled in, heaving his bulk into the room and falling into a vacant chair out of breath.

'What's afoot here?' he demanded.

'My husband, we have just planned the masked ball as per your instructions, and we are now going to put our plans into action.' Marie headed any direct question off.

'Pray do tell. Am I not required to approve any plans …hey?' he said in an angry voice.

'Your Lordship is surely too busy with events of state and government to be trivialised with a mere masked ball. It should be a surprise to Your Lordship and an enjoyable evening,' James Howell the Head Butler intervened.

'That as it maybe Howell, but I do wish to see who is coming to sup with me. I do not wish to meet any undesirables.'

'If your Lordship pleases, we have a list of invitees here.' Marie extended the written list to him.

He sat back on the creaking chair and through his slit eyes surveyed the list of names, making coughing noises, and a 'harrumph' every now and again. He took a long time to read the list as if his mind were elsewhere. At long last he handed it back to his wife.

'That is a list of the good and great neighbours, with three exceptions, wife. But I dare say you will have justifiable reasons for their inclusion.' He didn't say their names but inferred to Lisa's family.

Lisa bristled and moved uncomfortably in her chair at the rudeness of this crass man but remained dignified and silent. Her father would hear of this though.

He ignored her. 'Are you not considering any of the aristocracy from London, wife?'

'My Lord, I did consider this, but felt the journey would be too great for most of them and we cannot accommodate them for the time they would require,' knowing Henry hated having house guests.

He merely raised his big bushy eyebrows and waved at Howell and the footmen to help him stand as he wished to excuse himself.

Everyone gave a sigh of relief as he left the room, without questioning the cost or the numbers catered for. This would be a battle to be fought later, if required. Thank god, none of his cronies from London were coming ... she'd got away with that.

As the servants left them alone, Marie giggled at Lisa.

'Why the amusement dear friend?'

'I just had a wicked thought.'

'Pray tell!'

'We could ensure that His Lordship is well inebriated in the early part of the ball, so he can be placed in an antichamber to sleep it off whilst we amuse ourselves.'

'Mmmm … what an enchanting idea. We could wake him up for the fireworks and pretend he has been there all the time.'

'That would drive him mad. Not knowing if he had fallen asleep. We would need to ensure the servants kept their place.'

'Oh yes, let's plan on this. I believe your brother may give a helping hand?'

'How so?'

'He is able to obtain a sleeping draft which we can place him in charge of administering to His Lordship.'

'Great idea, Marie. I will take him into our confidence.'

Marie needed to rest, so Lisa called her coachman to take her home.


That evening, Marie dreamt of the Masked Ball and the fun she could get up to with Charles …

# 7

# Thursday

# July 2017

4am.

She awoke … sat up in bed and looked around her room in a daze.

Dawn was just breaking as the sun rose and filtered rays of bright sunlight through the flimsy material of her curtains filling her room with a shaded light as the breeze wafted in through the open window.

She had to shake her head to understand where she was.

She felt very moist and … satisfied. OMG … had she had an orgasm in her sleep?

She remembered the masked ball and her embrace with Charles in the Orangery, hidden behind the fern and foliage in her secret corner. She remembered the light touch of his lips as they brushed her open mouth, and the feel of his toned body against hers and his hardness as he took his pleasure.

That's why she felt as she did ... and she was embarrassed!

She felt fresh and rejuvenated for the first time in days.

She realised that today was her trip up to Flintwell Hall to meet Charles and the development team. The masked ball had given her an idea for the launch party. In fact, since her meetings with James and Randolph she had many different ideas about how to market the Hall as a boutique hotel.

She had a few hours before she had to get ready. Her train was leaving Kings Cross at 4pm, so she had plenty of time. Charles was meeting her at Newark North Street station for the thirty-minute drive to the Hall just east of Lincoln.

She reclined in her bed with her laptop and searched deVille family through Wikipedia and other search engines. The information she found added to what her father had told her last night. She dozed off with visions of the servants and people in the Hall in her mind.

At 8am Lisa and Clare burst into her room without knocking to find Marie looking fresh and healthy.

'Wow, didn't expect to see you looking so well. No dreams I take it?' Lisa ventured.

'You have a satisfied look on your face Marie – what have you been dreaming about now?' asked Clare.

'Ha-ha … yes, had a lovely dream last night. Not frightening at all. Mmmm … just ….'

'Just what?' demanded Lisa.

'Well it must have been good coz I woke up with a huge smile on my face … you know!!' she added with a wink and a smile.

'Well about bloody time, too. Thank God for that!' said Lisa.

They sat on her bed and asked her questions about her dreams last night and she answered some of them.

'This would make a great book my love. Get it down in writing before you forget about it,' Clare suggested.

'Aren't you meeting my brother at Newark today?'

'Yes. He is taking me to Flintwell Hall tomorrow to meet the owners and discuss the launch and marketing campaign.'

'Well, lucky you. When are you back?'

'Don't know. Probably a couple of days?'

'Better forewarn Charles then. Rampant bitch on the loose!!' and both the girls giggled out loud at Marie who was smiling, but secretly excited at spending some time with Charles.

On her way to the station Marie received a call from Rachel to say she was unwell and it would be better if she didn't come after all. But, she would be in the office to supervise any amendments. At Kings Cross station, Marie looked up at the departure board and looked for her train and platform. She checked her e-ticket and realised she had been booked in First Class. Oh boy … she was going to enjoy this.

Settling into her seat, she was offered a drink, so took a glass of prosecco and some sandwiches. She opened her brief and studied the couple of pages of the outline of what her agency were tasked to do. It was the first chance she had to look at this properly, as she had to complete and handover the current work on her existing clients to clear the desk for this project.

She read the brief. It was very well written by Charles, of course.

She stopped with her glass of prosecco half way to her lips … and stared at the paper in front of her.

She re-read the names in total disbelief.

FLINTWELL HALL – LINCOLNSHIRE WOLDS

OWNER -still in family hands and the current master is the 9$^{th}$ Marquess of Flintwell – Henry Bankes, 70 years old; divorced his 3$^{rd}$ wife two years ago. Member of the House of Lords, Conservative.

Henry Bankes has three children, all employed in running the family business in one form or another, and they make up the Board of Directors. Her jaw dropped as she read the names of the other board members.

Managing Director of the Hall: Randolph Blake

Commercial Director: James Howell

Services Director: Mrs. Elvira Cribb

Catering Director: Mrs. Patricia Pottage

Grounds and Farm Controller: Thomas Tilley

She knew them all but had never met any of them. A strange shudder went through her as she suddenly felt alarmed at the sheer coincidence of this situation. The very scary thought would be if they all looked like their characters in her dreams!! OMG! How the hell could that be??

Marie opened the brief outline her agency was given on the assignment to build a brand marketing campaign and the launch of the hotel.

*"The redevelopment of Flintwell Hall from a family residence into a boutique hotel is almost complete. The hotel will boast 20 en-suite, king-size bedrooms, all furnished to a very high standard but in a traditional 17th-century way. The décor throughout will reflect the Hall's past heritage and although modern and up-to-date it will lean towards the feel of a 17th-century atmosphere. The lights, for instance, resemble candles, so craftily give a dimmer light to the rooms both in daytime and at night, simulating the candles that would have lit the Hall back in the past times.*

*Cuisine at the Hall will be by a two-star Michelin chef, but will reflect the food of that century, served on wooden or pewter platters without cutlery. For those not wishing to be that authentic, there will be the usual silver ware available. Breakfast, for instance, will be cold meats, cheeses, Manchette bread and light beer or porter. The evening food will be very gamey and from the estate, but will also cater for special dietary requierments. The bar will offer beer from the Hall's 300-year-old brewery.*

*The landscaped 40 acres of land will offer a 9-hole golf course and tennis courts, as well as archery, crossbows, antique rifle targets and clay pigeon shoots. The Hall's stables will offer riding lessons for novices, or hacks for experienced riders. The Hall's four-acre lake offers fishing of all kinds. Built around the original servants' quarters is an indoor swimming pool together with a jacuzzi, hot tub, steam-rooms and a health SPA.*

*The main feature of the Hall is its 17$^{th}$-century magnificent original Dutch Orangery, including its secluded 'Loving' seats hidden by foliage such as fern, banana trees and other greenery."*

Marie knew that the next two days would be spent with Charles, taking in the atmosphere of the Hall and looking at every facet so that they would be able to fully appreciate the hotel's features. She was tasked with briefing the creative illustrators to produce a visual presentation of the marketing plan and launch. This would need to be with the team by midday tomorrow, as they had their first meeting with Henry Bankes, the 9$^{th}$ Marquess, and the management board on Thursday afternoon.

She closed her eyes and drifted off into one of her dreams. Charles was leading her into one of the 'loving' seats in the Orangery during the masked ball for an intimate embrace.

'Tickets, please.' The shout from the conductor brought her crashing back to her train journey and reality. Although Charles had split up from his girlfriend, Marie could not compare with or live up to the beautiful, luscious Leticia.

But there he was; tall, dark and handsome. He was standing casually with one hand tucked into his rear jeans pocket, open-neck shirt, dark Serengeti glasses, his perfectly cut short jet black hair shining in the sunshine, looking lean and mean against his open-top Jaguar XK.

*'My god, he is a hunk of a man. Why can't he be mine?'* she thought as she walked dragging her wheeled suitcase behind her, her attaché folder gripped under her arm, and feeling very dishevelled.

'Hello, you gorgeous thing,' he said as he walked casually towards her taking her case and portfolio. He bent down to give her a kiss on both cheeks.

*'He smells divine ... and he called me gorgeous!'*

'Hi, Charlie. Hope you've not been waiting long?'

'I would wait to the midnight hour for you my Frenchie.'

*"Wow, he called me Frenchie! He does that in my dreams ... the 17$^{th}$-century Charles I am having an affair with behind my husband's back".*

'Come along Marie, it's only a thirty-five-minute drive to the Hall. Thought we could stop off at a pub for lunch and just go over things before we arrive at the Hall. We are staying there as well, so you get the full experience. It's bloody fantastic!' He was so enthusiastic about this; his voice was confident and proud.

'What's your interest in the Hall? Are you a shareholder or just employed to develop it?'

'My company won the contract for the building work and I have headed the architects and designer teams. We also bought into the shares with a 30% holding. So, I suppose I do have an interest in the project.'

'How come you chose our agency over all the others? Were James and Randolph that impressive?'

'No,' he looked over at her, one hand on the walnut steering wheel, and raised his Serengeti's with his other hand, 'I wanted you on the project, so I told them that if you weren't in the team, we would go elsewhere.'

Marie was dumbfounded. She hesitated before replying, unsure whether this was a compliment or a proposition?

They reached a country pub just the other side of Lincoln, which would have been part of the Flintwell estate in the old days. It had a plaque over the front door stating it had been an inn since 1600 and a stone built into the wall was carved 1589. The two-storey building was long and built of stone with a slate roof. There was ivy climbing up the outer walls to the iron windows upstairs. The solid front door was of dense old oak with huge metal hinges.

Marie climbed out of Charles's car and hesitated as she looked at a very familiar building, having never actually been here before. She shivered in the 28 degree heat. Closing the car door, she followed Charles inside.

They took a seat inside the low beamed bar area and ordered drinks and food. It was quaint and very dark, a combination of musty old furniture, stale beer and chip odour wafting through the building. It looked like it was in private hands. As the landlady came over with their drinks,

Marie was curious.

'You have a lovely building. Have you been here very long?'

Hesitating before answering, the landlady stood and stared at Marie open mouthed, as if she had seen a ghost.

'It's been in our family for donkey's years. My ancestors were gifted the pub by the Marchioness of Flintwell back in 1651, soon after the death of the 1st Marquess of Flintwell.'

'How fascinating. How did the Marquess die?'

'That is a mystery. He was found in his bedchamber the next morning by the head butler. It was presumed that he died on his own bile following a night of heavy drinking. Plus, he was riddled with disease.'

'That is very gory ... just as we are about to eat as well, Marie,' said Charles, pulling a face.

'Sorry, did you say your name was Marie?' asked the landlady.

'Yes, Marie deVille ... why?'

The landlady had a very strange expression on her face, one of awe and bewilderment.

'Well, it's either a terrific coincidence or fate, because the Marchioness of Flintwell Hall was also called Marie deVille Bankes, and copies of paintings we have of her – look remarkably like you.' She was astounded as she stared at Marie for a while in disbelief.

'Please excuse me,' she said and disappeared behind the bar quickly.

'How about that then, Marie. Looks like you are famous.'

Marie became very quiet and she felt tormented by her dreams. This pub was so familiar it scared her.

'Let's talk about the project,' Charles said breaking her reverie.

'Tell me more about the family,' she asked.

'Henry Forbes Bankes is the 9th Marquess of Flintwell and inherited the title and lands from his father twenty years ago. He has had three wives, and three children from two of the marriages. The eldest is son is 30, a daughter of 25 and youngest son is 19. The family wealth had dwindled in the past century with death duties and taxes, coupled with bad investments. He lost a load on the stock market, or rather he was swindled out of a lot of money. So, his children have persuaded him to convert the Hall to a boutique hotel to save some of the family wealth. His staff are all very loyal and he has formed a board of directors with each taking key positions in the new venture. It's all a bit incestuous and I believe they need outside help to make this work. Which is where we, or rather you, come in.'

'How old is the Marquess?'

'I believe he is in his late sixties, but when you meet

him …'

'He will be overbearing, very rotund and drinks like a fish,' she answered for him.

'Have you met him then?'

'No, but I seem to know him from somewhere.'

'You are right … he is crass, rude and overbearing. Thinks he is right all the time. Thank God his eldest son has a solid head on his shoulders and a brain, too!'

'That's all very well and good, but can he control his father where the business is concerned?'

'Oh, yes. He is one of the few Bankes's that came out of university with a degree. A First in Economics and he went on and did his Masters. He has his father around his little finger where the finances are concerned and it's his idea to redevelop Flintwell Hall into a boutique hotel.'

'Are the family going to be in residence as well? I gather it's a huge house.'

'No, they own three houses on the estate into which they are moving. The Marquess is sadly losing his mind; they think he has the onset of dementia. Runs in the family.'

'So, what's the plan for this week Charles?'

'We will spend today looking around the Hall and the estate so you can familiarise yourself with the place. Tonight, we dine with the family and you get to meet them all. Tomorrow, HP will take us through his plans, if he doesn't tonight …'

'HP?' Marie asked with a quizzical look.

'Sorry, Henry Percival, or should we say Lord Henry Percy. He will become the 10$^{th}$ Marquess upon his father's death. He hates titles and likes to be called HP.'

'Sorry, I interrupted you.'

'We will spend tomorrow afternoon coming up with a launch plan that will work with your graphics team and present our preliminary ideas on Friday.'

'Who are the other siblings?'

'Lady Rosabella is his daughter who is 25 and The Right Honerable Arthur Henry is the youngest.'

'They all have a role in the family, do they?'

'You will find out later. Yes, they do but I can't quite remember what they do.'

Marie sat nursing her glass of chilled white wine thinking over her original ideas since she was given the assignment. She wanted to propose a masked ball for the opening event with a select guest list of celebrities. She could see the marketing literature in her mind but wanted to wait until she had seen the Hall and grounds themselves.

A cold shiver went through her as if someone was inside her and she recalled in her mind what the Hall looked like in 1648.

As Charles went to the bar to settle the bill, the landlady approached Marie with some papers.

'Here we are. Look at these. There is an uncanny likeness of you in these photographs of the paintings that hang in the Hall of the Marchioness. Sorry I stared at you earlier but it was as if you came in through a portal or something from them olden days.'

Marie looked at the pictures silently.

'Umm … err … thank you for showing me these. It is a huge coincidence I am sure. I will look into my family history. My ancestors on my father side are French.'

The landlady handed the papers to Marie, 'you can keep these if you want. They are copies, so I have others.'

Charles came back.

'You ready to go?' He looked at the prints of the paintings and stared at them. He looked up at Marie's face, then back to the prints and back to her.

'Wow … you have an uncanny resemblance to the 4$^{th}$ Marchioness. This is going to be interesting! Let's get to the Hall.'

They drove off towards Flintwell Hall.

They passed the huge lake she remembered riding around. The stone pillars of the entrance gate and the small gamekeeper's cottage built just to one side was still there, and inhabited by the looks of the well-kept little garden.

The long gravel drive wound its way through the

parkland. It was now tree-lined with oaks, which in her dreams were not planted. It was wide enough for one car and had passing places along the way. Up on the top of the slight rise was the magnificent hall, exactly as she had seen it in her dreams. She could see deer and sheep grazing along the edge near the woods that ran along the east side. Inher dreams through these woods would have been the first farm and a couple of cottages for the workers. Was it there in reality, she wondered?

Flintwell Hall was much wider in real life than her dreams. It seemed much longer than she remembered, with a massive frontage, four huge bay windows in sandstone and slate. It had three storeys, but the top floor had smaller windows set along the roofline. The covered entrance portico roof was held up by four giant pillars and the stone stairway reaching six steps up to the double front doors had a crimson red carpet. This had been changed over time, and she suspected the Hall had been built and extended by subsequent family owners over the last 300 years.

Charles drove under the huge entrance, just as a couple appeared at the door. Marie opened her door and stepped out of the car looking up at the building in awe. Her gaze fell on the couple standing at the opened front door and all she could do was stare.

'Welcome to Flintwell Hall Miss deVille,' the man

said.

Marie hesitated to take his hand. He was so familiar but dressed in a modern dark grey suit, white shirt and red tie.

'Mr Howell ... Mrs Cribb, so pleased to meet you.' They were both staring at her as well.

'Please may I take your bag Miss deVille and we will have it delivered to your room. Hello again Mr Dashwood.' James Howell regained his composure, but Mrs Cribb was dumb-struck. She walked away without saying anything.

'Please it's Marie, nothing formal Mr Howell.'

Charles took Marie's arm and led her into the Hall's main entrance. She stopped and looked around expecting Lisa to pop around from behind one of the pillars. The spacious hall was magnificent and had the massive stone staircase leading off from the righthand side in a gentle semi-circular form to reach the first-floor landing. The marble balustrades were highly polished and gave a depth to the setting. There were three huge doors that led off the hall on the ground floor; one in front was opened and led into the first anti-room, where an antique reception desk was placed. Off this was another door, and Marie was ushered into a large high-ceilinged room with antique chairs and tables, lined with very old oil canvassed portraits.

From a door at the far end hobbled a huge, portly man with an elaborate walking stick and a red setter by his side. He had receding ginger hair, bulging red eyes, and a ruddy complexion. His rotund stomach oozed over his tight plus-four pants as his shirt tails dragged behind him. He was wearing shooting clothes but had discarded his jacket.

He stood still in front of Marie, his eyes searching her face, his ginger bushy eyebrows raised so high, his forehead distorted the loose skin on his face.

'My, my … are you a ghost!' were his opening words as he stared at her in a bewildered gaze.

'My Lord. It's good to meet you at last.' Marie extended her hand.

He glared at her refusing to take her hand.

'Marie deVille. I have come with Charles Dashwood to plan and discuss the opening of your new venture.'

He still said nothing but just stared, and it was starting to unnerve her.

The other side door opened and in walked a thinner younger version of the 9$^{th}$ Marquess, with a very pretty woman at his side.

'Marie, may I introduce Lord Henry Percival Bankes and Lady Rosabella Bankes, Lord Flintwell's family.'

'Please … its HP and Rosa. We don't stand on ceremony here with all that aristocratic bullshit … eh Charlie?'

'A pleasure to meet you both.' Marie again extended her hand.

'My God ... you have succeeded in confounding my father and I can see why,' he said.

'Please come with us,' Rosabella took Marie's hand and they led her through a third door to a very long gallery, and stood looking up at a huge portrait at this end.

Marie gazed at it with her mouth open. It was her. The 4th Marchioness Flintwell. The name plate stated:

"Marie deVille-Bankes, 4th Marchioness of Flintwell 1649 by Peter Lely."

'That is surreal!' exclaimed Charles.

Everyone was staring at the painting – then at Marie.

She felt nervous and vulnerable, uncomfortable to be standing next to a life-size painting of her double. And even more disconcerting was the fact that this painting was in her dreams as she sat for the painter in the Orangery.

The Orangery!!

'Is the Orangery still here?'

'Why yes, how did you know about that?' asked Rosa.

'Um ... I ... ahh ... saw it in a brochure on the Hall.' she stammered.

'Come this way. It's magnificent and my favourite part of the house. HP, Arthur and I used to play hide and seek and other games in there, but we gather from days of old it was used for other purposes.' Rosa was especially excited about the Orangery.

Lord Flintwell was left seated in the anti-room, a glass of something red placed in his shaking hand. He was still speechless.

The wooden Orangery was as elegant and mysterious as Marie had envisaged it to be. It was a white, painted structure, spanning three quarters of the rear elevation of the Hall, facing south. It reached the length of the Long Gallery and the glass panes held in by lead work reached from the ground up to the top of the construction. Huge carved pillars separated each window expanse holding up a pitched glass roof. Outside, it had doors either end, east and west, and inside the roof trusses were ornately carved and enhanced by iron-work. The floor was a cream marble tiling that shone brilliantly as if highly polished and in each of the huge glass panes were seats of a strange construction. They were more like 'loving couches' and although the seating area was carved out of a solid marble block, they looked very comfortable. There were enormous grey, black and white pots on the floor each holding a different variety of exotic plants, from giant ferns to banana plantains, orange and lime trees. These were placed in such a way that they would partially hide the people in the seats. It was a warm day outside but curiously the temperature inside the Orangery was cooler, with that rich aroma of green foliage.

It was incredible to think that this had stood here for over 300 years, relatively unchanged and built by a Dutch specialist at her ancestors' demands.

Marie's mind was maxed out as she thought of multiple different possibilities, for both the marketing and the masked ball. The Orangery had to be the main feature of whatever they ended up doing.

Mrs Cribbs entered the Orangery with another woman who was very familiar to Marie, Mrs Pottage; carrying trays of teapots and a pair of cake-stands loaded with delicately cut sandwich triangles, scones, eclairs and Victoria sponge cake.

'I want Marie to capture the atmosphere of the Hall and visit the facilities this afternoon, then we can get a better idea of how we can launch the Hall to its best advantage.' Charles outlined this once they were sat in the middle of the Orangery with HP and Rosa.

'Of course, we can tell you all about our sordid family tonight over dinner. Hopefully papa will be too inebriated to join us. Dinner is at 7.30 … that's right Mrs Pottage?' Rosa said.

'Until later tonight then,' said Marie.

'Casual … we are always casual for dinner,' HP said.

They left the Orangery and went for a walk around the huge Hall and then part of the vast 40-acre grounds, taking in the tennis courts, the first tee of the golf course and the pool/SPA buildings. It was a complete package and all had been expertly redeveloped and built.

Charles left Marie outside her bedroom door on the first floor. She entered a luxurious bedroom. The walls were lined with feltlike material in deep maroon and gold, with a royal blue, thick pile carpet. It was dark and ostentatious, with an imposing double four-poster-bed complete with net curtains. A chandelier hung from a wide ornate ceiling rose in the middle of the room, giving out a dim light. Both bedside lights were on, giving a warm, cosy feel to the room. The bathroom was half as big as the bed room, with an old ceramic bath wide enough for two people, the throne, bidet, and a double pair of wash basins. The floor was highly polished wood and the window heavily curtained.

She walked to the window and looked out at the rolling parkland as her bedroom faced the front of the Hall. She ran a hot bath and found a bottle of sparkling chilled water in the fridge.

She planned to remain professional tonight so despite the casual dress code Henry had advised, she chose to wear a blue Dior dress and heels. She bought the posh dress from a charity shop in Marlow a few weeks ago. Marlow has a reputation for having the best deals on exclusive dresses worn only once by the rich and famous.

At 7.15pm there was a knock at her door, and Charles looked ravishing in designer jeans, an open-neck pale blue shirt under a dark blue linen jacket.

'You look ravishing, Frenchie,' he said as he gazed at her, extending his arm for her to take.

They walked down the corridor to the wide main staircase. On reaching the bottom a footman offered them a glass of champagne and escorted them into an anti-chamber to the main dining hall. HP, Rosa and Arthur were already there, all in jeans and shirts or sweaters. Arthur was still in jodhpurs from the stables. Marie felt overdressed.

'Wow, Marie. You look stunning, but we don't tend to dress up here,' said HP.

'Dress up?' she laughed. 'This is what I normally wear in the evenings,' and threw her head back and giggled.

'I like you,' replied Rosa clinking her glass.

'So, what do you make of this money pit?' asked HP.

'It's a magnificent building and your grounds are perfectly manicured with super facilities. A highly marketable bijou hotel,' Marie answered.

'Trouble is, we want to launch a boutique hotel, not a bijou one,' Arthur said sarcastically.

HP coughed loudly. 'Arthur!' he said staring at his younger brother.

'Please excuse my brother. He runs the stables and shoots so has a warped view on what we are trying to achieve.'

'Is His Lordship not joining us?' Charles asked.

'Doubt it. One never knows with my inebriated father. He is a liability, and if he does make an appearance, please can we apologise now,' replied HP.

A gong sounded.

'Dinner time. Let's see what Mrs Pottage has caught and cooked tonight. Shall we?' Rosa escorted them through to the dining room.

The room was huge. The table itself could seat over 30 people so they were all seated at one end. There were three chandeliers hanging from a painted ornate ceiling in the centre of the room. Tapestries and paintings adorned the green painted walls. One was of the 1st Marquess and his younger 4th wife.

*"It's a very odd feeling seeing yourself staring back from the wall,"* Marie thought.

As the soup starter was served, Rosa, who was seated opposite Marie next to HP, asked, 'I gather your family is as old and as mad as ours, so Charles tells us?'

Marie looked around the room and gave a nervous laugh.

'Yes … I suppose so. From what I can gather, my family were French aristocracy, before they were all kicked out following the revolution. At the time of the Marchioness there.' pointing up at herself on the wall, 'her father was a wealthy land owner in the Loire valley, famous for his wines and champagne. He was Louis Bernard de Ville, the Duc de Touraine, and was a close advisor to King Louis XIII and Queen Anne. At the time Marie was born and raised in France, she studied English amongst her music and Latin lessons, but following the death of the king and the accession of the Dauphin King Louis XIV at the age of 10, he wanted his daughter to be safe, so arranged a marriage with your ancestor the 1st Marquess.'

'You know your subject Marie. I am impressed,' said HP with a smile on his face. 'But you know what happened to him, don't you?'

'Who are you referring to HP?'

'That braggard Henry Fortescue Bankes. He died five years after he married Marie Celestine, found dead in his room from consumption or alcohol abuse, choked on his own vomit.'

'What happened to Marie after that?' asked Rosa.

'As a widow, she became free to marry her sweetheart Lord Charles Dashwood, my great, great grandfather,' answered Charles with a twinkle in his eye, winking at Marie at the same time.

'So, we are all related then?' Arthur asked.

'Not quite. Marie Celestine did not have any children with Henry Fortescue, so there is no family ancestry there. We believe that there must be a distant relationship through the Dashwood line, eh Charles?' HP explained.

'Well, yes … it's a very distant possibility but we don't actually know if she and Charles Dashwood did marry in 1653. There are no records of this and in fact we know that Charles Dashwood was married to Elizabeth Failsworth in 1654, nine months after Marie's death.' Charles added, 'you know, it is very weird talking about this with both of us sat here.'

The main course of lamb and all the trimmings was served by the waitresses, and HP poured out wine to go with it. He raised his glass.

'Welcome all to Flintwell Hall. Here's to our successful venture."

Just then the tall double doors to the dining room crashed open and in staggered a very inebriated Marquess. He had spilled most of his red wine or port down the front of his tartan waistcoat, his dirty pale blue shirt sticking out of his trousers, his huge belly held in by a wide brown leather belt and his collar undone so that his treble chin could allow him to breath. His teeth were yellow and uneven and his face was bright red.

'What the hell is going on in here?' he shouted in a drunken fury. 'Who gave you permission to eat in my hall, at my table without my invitation … eh … eh?' as he said this spittle flew from his mouth, he staggered from one chair back to another until he was facing everyone down the table.

A maid pulled out a chair for His Lordship to sit on, and helped him onto it. He sat heavily and the sound of the chair groaning under his colossal weight could be heard by all.

The dining room fell silent.

HP stood and walked to the door and shouted for help. In came an older man in plus fours shooting dress along with a younger boy.

'Yes HP, what can I do for you?'

'Can you remove His Lordship and take him to his room. He is out of his mind and disturbing our guests. Thank you, Thomas and Abel.'

'Yes HP.' He walked up to His Lordship and without asking put his arm around his waist, his Lordship's arm around his shoulder and between them both the hauled him onto his feet.

'Come along Your Lordship. Let's get you to bed.'

The Marquess tried to fight them off at first, then stopped and stared at Marie. He stretched his free arm and pointed at her.

'She has risen from the dead. She is the witch who killed my ancestors, the French whore. What is she doing here, and who invited her here? Get her out of my house now.' He shouted in a incoherent bellowing deep voice, as if possessed.

As he was dragged away, Marie could smell his body odour, a mixture of sweat, stale urine and alcohol. It was the same smell as she had had in her dreams.

She shuddered.

Rosa, Arthur and HP saw her reaction. She sat very still and tears slipped from the corners of her eyes.

Rosa came and took the chair next to her and placed her arm around her.

'Please ignore our father. He is always in a state of drunkenness these days. And please accept our apologies for his behaviour. He really doesn't know what he is saying or doing.'

'He should be locked up in an institution for the insane, HP. Told you this before. He will ruin our plans for the redevelopment of the Hall.' Arthur had no love for his father.

He turned to Marie. 'My sister is right. Please don't take anything he said to heart. He is a very cruel man and we have had to put up with him all our lives. He is a huge burden on the family. We can't wait for HP to take over the title, but we are stuck until the bastard is dead,' Arthur said this with hate in his voice.

'Please calm down Arthur. We all know how you feel about Pops. We just have to wait until he gives up the will to live, sadly.' HP was very sad.

'Has everyone lost their appetites?' asked Rosa.

'No, I am famished so let's eat.' Charles announced, trying to change the subject.

The rest of the evening passed relatively quietly as the Bankes family elaborated on their long history, and the plans to convert the Hall to a hotel. All three had very fixed ideas on what they would be offering their clients in terms of luxury, food and entertainment. They were investing quite a lot of the family's cash into this, and explained that they had already moved out of the Hall, except their father, who still lived in the far wing of the house. They planned to rehouse him in what was the land agent's house, the Manor House, which stood the other side of the woods. But it was obvious they all hoped His Lordship would not last too much longer.

After dinner, HP took Marie into the Orangery and offered her a glass of champagne from the bar in there. Rosa and Charles followed.

'I do apologise once again for my father's outburst. You see, he is riddled with cancer and his drinking, together with a small quantity of opium, dulls the pain. But he is uncontrollable and one day we fear he may fall down the stairs or worse.' HP was very sincere.

'That is totally understandable. No need to apologise HP.' She turned and looked at the Orangery.

'Just as I dreamt about it,' she said aloud.

'Sorry ... did I hear right? Have you dreamt about this?' he opened his arms and turned around the orangery.

Marie blushed, she had not meant to vocalise her thoughts. 'Yes, when I read about the Hall in the brief I wondered what it looked like. It's marvellous, isn't it?'

'Back in the 17th century, they apparently held indiscreet parties in here, when the 1st Marquess was in London. Your namesake and a lady called Lisa Dashwood, probably a relative of Charles' here, had men and women over for riotous alcohol-fuelled scandalous parties. Apparently, Marie deVille was quite a highly sexed woman at 25 years of age, and encouraged illicid liasons. But she herself only had eyes for the dashing Lord Dashwood.' HP's knowledge of his ancestors and the Hall's history was complete.

'I have an idea to hold a masked ball as part of the opening celebration. We invite high value celebrities, we can cash in on a magnificent party here on opening day, inviting them all to stay. Plus of course the journalists from all the best monthlies and high-end travel magazines. We want this in as many celeb magazines as we can get. Some will want to negotiate exclusivity, but we want it broad and international, if we are to attract the rich and famous here.'

'I see you have it all worked out already. Charles said you were the best.' HP raised his glass and chinked hers as he smiled at her. 'Tomorrow then you are going to look at all of Arthur's domain; the stables, golf, archery, pool SPA, etc.'

'That's the plan.'

Marie saw the man dressed in plus fours enter the Orangery from the East door. HP excused himself and walked down to meet him. They had a quick conversation that ended with HP patting him on the back.

'Who is that?' Marie asked, 'Is it Thomas Tilly, the Gamekeeper?'

HP looked at her astounded.

'Yes, but he is our Farm and Estate Controller. Back in 1649 there was a Thomas Tilley, who was the gamekeeper. We often pull his leg about it, but he swears he is not related. It's just pure coincidence he has the same name. His side kick is Abel Jones who is our stable groom, he also had a double who was a gardener.'

Marie bade them all goodnight and retired to her room. She lay on the bed and reflected on the evening, totally bewildered, confused and slightly frightened at all the coincidences. She slipped into her PJ's and snuggled into bed, hoping to have a good, peaceful night's sleep.

# 8
# JULY 1649

The preparations for the masked ball in a few days time progressed. The Hall had been made ready and more serving staff had been recruited from nearby villages and farms. Marie oversaw the menu for the feast, the wines from her family estate, and the arrangement of the new trees she had ordered for the Orangery. There were two lists of guests, one for His Lordship which he had approved and the actual one of all her friends. Invitations had been sent out and most replies received. There would be around 100 of the local gentry here on the night. She planned to drug her husband with the vial of sleeping draught that Charles had obtained, so he would stay comatose in his apartments all night.

The one person who watched her every move was Thomas Tilley. Fortunately, he could neither read nor write, so would not know that there were two lists. But he was a spy in the household camp, who had everyone in fear of him. He was watching her when she went out riding, whilst she greeted the farmers on her land, and when she met her friends for tea in the Orangery. She caught him up ladders seemingly repairing the windows of ladies' dressing rooms and questioned what he was doing. He always had an answer. And, most disturbing of all, her husband dismissed her complaints with a comment that she was being a silly little girl.

The Hall would be full of guests the night of the ball and it was going to be mayhem for the servants. The stable block had been temporarily expanded with wooden and canvass structures erected by the woodsmen. The cellar was full of casks of beer, brewed over the last three weeks, and there had been three cart loads of wine casks and bottles of Champagne delivered from Dover.

The huntsmen had shot deer, swans, pheasants, partridge and pigeons, and the farmers had supplied plenty of sheep, pigs and bulls for the kitchens. The whole Hall and estate were working overtime to fulfil the quantity of food Mrs Pottage requested to feed every guest. Downstairs in the kitchens it was hot and sweaty, the air filled with swarms of flies and other insects as they attacked the raw meats and other food materials left out in the open. The workforce in the kitchens got used to the smell of rotting flesh mixed with spices and food cooking in the ovens. The brick and tile-lined floors covered in straw were filthy as a team of people set about their individual tasks of making elements of the gastronomic delights to be served later.

Marie asked if her best friend Lisa would stay with her as she feared her husband's moods. He did not like the idea of the Dashwoods coming to the masked ball. She understood that Thomas Tilley had been filling his head with talk of her 'friendship' with the Honourable Charles Dashwood, and he was incensed.

The day of the masked ball arrived and the whole Hall was buzzing with excitement. They had never had such a party before and the anticipation of the arrival of the guests made everyone dizzy. All throughout the day, horse and carriages arrived at the Hall as guests made themselves at home in every room as well as the bedrooms they were appointed to. Some of the aristocracy were very demanding of food and wine.

His Lordship refused to come and greet his guests as he did not want his house filled with people he didn't know or like. He stayed in his chambers drinking porter. It was left to Marie and Lisa to greet everyone as they arrived and send them to their rooms with several footmen who carried their heavy bags and travelling chests.

She bathed that afternoon in flower-scented water and started her preparations to get into her costume. She was going as a vestal virgin as His Lordship had requested and she did not dare object for fear of his public humiliation of her.

At six that evening she went to his chambers with the vial of sleeping draught hidden inside her skirts. His personal valet opened the door for her and as she entered the room she had to suppress a gag as the putrid smell of decay hit her nostrils. The room was stale and airless as if the windows had not been opened all summer. This was her worst experience as he seemed to be oblivious and his valet, butler and footmen carried out their duties without complaint. He was very drunk and dressed as the devil with red paint all over his face. He sat in his reinforced chair and stared at her.

'Come here you French tart,' he demanded.

She stood her ground.

'Damn you whore, I said come here. Do as your husband commands.' He was shouting this at her, his face mask of the devil making him more evil.

'Is my husband joining me in greeting our guests at the masked ball? I have dressed as your Lordship requested.' She stood her ground.

'I will not be commanded by my French whore of a wife … you hear me …eh? …eh?'

'You requested the masked ball my Lord, so it only seems right that we greet our guests to open the ball, and then you can retire if you so desire,' she said in a monotone voice. The servants stood very still, knowing what was to come.

His eyes bulged out of his face, foaming spittle ran down the corners of his mouth, his face a beetroot colour. He stood unsteadily on his feet and took a few steps towards her, panting and trying to catch his breath, his huge belly overhanging his doublet. He was unable to speak he was so enraged and began pointing at her with his shaking left hand. His righthand gripped his walking stick as he continued to stagger towards her. His valet and first footman followed behind him, two others carrying his chair in case he fell. She turned and opened the double doors to his bedchamber and walked slowly down the long corridor that led from his quarters to the main staircase. He followed shouting after her.

'French whore … ungrateful witch … you will be sorry.'

At the top of the marble staircase, she looked down at all the guests, gathered in the grand hall to greet their host and hostess. The spectacle was magnificent as everyone looked dazzling in their masks and fine clothing. As the Marquess appeared next to his wife, she signalled to Mr Howell who rang a bell to silence the tittering voices of the congregated guests. Silence fell in the hall.

'My lords, ladies and dear guests, may I present to you His Lordship, Henry Fortescue Bankes, the Marquess of Flintwell.'

From below the sound of gloved clapping and the odd 'Hurrah' continued for some time. Henry Bankes composed himself and said in a low voice, 'you are in serious trouble whore.'

'My Lord, would say a few words,' she said out loud to the audience.

He cleared his throat, put his hand out to a footman for his glass of porter, took a huge gulp of wine, and with red liquid dribbling down his chin he opened his arms to everyone and gave a false laugh.

'Welcome one and all to Flintwell Hall's first and last masked ball. I hope you all die of consumption, poisoning or Mrs Pottage's cooking.' With that he lost his balance and was caught by his footmen in his chair.

Below the guests were unsure as to how to receive this greeting and there was a hubbub of rapid whispers.

'Dear friends,' Marie raised her voice, 'my husband has been unwell and is not of his mind. It was good and brave of him to come personally to see you. Please enjoy your time here and partake in good food, wine from my father's estates and beer from our own brewhouse. Howell and the servants will show you through to the long gallery and the Orangery. Music please, Howell and I will join you shortly.'

They all clapped and started to push their way into the long gallery for food and drink. Marie heard the musicians start to play and turned around to face her husband.

'Take him back to his chamber and see to it that he does not leave. He is unwell and this medicine will sooth his ailments. Please make sure he drinks it all in his wine.'

'Yes, my Lady.'

And with that the fat, semi-unconscious, inebriated Marquess was carried by five footmen back to his rooms. His valet took the draught and promised to give it to him. Anything for a peaceful night.


In amongst the crowded hall was a tall gentleman in odd clothes behind a mask of feathers and antlers. His odour was unpleasant and he did not act like a gentleman. Lord Wentworth approached him and asked who he was.

'Sebastian Holliday, your Lordship, at your service,' and he bowed.

'What household do you belong to? I have not heard of the Hollidays around these parts.'

'No, your Grace, I am up from London. In the House with His Lordship the Marquess, here by his invitation.' He bowed again and turned to leave.

Just at that time Charles Dashwood approached him.

'Your Lordship, it was good of you and your family to come this evening, although we won't be seeing much of the Marquess.'

'Indeed, young Charles, my son is here somewhere, so

you had better keep an eye on your sister,' he laughed.

'They would make a good match and father would approve, your Grace.'

'Charles ... what do you know about the Hollidays?'

'Never heard of them your Grace. Why do you ask?'

'That gentleman in the white feathers and antler mask is no gentleman by his odour. Nor is he a member of Parliament as he just tried to make out. I think we have an imposter in our midst ... implied he works for the Marquess.'

'I will make enquiries my Lord. I will need to find your son to help me. By your leave, My Lord,' he bowed and retreated to find Henry Wentworth.

The night progressed as all the guests feasted on the mounds of finger food laid out in the dining hall and had their fill of ale, wine and champagne. Dancing was held in the main ballroom; the long gallery was full of people talking and the Orangery was alive with whispered titters and girlish screeches as couples took advantage of the discreet corners of the room. The party flowed outside into the garden as it was a very pleasant and warm evening. A fireworks display was planned for 10 pm and the servants were warned that the function would go on long into the night.

Charles found Henry with Lisa and explained the predicament. They agreed to look for this character and observe him from a distance.

Marie dutifully spent some time with each guest, talking about the estate, the Marquess' health and her family. The main topic of conversation was the future of the Commonwealth under Cromwell and government by the Long Parliament. In January, King Charles the 1st had been beheaded outside the Palace of Whitehall. Would the country survive without a royal family? Charles, Prince of Wales, had declared himself King Charles II of England, Scotland and Ireland, but would he be recognised as our King in London?

She did not care for politics, nor was interested in the Royal family, as she had concerns over the safety of her own family in France. Her discussions were always superficial and she moved on to another couple when talk turned to politics.

Charles watched her work her guests. She was bright, happy and in his eyes beautiful and he was so much in love with her. But her marriage to the old buffoon was the biggest obstacle he must cross. Get rid of the Marquess and she would be his to wed.

He saw the imposter and followed him at a distance, signalling to Henry Wentworth. The man was helping himself liberally to food and wine but held no conversations with other guests. Charles realised that he was stalking the Marchioness and became alarmed.

As Marie entered the Orangery, she was grabbed by strong hands and pulled into a vacated alcove, hidden by large fern trees. At first, she thought it was Charles, but then the odour hit her nostrils as she turned around to see a stranger in a most awfully made mask. He stank of stale body odour and wine.

'His Lordship said I could take you, so bend over my lady as I wish to have my fill, French whore.'

With that he grabbed her shoulders, spun her around, pushing her onto the marble seat and tried to raise her skirts, just as a someone in a cloak pulled him backwards.

Marie cried out in shock … just as her attacker was man handled off his feet …

# 9

# FRIDAY

# JULY 2017

4.30am.

Marie cried out and sat up in bed. Soaked in sweat again, she tried to focus on where she was.

This time she was shaking with fear.

That recurring nightmare.

The four-poster bed was huge with its heavy drapes. The room was in darkness and the heavy floor to ceiling curtains covered most of the window. There was an open edge that let in a little light as the night-time turned into dawn breaking at 4.30am.

She remembered where she was. Flintwell Hall.

She remembered the meal and conversations last night. It had been fascinating hearing about the Bankes family history, intertwined with her own.

She reached for her glass of water and took several sips.

Thomas Tilley was the masked man who attempted to rape her in the Orangery. Did he succeed? Who was the shadow who appeared just before she woke up?

God, it was going to be a very long day if she didn't get back to sleep.

She went to freshen up in the bathroom and splashed water over her face.

Looking in the mirror she wondered what the meaning of these dreams was. Was it a total coincidence that every night she went back to the same period?

What would a shrink make of this?

Was there a message being delivered to her?

Why is this about her and her ancestors and why here?

She became angry at herself for her lack of willpower. Should she take a sleeping pill to knock her out? But then, she had arranged to meet Charles for breakfast at 8.30 am – five hours' time.

"*Go back to bed young lady and sleep ... please*" she said to herself in the mirror.

Turning the bathroom lights out she went to the window and looked at the beautiful sight of the dawning light across the parkland that stretched out before her. She grabbed the curtains and pulled hard to block out the remaining light and crawled back up onto her huge bed and snuggled down.

She soon drifted off ...

# 10
# JULY 1649

… it was Charles who grabbed the man and pulled his mask off. Henry joined to restrain him.

'Thomas Tilley. What do you think you are doing?'

They manhandled him out of the west door of the conservatory and out into the grounds.

Lisa took Marie into her arms and held her tightly, then led her away into her private chamber. None of the guests noticed as they were either too intoxicated or they thought it was one of the fools acting.

Sometime later Charles and Henry knocked at her door and Lisa let them in. Charles came straight in and kneeled down in front of her, taking her hand as she sat on her chair.

'He is dealt with. You no longer have worries from those quarters.'

'What have you done Charles?' she said with tears in her eyes.

'No need to trouble yourself over him. He will never harm you again. And, my Frenchie, we must never speak of this again to anyone. Are we all agreed?' He looked at Lisa and Henry who both nodded.

With that he took her into his arms. Lisa and Henry made a silent exit, leaving them alone.

The next morning, Marie woke with warmth in her heart. She had her lover beside her sleeping soundly. He was utterly gorgeous in her eyes. She was for once a very happy Marchioness.

The guests who stayed at the Hall were gathering in the dining room for breakfast, all looking very jaded. The servants also looked worn out. Breakfast of cold meats, cheese and Manchette bread was laid out on a long table, with small beer and cow's milk to drink.

His Lordship was indisposed in his bed chamber, still asleep from the draught given to him by his valet and his personal staff were grateful for the peace.

That morning several activities were planned to entertain the guests. There was a hunt for those with horses, archery and crossbows on the main lawn for the ladies and, of course, bowls.

There was a small commotion in the servants' quarters as one of the stable lads ran into the Hall to see the estate steward Randolph Blake. He in turn spoke to James Howell requesting an audience with His Lordship on a very urgent matter.

Marie asked what was going on.

'My Lady, we need an urgent audience with His Lordship. I am afraid to say that Thomas Tilley has been found drowned in the beer vat. He must have fallen in last night.'

Marie put her hand to her mouth to express surprise.

'His Lordship is still asleep Mr Blake, so can you leave the news with me. What were Mr Tilley's duties today?'

'He needed to organise the hounds and horses for the hunt this morning, your Ladyship.'

'Is Abel Jones capable of these duties in Mr Tilley's absence if you supervise him?'

'Yes, My Lady. I will see to it.'

'Mr Howell, could John Bedlan organise the ladies' activities on the front lawn?'

'Yes, My Lady.' He doffed his forehead and went to speak with Bedlan.

Marie sat in her chair musing over last night. It must have been Charles and Henry who disposed of that horrible man. Well good riddance!

Charles entered her room.

'You have of course heard the news, or know of it, Charles?' she asked with a wry smile on her face.

'What news my Frenchie?' he asked, as he knelt in front of her. They were alone and unlikely to be disturbed unless someone knocked on the door. He kissed her hand and looked up into her sparkling eyes, his were full of love and adoration.

'You tease me my Lord. You had a hand in it, I take it? You and Henry … last night?'

'I am at a complete loss as to what you are referring to, my love!' he said with mischief in his eyes.

She laughed and kissed him on the forehead, 'well, thank you anyway. It gets rid of a horrible man and a known retainer of the Marquess.' She was happy.

A knock on the door. Charles stood up and to one side of Marie.

'Entrée,' she said.

There was a rush of people headed by Lisa Dashwood and Henry, plus Mrs Cribb and some close friends of the Marquess, all chattering at the same time.

'Oh Marie, the Marquess is asking for you. There has been a terrible accident. It appears that Mr Tilley the Gamekeeper had one too many dips of his ale pot into the beer vat and has fallen in and drowned.' Lisa said in a rush, then winked at Marie when no one was looking.

'Yes, Mr Blake and Mr Howell have informed me. An unfortunate accident. I take it his body has been removed and the brew disposed of and a new brew ordered immediately.'

Everyone was surprised at her cold efficiency. They

all knew there was no respect by either party and Thomas Tilley's demise would not be mourned by the Marchioness.

'My Lady, His Lordship is demanding you attend him now,' Mrs Cribb said.

'Yes, yes … I will go to him now. What mood is he in?'

'No different Ma'am. He wants to know who was responsible for Mr Tilley's demise.'

'Who was responsible?' she repeated in an incredulous voice, 'well the stupid fool himself was responsible. Serves him right helping himself to His Lordship's brew.'

She stood and walked towards her husband's stinking rooms for her castigation. It would of course be all her fault.

'Would you like me to accompany you My Lady?' asked Henry Wentworth.

'That's kind of you. Mrs Cribb, have you a pomander for Lord Wentworth to use as the stench in my husband's quarters is vile,' she said openly for all to hear.


Mrs Cribb, James Howell, Lord Henry Wentworth and Marie all walked solemnly towards the Marquess' quarters. His valet opened the doors to them, and they stood still for a while acclimatising to the putrid air of the room.

'Ah … there you are! What took you so long? I

requested your company some time ago,' he said in a sober voice.

'My apologies my husband. I have been organising the servants and the activities for our guests this morning in the absence of Mr Tilley. Mr Blake and Able Jones are running the hunt and I have asked John Bedlan to organise the ladies' activities on the front lawns. I hope that meets with Your Lordship's approval.' Her voice was loud and even.

'No remorse from you then my wife?' he asked in a menacing voice, staring at her.

'It is regrettable but the stupid fool's greed in stealing your Lordship's brew, causing him to fall in, is nothing to be remorseful for. He has cost us a full vat of beer, which I have instructed be poured away and remade.' She stood her ground.

Henry Bankes stood still and looked around at everyone. His eyes stopped at Henry Wentworth. He knew she had not come alone so he would not be able to blame her.

'Wentworth, what say you about this … eh?'

'My Lord, it is very regrettable that you should lose such a talented Gamekeeper, but The Honourable Charles Dashwood and I caught him impersonating a gentleman with the false name of Sebastian Holliday, posing as a Member of the House, and wearing a mask made of feathers and antlers. He presumably had no instructions from your Lordship to act in this way, and simply became intoxicated.'

'The stupid fool. See to it he has a decent burial and find another Gamekeeper. Now away with you all.' He waved them away as he turned to his pewter jug of porter for his first drink of the day.

'Will your Lordship be joining his house guests on the front lawn for games, Sire?' Marie asked directly in a loud voice so all could hear.

'I am afraid I am too busy today, so you will have to attend on my behalf.' And he turned his back on his wife.

She felt relief and the group walked back to the central part of the Hall to mingle with the house guests. As she walked back she took Henry's hand.

'Thank you, Lord Wentworth, for your support. I am in your debt.'

'It was my pleasure to see the old scoundrel put in his place. You did well to stand up to him. My god he looks unwell.'

'At least he was sober this morning.'

Charles was waiting for their return. He smiled at her and it made her heart jump. God how she wished she was free to be with this man. She was not an ungrateful or spiteful woman, but her marriage to this tyrant was not of her making and she wished that the sooner he drowned himself in his wine the better. At least that horrible spy Tilley was gone and her husband had no other eyes and ears in the Hall. Last night's liaison with Charles was wonderful. She never knew that making love could be so gentle, sensuous and romantic. She had never experienced those tumultuous tremors and the rush of blood to her head as they both climaxed in ecstasy. Oh, to be living with this man to experience that as often as they wanted. She sighed.

There was a bell ringing, a strange buzzing sound like a giant bee, and a vibration she had never experienced before .

# 11

## FRIDAY TO SATURDAY
## JULY 2017

8am.

Her mobile phone alarm buzzed and vibrated on the bedside table. She slowly came out of her deep sleep.

She sat up in bed.

God, she was exhausted.

She looked to her left to wake up Charles, but he was not there. Then she remembered the dreams.

She felt wet … and sensual! But she realised that she hadn't made love that night. It was her dream!

She dragged herself out of bed and walked into her bathroom and turned on a cold shower to wake herself up. She washed her hair and stood under the vertical downpour of water from the huge shower-head.

As she descended the main staircase, the aromas of a cooked breakfast, fresh coffee and toast emanated from the dining room. Charles, HP and Rosa were already eating, and Marie went to the serving table to look at what was on offer.

'Good morning everyone,' she greeted them with a smile.

'Hope you slept well and didn't meet any of our ghostly ancestors,' HP joked.

'Yes, slept very well. The bed was so comfortable and cosy.'

'Lots to do today, Marie. We need to show you the grounds and start to pull together some of your ideas for the launch and the marketing.' Charles was as ever on the ball.

'That would be good. I would like to get back to London tonight to use the programmes we have in the office tomorrow morning, then come back up tomorrow evening, if that's OK?

'Whatever you need. I was thinking of inviting Lisa, my sister up for the weekend, HP if that's okay with you? She is a medic but she has an eye for this sort of thing and I would value her opinion.'

Marie stared at Charles in surprise at his suggestion. Why? Did Lisa know? It would be great fun to have her bestie here for the weekend and to be present at the big reveal.

Arthur walked into the dining room, picked up a plate and started loading it with cooked food.

'Morning everyone,' he said cheerfully.

'Going to show you around my domain this morning Marie. You are in for a treat!' he said smiling as he took a seat next to her.

'Yes, looking forward to it. Where are we starting from?'

With a mouthful, he said, 'Mmm … this is yummy. I love Mrs Pottage's breakfasts. I thought we could look at the golf course, the archery field and that pool Spa. I gather that Charles' sister Lisa is coming up this weekend?'

'Yes, that's right.'

'Good, well we will leave the stables to Saturday then and both of you can go for a hack, unless you would like a guided tour on horseback.'

'Why not, that would be brilliant Arthur, but I need to get back to London tonight. I think a riding tour of the estate would be perfect today, and it's forecast to be a sunny day, too!'

HP sat silently listening.

'When do you plan to present your ideas for marketing and the launch Marie?' he asked.

'On Sunday afternoon, if that's okay. Will His Lordship be present at the meeting?'

He gave a half laugh. 'Now that is an unknown quantity. If he is sober enough, he may join in, but heaven help us if he does because I can tell you right now, that he won't like anything.'

Marie secretly hoped that the Marquess didn't attend.

'Marie, why don't you go with Arthur on the visit? I

have some building work details and finances to go through with HP and Rosa, so will see you for lunch. What time will you be heading back to town?'

'I thought about threeish. Can someone drop me off at Newark North Gate station?'

She called Lisa, then Clare to tell them she would be working late at the office but would meet them in their local pub at 8pm for a catch up.

The tour of the recreational facilities impressed Marie. Every aspect had been well thought out and the support teams, equipment and quality of each event was very professional. They had built facilities to cover a 9-hole golf course that could be played as 18 holes, four tennis courts, a croquet lawn that also had traditional bowls; and the archery was held on the main rear lawns next to the pool and SPA facilities. The stable block and tack rooms were further away from the Hall near the garages and old servant quarters, and there were eight stables each housing fine-looking horses.

Arthur was so enthusiastic about every aspect, he knew his subject well and could play golf, shoot clays and wield a bow and crossbow like a professional. Marie had an hilarious time trying to hit her targets with bow and arrow, but she preferred the crossbows. Arthur was a very good and patient instructor.

Marie made plenty of notes and took pictures on her work's camera to include in the presentation.

She found Arthur to be a very open and friendly person, totally different from his brother and sister in both character and outlook. Marie warmed towards him during the three hours they spent together.

He dropped her off at the railway station.

'We will see you tomorrow then Marie. Just text my mobile when you get to Grantham and I will come and collect you. Doesn't matter what the time is.'

'Arthur, thank you so much for spending this morning with me. I had such fun and your facilities are to die for. You have done a brilliant job and I am sure they will be very well received by the paying guests.' She leaned over and kissed his cheek, it made him blush.

'See you later,' he said.


She watched him drive off in his soft-top Porsche 911 before she went over the bridge to the southbound platform.

On the train she worked on her laptop, pulling the main story together ready to upload into their systems at her office that she would produce the glossy brochures and Powerpoint presentation for Sunday. She went straight to her offices in the city and worked until 7.30pm.

Shattered she made her way to the local pub to meet

her housemates and have something to eat. She did not want to drink too much as she still had work to do on the final marketing plans and she had to run through them with Randolph and James before setting off back to Flintwell Hall. She could not have a hangover!

Lisa was excited about going to Lincolnshire with Marie the next day and Clare was insanely jealous, complaining that she didn't get an invite. They wanted to know what HP and Arthur were like and if they were single.

'Come on, Marie, you can get us an invite to the opening launch party, can't you?' Clare pushed.

That night Marie hoped to have a good clear night's sleep. She dreaded closing her eyes again, but was so shattered after all the activity and work she had done that she drifted quickly into a deep sleep.

♦♦♦

Both Lisa and Clare were already in their tiny kitchenette having breakfast, the smell of toast, grilling bacon and fresh coffee assailed her nostrils as she walked in, hair still wet and just in her PJ's.

'OMG, Marie, you look like you've had a night with Brad Pitt. You look very happy,' said Lisa.

'Ha-ha …more like satisfied … so what time did he slip out of the house?' asked Clare.

'Umm … what? … no … I mean I didn't have anyone to stay last night,' a bemused Marie answered sheepishly.

'Well, you could've fooled me, babes,' snorted Lisa with a cackle. 'The noises coming from your room at 3am woke me up. God, it must have been some fantastic dream you were having.'

'What do you mean?' she asked innocently.

'That sounded like one hell of an orgasm you had last night, missy … so you can't fool me!' Lisa teased.

'Any spare bacon going, I'm famished?' Marie asked.

'See, that's a real sign you have been having very naughty dreams again … my brother I take it?'

She blushed.

'Oh, Lisa please. It was the same dream again. You know the one in 17$^{th}$ century … only …' she hesitated.

'Only what?' both Lisa and Clare stared at her.

'Well you are not going to believe this!'

'Go on …'

'You know this assignment I have with Charles in Lincolnshire … the one where we are relaunching an old family hall as a boutique hotel?' She paused, both the girls hung on her next words.

'It turns out it's the same Hall as in my dreams, with the same people, names and everything, except it's in the here and now. I can't believe it. It's really scary.'

'You are kidding, babes?' Lisa stated with a mouthful of bacon sandwich.

'Have you told Charles of your dreams?' Clare asked.

'No, I haven't said anything. And the scariest thing of all is that my portrait is hanging in the Long Gallery, painted in 1648 by some guy called Peter Leley. She is my great, great, great aunt I suppose. Marie deVille Bankes, Marchioness of Flintwell. And it's bloody me to a tee!'

'You are shitting me! Has Charles seen it?' Lisa asked.

'Oh yes. He was astounded, as were the Bankes family and all the staff there. It's very, very, weird. But why these dreams, that's what I can't understand?' She was clearly distraught about the whole thing.

'So, what you are telling us is that those very vivid dreams you've been having are all about this Lincolnshire Hall and family in the 17th -century?' stated Clare.

'Yes. It's totally unbelievable. The whole family and staff up there are those in my dreams. I am getting really freaked out about it, so much so, that I dread going to sleep at night.' Marie looked scared.

'You need professional help, my love.'

'I know, I haven't got time to see anyone. I have a deadline to produce the marketing and launch ideas by Sunday, so, I am going into the office this morning to collect the final presentation. Lisa, I'll meet you at Kings Cross at 3pm?'

'See you later hon. I plan to have a good time this weekend!' Lisa answered as Marie grabbed her keys and bags and went to leave the house.

Her office was buzzing, not normal for a Saturday. It seemed to be in chaos as everyone had an element of the marketing plans and launch for Flintwell Hall. Randolph and James told everyone to drop what they were doing and concentrate on completing the presentation package based on Marie's brief. Graphic designers were pulling images and creative ideas into visual formats; copy-writers were putting the words together and James oversaw the finished article. The printers were on standby to produce brochures for the presentation, and Randolph was completing the financial package.

Marie walked into the partners' office.

'Good morning.' She was bright and motivated.

'Hi Marie. Your brief was excellent; give us an hour and we should be able to have a run through. It's going to be costly, based on what you have proposed, but I take it these guys have money?' Randolph was as ever on the money. 'Do you need James or I there on Sunday? One of us would like to meet your clients.'

'Yes, of course Randolph. The presentation will be at

3pm, followed by a working high tea to cover any questions they don't raise in the meeting.'

James walked into the office.

'Hi superstar. What time are you leaving today?'

'Hoping to catch the 3pm from KC.'

'Right, will have the package ready for then. I love your idea for a masked ball in the Long Gallery and Orangery. Can't wait to see the Hall. Randy told you about Sunday? You don't mind?'

'James, you both own this agency, I don't ... so of course you should be there. Besides you can answer the hard questions ... you know ... money!'

James laughed and patted her on the back.

They went through the invitation list for the masked ball to discuss the benefits of each guest. There were a handful of local politicians, members of the judiciary, the Chief Constable of Lincolnshire, and all the aristocracy and wealthy who lived within fifty miles of the Hall. These were deemed as travelling guests, then there was the elite list of guests who would be invited to stay the night in the rooms. These were their target audience as well as local families. Some of the celebs on the list made Marie's eyes widen.

'Can you really get them to come?' she asked James.

'Of course, my dear. You don't go to Eton and Oxford

without picking up a few contacts. Besides, they will come if it's free,' he said in an ironic voice head on one side to illustrate a point.

She met Lisa at Kings Cross and they boarded their train in First Class.

'Well, kiddo, what are we going to get up to this weekend?' Lisa asked as they sipped their first G&T of the day.

'I want to go riding tomorrow morning and get a feel for the place. There is a huge lake I want to see, and also I need to check out the local hacks. Then the pool and SPA is on the list to confirm everything I am saying on Sunday at the presentation.'

'Any dishy guys there?' her grin said it all!

'I am working, Lisa Dashwood, so I am not going to be flirting with anyone; besides your brother's idea is that you are there purely as a distraction. So, look glam and lap up the opulence.'

'Oh, come on? What's the Marquess like?'

'Old, fat, smelly and drunk most of the time!'

'I meant his successor, the future 10$^{th}$ Marquess, and he has a brother as well, both single I presume?'

'Lord Henry Percival and Arthur Henry are both single, and they hate their titles. So, they are just HP and Arthur. Arthur is a bit young for you Lisa,' she said sarcastically.

'So, HP is game, is he? You are after my brother, aren't you?' she had an enormous toothy grin as she said it.

Marie blushed at the mention of Charles. She had had a crush on him since she was a little girl.

'You will find the family are very nice, especially Rosa their sister. The father is horrible and is permanently drunk, so hopefully we won't see much of him. Oh, and I must warn you that there is a huge portrait hanging in the Long Gallery of my great, great, great aunt … well I think she was. Well, it looks like me.'

'Yes, you have already mentioned that.'

Marie sat in silence and shivered.

'Are you cold?'

'No … just …. this place gives me the creeps.'

'Hey honey, tell me about your dreams again and how this is a coincidence with this place we are going to?' Lisa had her serious, engaged face on, so Marie told her the whole story of what had happened up to now.

The train journey went quickly, as did the four G&T's enroute.

Arthur was there to meet them, and he took a shine to Lisa straight away. Her eyes widened when she saw the family Porsche Cayene car he arrived in, and she jumped into the front seat before being asked. Marie tutted and sat in the back.

Arthur chatted away to Lisa all the way to the Hall. Marie sat in silence in the back, half listening to their random conversation. It was clear that Arthur was besotted by Lisa. When they reached the arched stone gateway and she saw Flintwell Hall standing on top of the hill, half covered in evening sunshine, Lisa exclaimed, 'OMG this is fantastic!'

Charles appeared at the front doors to greet his sister and Marie. HP came up to say hello with Rosa. Lisa did a small curtsy to her brother's embarrassment.

'Sorry HP, my sister was dragged up … she thinks you are royalty.'

They all laughed at Lisa's embarrassment.

'Here, let me take you to your room Lisa,' said Rosa taking her hand. Lisa's eyes widened as she walked into the huge hall and up the stairs to the bedrooms. Rosa was telling her about her family's history.

Charles gave Marie a gentle kiss on her cheek as she entered the hall. HP took her hand and kissed it.

'Cocktails in the Orangery,' HP shouted up the stairs to Rosa and walked off into the back of the Hall.

Charles leaned over and whispered in Marie's ear.

'Think he rather fancies you Frenchie. I've got competition!' and he smiled at her as he took her hand and led her into the Orangery. Someone took the bags to their rooms as if by magic.

Everyone was gathering in the Orangery, when they all heard Lisa's voice.

'Fuck me, it bloody is you Marie!' and she walked into the Orangery, 'this place keeps on getting better. WOW.' she exclaimed as she did a circle on her heals looking all around.

'Oops ... sorry about the language. But have you seen that picture of you in that long room?' she was pointing backwards.

Everyone laughed at her naivety.

HP handed her a cocktail.

'Manhattan. Hope you like it. Cheers and welcome to my humble home.'

They toasted Lisa's arrival.


Mrs Pottage came into the Orangery.

'Dinner is served, My Lord,' she said to HP.

'Very well Mrs Pottage ... shall we?' he led the way into the dining room.

As they passed the portrait, Arthur said to Lisa.

'It's a very uncanny likeness to Marie. Scary really!'


The evening passed in a lighthearted banter where the Bankes' delighted in telling Lisa some bawdy tales of their ancestors including the 1st Marquess of Flintwell and his fourth wife. Although she had heard most of this from Marie, she was still intrigued with the embellished version. They spoke briefly of their father as well with a word of warning should he appear.

The food and alcohol flowed. Marie and Lisa climbed the stairs to their room, gone midnight.

'See you at eight sharp. Breakfast before the ride?'

In her room, Marie filled the bath with hot water and a perfumed foam gel, then poured herself some chilled water, sliding in to relax before bed. She hoped that she would sleep soundly tonight without any nightmares. The hot scented water penetrated every joint and eased all her muscles. Closing her eyes, she allowed herself to drift into a state of calmness, clearing her mind.

Naked and barely dry, she climbed up onto the high bed in the vain hope that she would drift into a clear soundless sleep. She switched off the dim bedside lamp, closed her eyes and saw stars twinkling inside her eyelids. She tried to clear her mind and slowly sank into a comfortable state of peace.

*'... he took her hand and gently pulled her into a secluded corner of the Orangery, hidden by a large fern and some overgrown bushes planted in huge earthen- ware pots. Behind the foliage was a cool smooth seat carved out*

*of the marble, where two people could sit in total privacy, unseen by any passerby. She wore a lowcut light summer frock with a single underskirt, her arms and hands bare. His hand gently covered the back of her long neck as he pulled her towards him, his moist lips just brushing hers.*

*He smelt of a heavy man's musk, not unpleasant, and his lips tasted of sweet wine. His tongue caressed her lips and explored inside her mouth searching for hers. She gasped with the pleasure of this unexpected experience, her breath coming in short bursts as she felt other intimate areas of her body reacting to his strength. His other arm held her gently around her lower back. He pulled her to her feet and his arm circled around her waist as he pulled her tightly into his body. She could feel his hardness pressing out of his breeches, wanting to escape. She wanted more. She wanted him. She hoped he would explore her further with his hand. She felt a wetness ... a glorious pulsating ache between her legs ....*

*Suddenly, making them jump, the big fern was pulled aside and her husband the Marquess stood sword in hand, swaying, eyes bulging out of his crimson face, totally inebriated, in a rage and foul smelling, he could hardly form the right words.*

*'You sire are a cad, and a blighter. Leave my French whore of a wife alone and face your death.'*

*He brandished his sword and fell over onto the marble*

*tiled floor in a drunken heap. Footmen and servants ran to his aide, but Marie stepped over him and said, 'take him to his chamber and lock the door until he is sober,' then turned and took Charles' hand and led him to her bedchamber ...'*

She sat bolt upright in bed.

Totally wet again.

Caught her breath and looked around the dark room. She was alone.

Getting out of bed, she walked to the window and pulled the heavy curtains to one side. The full moon shone out of a clear dark sky and lit up the lake at the bottom of the parkland front leading up to the Hall. She peered closely as she saw a couple of figures walking around the edge of the lake in the moonlight.

She shuddered, drank some water and climbed back into bed, laying on the other dry side of the huge king-size bed.

She was so exhausted, she closed her eyes, she drifted off into another deep sleep ...

At some point in the early hours of the morning she sensed someone was in her room, but dared not break the experience she was dreaming of. She could smell a musty, stale acrid odour ... but thought that it was in her dream.

# 12
# 1650

She woke to find herself on top of her bed fully clothed. She knew she had laid with Charles that night after being caught red-handed by her drunken husband. Now she did not care. She and Charles had sealed their union and her only thoughts were of how to free herself from her husband.

Charles would inherit his family title on the passing of his elderly father, so her position in society would be maintained, and her father should not object.

She cared not what society thought of her, she was in love with Lord Charles Dashwood, and would become his wife at some point in the future.

Her bedchamber door burst open, and her husband the Marquess stood in the doorway. He was more sober than last night but still had difficulty walking due to his immense bulk. He stank. She could smell him from that distance. That acrid odour of stale sweat, dried faeces and piss, together with rank wine. He still held his sword in his hand, using it as a walking stick.

He waddled in and approached her bedside.

'I will not abide your disloyalty to me you French whore,' he stammered, his mouth frothing and spittle ejecting with every word spoken.

He pointed the sword at her.

'I will have you hung in the village square for your unfaithful actions, if you do not give me your word that you will not see that braggard Dashwood again … eh? … eh? … what do you say French whore?' His eyes stared at her through his reddened face, his cheeks puffing hard on every intake of air.

She was not afraid.

'I take it that you too will cease your whoring in London as well, My Lord?' she said boldly.

He went into a rage, wielding his sword above his head, slashing at the four posts of the bed and the mattress.

Servants and footmen rushed into the room, thinking he had gone mad. James Howell, John Bedlan and Mrs Cribb arrived to see his Lordship in such a state.

James approached behind the Marquess and grabbed him in a bear hug, as John Bedlan relieved him of the sword.

'Are you all right My Lady,' asked Mrs Cribb.

Marie said calmly, 'yes, thank you Mrs Cribb. Master Howell … would you be so kind as to place my husband in secure irons and take him back to his bedchamber, locking the door. He is not himself and is suffering from a mild madness. Can you also call the physician to attend my husband as well?'

'Yes, my lady.' James Howell disliked the Marquess immensely, as he was a cruel man when sober and a liability when drunk, so he was pleased to take him away.

Later that morning, whilst out riding with her best friend, Lisa Dashwood, Marie took her friend into her confidence and told her about her assignation with her brother last night and the reaction from her husband this morning.

As they rode around the lake, Lisa saw a huge log, drifting in the centre of the lake.

'What's that Marie?' pointing to the floating object.

Marie looked and pretended she couldn't make it out at first, then saw bubbles escaping around the object.

She reigned her horse to a stop and stared at it. Then put her hand to her mouth to feign surprise, as she said.

'My God, it's a body. Look Lisa it's a man's body.'

'You are right, and the clothing is familiar as well. I have seen it before. Quick, we had better ride back to the Hall and summon some help.'

They galloped back to the stables and asked for Randolph Blake to investigate.

As she entered the Hall, the physician Dr Melder was just leaving. He bowed deeply in front of her.

'My Lady.'

'How is my husband?'

'He is unwell, My Lady. I have attended his humours and bled him with leeches and maggots to remove any bad bloods, but His Lordship does not help himself with the amount of alcohol he consumes. He is to be kept in a quiet state for the time being and I have asked Howell to refuse him porter.'

'Thank you Dr Melder. I will attend on my husband.'

She decided not to call upon him just yet as his mood may still be sharp after his ordeal with the physician. Instead she sought out Mrs Cribb to discuss the next month's entertainment plans.

A footman approached Mrs Cribb and whispered in her ear.

'My Lady, Lord Dashwood has arrived and is requesting an audience with you. He is in the Orangery.'

'Thank you, Mrs Cribb. I will leave you with the arrangements for Lord Harwood's visit next week.'

In the Orangery, Charles was pacing up and down in his breeches and riding boots. It was a warm day and it was obvious that he had been riding hard to get here from his house, which was a good two hours away. Marie paused at the entrance to look at him as her heart missed a beat. She looked around for any servants, but they were all elsewhere occupied

'Charles.' She rushed into his arms.

'Marie ... please we need to be a little discreet.' He was cautious and seemed nervous.

'What is it my love,' she asked, concerned that he seemed out of sorts.

He surreptitiously handed her a small glass vial containing some white powder, looking around to make sure they were not seen. She took the vial and popped it into a small pocket inside the waistband of her gown.

'This needs to be mixed into Henry Bankes evening drink. Preferably water, but it should dissolve in wine as well.'

'What is this Charles?'

'Something to make him sleep ... permanently! It should not be discovered and he will give all the indications of a seizure.'

'I will wait until the right opportunity arises before administering this to him. We walk on dangerous grounds, my love.'

'We do ... but it will be worth it. In the long run.'

There was a slight cough from the Orangery door and Randolph Blake stood waiting for Marie to finish her conversation.

'What is it Blake?' she asked.

'My Lord,' he greeted Charles doffing his brow.

'Blake, what news have you of that unfortunate soul in the lake?'

'My Lady, it was master Able Jones, the gardener. We suspect he fell into the lake last night after consuming too much beer. We caught him with a couple of barrels of the beer you ordered destroyed after Master Tilly fell in and drowned. Jones must have helped himself to some before following your orders. We understand from the servants' quarters that he was unsettled with Tilley's demise and blamed His Lordship.'

'When did this happen Blake?'

'Late last night my Lady, or in the early hours of this morning as far as we can tell,' he hesitated … struggling for the right words.

'What is it Blake?'

'We also discovered that he had forced himself on one of the kitchen maids last night. She was also found this morning … alive, but in a very bad state. It appears that she tried to resist and fought back but was beaten for her troubles. We believe she may have pushed him into the lake after he had finished with her. She is asleep, so we cannot question her yet.'

Marie was moved by this horrible outcome to the

maid servant. She instantly blamed Thomas Tilley for leading the young lad astray, but the vile man had met his comeuppance, too.

'Thank you, Blake,' she said ending the discussion.

He still hesitated, standing still. He coughed ...

'We must inform His Lordship, Ma'am, as this is the second death on the estate. The Sheriff of Lincoln should be appraised of this as well. Both were self-inflicted so there will be no detriment to the estate.'

'I will tell his Lordship later, Blake. Now he is unwell with his tumours and must not be disturbed.'

'Very well my Lady.'

He bowed to both and went back to managing the Flintwell Estates having discharged his duties to her Ladyship.


Once he had gone, they were alone again.

'Well that's a surprise. My husband will not take the news well, I fear. He will again lose his temper, no doubt taking it out on me again.'

'Why don't you use the opportunity to give him a draught to settle his temper.' Charles indicated the vial.

He took her hand and pulled her gently into the alcove of the Orangery. Behind the wall of foliage, he put his arm around her tiny waist and pulled her close to him. His lips hovered over hers, just brushing the corners of her mouth, his tongue exploring the edges of her lips. She reached up on her tiptoes and opened her mouth wanting to devour his lips. They held each other tightly for what seemed to be a long time, before he released her, stepped back, bowed and kissed her hand.

'My lady, please excuse me,' was all he said as he walked out of the Orangery door and rode away at a gallop down the long lane.

Mrs Cribb appeared around the foliage, with a tearful Mrs Pottage.

'Mrs Pottage, I have just been made aware of your ward's horrific experience at the hands of Able Jones. She to is be seen by the physician as soon as possible and given bed rest in the Hall until she is recovered. I will inform His Lordship later today. In the meantime, can you hire more help for her duties in the kitchen. Please tell her not to worry about her position here, I will visit her when she feels better.'

They both bowed, and Mrs Pottage nodded and left without saying a word.

'Ma-am, if I may indulge your time?.'

'Yes Mrs Cribb.'

She hesitated … a worried look on her face.

'I am sorry to bring this up My Lady, but there are rumours below stairs of His Lordship's illness, and there is talk that Master Tilley was pushed into the beer vat by someone outside the household. Now that Abel has also lost his life, through his own fault, there is some unrest.'

'Thomas Tilley fell into the vat of his own drunken accord and was caught impersonating a gentleman at the ball, helping himself to his Lordship's generosity. Jones was ordered to pour away the contents of the beer but instead decided to steal some for himself and in his drunken state took that poor girl against her wishes. I will not stand for any nonsense Mrs Cribb, by the servants. I will address the matter later today, once I have informed his Lordship.'

Marie was very forthright and stern with Mrs Cribb. She knew this message would be repeated in the servants' hall. But she fully intended on calling in on the servants hall when they all ate. She also knew her kindness towards the kitchen maid would reach them all as well.

Now to see her husband.

She saw his footman outside his bedchamber door. The look on his face told her his Lordship was in a foul mood again. He opened the door for her, she took a deep breath and walked calmly in as serenely as she could.

He was sat in his chair, papers in one hand and a pewter mug in the other. He looked up.

'What took you so long wench? 'he spat out as he leered at her.

'I had household matters to deal with, my husband.

Master Jones has fallen in the lake after taking a poor kitchen maid by force. That's two more servants we need to replace. Mrs Cribb is once again doing her job well.' She stood her ground ten feet away from him, arms in front of her, hands together. She was holding back the urge to gag with the stench of his room.

'I have been made aware of this already by Howell. Master Blake came to see you earlier, yet you failed to report this to me first. I find that unacceptable from my wife. Your first duty is to me above all else, you French whore.'

'If your Lordship continues to insult me using those terms, I will need to inform my father the Duc, who will no doubt cut off your supplies of wines and port. It is no wonder I do not wish to put you first, and can't you open a window and let this stench out?' She felt bold and reckless, knowing he would blow a fuse.

His face became fiery red, his small eyes seemed to bulge out in his growing rage, as his body trembled. He grabbed the arms of his chair to elevate himself out of his chair and stood up unsteadily. He pointed at her unable to form the words as red bile dribbled down the sides of his mouth. He was shaking in anger. His footman did not know what to do so stood still as he watched her Ladyship just stand and stare at her husband.

He lost his balance and fell back in his chair, caught in

time by the footman.

'I shall resume my duties, My Lord and take my leave,' Marie said firmly to a stupefied Marquess.

Before she left James Howell silently entered.

She said to him and to the footman.

'See to it that that window is opened and left open all day to change the air in this room. It cannot be good for his Lordship to wallow in such disgust. Howell, run his Lordship a bath and see to it he has a change of clothing, his stench is offensive to all of us.'

'Yes, Your Ladyship,' a confounded Howell answered. He had just been given an impossible task.

# 13

# SUNDAY

# JULY 2017

The sound of barking dogs broke the silence. A strong shaft of bright sunlight streamed through the break in the curtains, billowing in the gentle breeze from the open window.

She remembered that she was at the Hall and this afternoon would be the big presentation to the family.

Last night's dream was as real and vivid as the other nights. She was becoming aware that her dreams were somehow linked to the present, being a forewarning of what was to come.

A double murder? Did she kill young Able Jones? Surely not!!

She dismissed it and got showered and dressed for her ride with Lisa after breakfast around the grounds.

They were all in the dining room eating the wonderful breakfast spread made by the kitchens. The chef used it as a trial to show the family what would be offered to guests once they were up and running as a hotel.

HP looked up when he saw Marie enter the room and

smiled at her; there was a look of surprise in his eyes as he noticed her figure in jodhpurs and tight-fitting T-shirt. Charles noticed HP staring at her and wondered again if he had competition. Then, Rosa placed herself next to Charles and was trying to engage him in conversation.

Lisa was also at the table dressed in jeans and a bright yellow Polo shirt.

'Good morning everyone,' she breezed in.

'Good morning Marie. Trust you slept well?' HP pulled the chair next to him indicating her to sit next to him. She helped herself to some food and sat down.

'HP, do you have any records in the Hall of a body being found in your lake in 1650? Was it one of the gardeners called Able Jones?' Marie couldn't resist asking.

'That's a very strange question, Marie? Why do you ask?'

'Oh, just some research into my ancestors. I am fascinated by the family connections, that's all.' She didn't want to give away that she had been having the dreams ... well not just yet.

'Please feel free to use the library at any time. I am sure there are records in there of the time your ancestor Marie deVille Bankes was here. From memory, that was a very strange time; it's when I believe the gamekeeper fell into a vat of beer and drowned and there was something to do with his sidekick, but I can't remember. Still it will be fascinating to know!'

'That's very kind of you HP, I will look, if you don't mind.'

'Are you and Lisa riding this morning?' asked Arthur.

'Yes. I am going to show her around, the same as we did yesterday. Are you going to join us?'

'I would love to come riding today, if I may?' Rosabella announced. 'I can show you around as well.'

Rosa left to change into riding gear and met them at the stables.

Thomas Tilley was at the stables getting the horses ready.

'Morning Thomas. Have we got some good horses today? Marie and Lisa are proficient riders so the ones with character and my Bess, today please?' Rosa knew Thomas for a long time. He had been with the family since she was little.

'I have Miss Rosa. Saddled Hardwick, Troy and Bess ready for you. Miss Marie rode Hardwick yesterday with Master Arthur.'

'Lisa, you are in for a treat with Troy. He is a little headstrong so needs reigning in a bit. Keep him on a short rein,' she advised.

Marie found it strange that Thomas Tilley was still

here, as he was a different character in her dream. This Thomas Tilley was a pleasant man in his early thirties and respected by the family by all accounts.

They mounted their horses and trotted out of the stable, pushing into a canter, then a gallop down the main rolling parkland that reached down to the lake. They went around the lake front and out onto the small track that led to the woods. The very tall trees planted closely together formed a dark canopy of leaves and made the light very sinister. The single file track wound its way through the woodland floor of bracken and other vegetation. Marie remembered riding through this in her dreams whislt Thomas Tilley and Able Jones spied on her and Lisa. There was one big old tree, but the others were just saplings back then and the ground was open grazing land on the hill top. She became silent and shuddered in her saddle, shuffling nervously.

'What's up babes?' Lisa asked, knowing her best friend's body language well.

'You know the dreams I have been having?'

'Yes, go on?'

'Well it was here that Thomas Tilley spied on me.'

'He was a vile man.'

'What dreams are these?' asked Rosa.

Lisa and Marie had forgotten that Rosa was with them. Marie nodded at Lisa to indicate she was going to tell her.

'I have been having strange, very vivid and lifelike dreams about my ancestor in 1648 to 1650. They feel so real that it's a weird and scary coincidence that you and your family are exactly as I dreamed about.'

'So, your interest in the body in our lake in 1650 is not just a mere coincidence?'

'Not exactly.' ... she proceeded to tell Rosa the story so far. They rode around the estate side by side by side, Marie in the middle and Rosa one side, Lisa on the other.

By the time they reached the end of the bridlepath, they were on the other side of the lake. Marie screamed out aloud, making the horses jump nervously. Lisa's horse reared and it took all her riding skills to stop Troy from bolting, and Rosa, used to Bess, just stopped next to Hardwick. Marie was pointing towards the middle of the lake at what looked like a log. Rosa called the Hall on her mobile and asked them to call the police; she would meet them at the lake.

Marie was shaking ... it was her dream come true, in the worst circumstances. She had a presentation to make this afternoon and her bosses were coming, too.

Was it just a log or a body? Lisa had ridden around to the other side to get a better look. She galloped back.

'Someone has fallen in and is face down so can't tell if it's male or female.'

Within minutes a Range Rover Discovery came racing across the meadow stopped abruptly and both HP and Thomas Tilley jumped out, running to the water's edge. Arthur and Charles arrived in a four-wheeled buggy. Police sirens were heard in the distance, then a couple of cars with lights flashing pulled up next to the Discovery and buggy. Arthur was holding the horses' reins keeping them calm.

'Who discovered the body?' the police officer asked.

'Well, I suppose I did,' said Marie shakily.

HP gave her a very strange look remembering her strange question this morning.

'Who is it officer?' he asked.

'We will recover it soon. Waiting for the underwater rescue team. But I need to question you all at the Hall.'

'Please feel free to use the study, officer. We have a meeting planned for 3pm this afternoon, but I recognise that this will take priority,' HP offered.

'Thank you, my Lord. Perhaps you could take the horses back to the stables and wait for my team to come. We will be as quick as we can once we have identified who it is.'


They all left the lake side. Marie was still in shock so she went back with HP in the Discovery, whilst Rosa, Lisa and Arthur rode the horses back to the stables.

When they had all gathered in the Orangery, awaiting the police, HP asked, 'Marie … strange that you were asking about a body in the lake this morning. Is this a pure coincidence?'

'Yes … and no,' she answered straight away. 'I had a strange dream about it last night … it's a bit weird really.'

Charles and Lisa both looked at Marie and nodded at her, as if to say, '*you had better tell them'*.

But Marie shook her head to say no. She didn't want anything to disrupt the presentation that afternoon … if it was still to go ahead. She had James and Randolph arriving at 2pm and the room to set up ready for the powerpoint presentation.

The police were in fact very good and simply took statements from everyone. They were finished by 1pm, so Marie and Lisa set up the presentation and brochures in the library. Charles was despatched to Newark to collect James and Randolph.


Marie went to her room to compose herself and to run through her presentation. Lisa knocked on her door and let herself in.

'You okay babes?'

'Yes, thanks. Come and listen to this and tell me if it's

crap.' She sounded as if the last few hours never happened. She went through her presentation for twenty minutes. Afterwards Lisa knew why her best friend was so good at her job.

'It sounds fantastic Marie. I would buy it. Gosh ... didn't know that the Hall would be such an exclusive hotel ... and pricey, too!'

'They don't want riff-raff in, so by making it effectively six-star it will only attract those that can afford it. But the Hall and its facilities have to give the top end service a well.'

'You sound doubtful that the Bankes' can deliver the service?'

Marie was silent for a while. She was reflecting on her dreams and what they were trying to tell her.

'The Hall is fantastic and the facilities are top of the range. Charles has done a fantastic job with the re-development and no expense has been spared. Don't get me wrong Lisa, I think they can do it ... it's just ...'

'What ... you mean your dreams?'

'Well yes. I think they are telling me something. The old Marquess is gaga and quite scary and the death in the lake ... well ... it all actually happened three hundred years ago.'

Lisa could see that her friend was troubled by her dreams. It did feel very strange being here, knowing that the family could trace its history back to the days of Cromwell and King Charles 1st. Her presentation was based on the family history and the launch idea was simply inspired.

'You will just have to put your dreams behind you and go with this. It's a fantastic presentation and the graphics are superb.'

There was a commotion in the entrance hall, and Marie heard James's raucous laughter and Randolph's deep baritone voice. Marie left Lisa in the library to go and greet them. HP was already there as Charles and Rosa appeared from the Orangery.

'Here she is, our superstar,' James greeted. 'Wow … this is some place you've got here HP.' He was looking up at the ceiling and turning around on his heels. Randolph was very quiet, a sign that he was overwhelmed. They took them through to the Orangery. James Howell and Mrs Pottage came in with trays of canapés and glasses of champagne. There was a noisy echo of voices in the Orangery as everyone was talking at once.

A bell sounded in the Long Gallery, and Mrs Cribb announced that they were expected in the library for the presentation. As they approached the Long Gallery, James stopped suddenly and stared up.

'Fuck me … it's Marie our French marvel.' Pointing

at the huge portrait of Marie deVille Bankes. He peered at the name on the bottom.

'Bloody hell, there's been two of you then?'

Everyone laughed at his expression. HP explained that Marie's ancestors used to own the Hall in 1649. Randolph just raised his eyebrows with the hint of a smile on his face.

Marie was anxious to start the presentation before any other interruptions. She was worried about the Marquess and hoped he would stay in his room. But the noise everyone was making may spike his interest and he may venture out to see what was going on.

She took Rosa to one side. 'Your father won't make an entrance, will he?'

Rosa laughed, 'not with the sedatives we have just given him, no. He will be comatose until tomorrow morning when the doctor is due to see him.'

That was a relief at least.

Everyone was settled into the horseshoe arrangement of chairs in the library, each with a small table, surrounding a plasma screen. The atmosphere was perfect, the library was not one of the largest rooms in the Hall, but it had very high walls, lined with old books, that created a musty smell of old leather and paper combined with stale cigar smoke. This was part of the original library and contained books dating back to the 1500s, worth a mint. The deep red carpet complemented the heavy golden silk curtains that draped the full height lead glass window. The double oak doors were closed and a silence settled in the room. Present were the family, Charles, Lisa and the board of directors,

James stood up.

'What a fabulous place!' he exclaimed. 'And to see a full-size mirror image of our star, Marie, here, just made my day.'

Everyone laughed.

'Although Randi and I own the agency, we have to be up-front and say that this is all Marie's work. She has created the idea, worked with our team in London and produced what you are about to see. As an agency, this has been the most exciting project we have ever worked on and our thanks go to Charles and the Bankes' family for inviting us into your confidences. Right, enough of my diatribe … Marie … it's all yours.' He resumed his seat.

Marie stood and silently looked at everyone. But her gaze rested on HP, Rosa and Arthur, the key decision makers.

She pressed a button on the remote and a trailer started. Randolph's voice came on, a deep baritone, traditional English public school accent which opened the video. It was welcoming and gave a brief historical setting to the Hall, bringing it into the modern day boutique hotel. It started with an aerial shot giving the impression of an arrival by helicopter. Marie had cleverly used a drone. It swept up the drive from the entrance gates right up to the front portico. It swept through the main hall, the Long Gallery into the Orangery and out through the back into the grounds. It covered all the services and sporting events, finishing with the Spa and pool area. There were people in the video dressed in 17$^{th}$-century clothes in the Orangery and out in the grounds, transforming into elegantly-dressed beautiful women in the modern day outfits.

Another view of the Hall from the air swept around the outside only a few feet above the roof top, showing off the magnificent building. There were single shots of the bedrooms, fading in and out, the bathrooms, the library and dining hall. It made Flintwell Hall a place you would want to see for yourself.

'Where on earth did you get that from, and who are these women? I never saw them!' HP exclaimed.

Marie was pleased by the expression on everyone's faces.

When the video had finished, a slide appeared on the screen. It was a picture of her portrait.

'I feel a real affinity with the Hall. My great, great, great aunt lived here, well that's what I presume she was, as she never gave birth from what we can tell. My father confirmed this morning that our family has distant ties with the Bankes.' She hesitated to let everyone settle down.

'It is with the greatest honour that Charles asked me to work on this. Discovering my connections with the Hall and the family gives me a unique insight into what the Bankes' are trying to achieve ... and it will be THE MOST exclusive boutique experience, anyone who can afford it, will have in their entire lives.'

Shots of all the current day aristocracy and famous stars from film, music and books came onto the screen together with the top ten destinations in the world, with a caption "The Best Exclusive Luxury Hotel ". Everyone murmured at the caption. Marie added, 'Well, as the saying goes, *"if you have to ask, you can't afford it."* Everyone tittered their approval at this.

There was a flurry of words and expressions as everyone recognised the famous faces and the destinations. She did not have to say anything at all as these images portrayed what she wanted the Hall to be.

The next image on the screen was a picture, also hanging in the Long Hall, of the infamous masked ball of 1650.

Then a list of names appeared on a rolling tape, all were famous artists, aristocracy, the in-people of society, a few politicians, the Local Chief of Police and the Bishop of Lincoln.

'We are proposing to hold a masked ball in the Long

Gallery and Orangery to launch the new Hotel, inviting all these potential customers as our guests. The ball will follow similar lines to the last one ever held here in 1650. It will be elaborate, extravagant and will be such a 'must have' invitation, that more people will want to be invited than we can accommodate. It will be the talk of the month in Monaco, Nice, Paris, New York and London. Those not invited will be jealous, envious, annoyed and will know that they are not the elite in society. After the ball, your bookings will soar for the next four years as everyone will want to experience even one night here.'

She ended her presentation with a firework display on the plasma screen.

There was silence at first, as everyone in the room took in what had just been presented to them, then all at once they spoke, cheered and congratulated everyone.

It was a success.

The double doors banged open, startling everyone.

There stood a half-naked, inebriated, half-drugged Marquess.

'What the blithering hell is going on here?' he said in a very slurred voice on unsteady legs.

Mrs Cribb, James Howell and HP jumped up and took the Marquess back to his room, soothing his loud demands to be left alone.

'This is still my house you know! You won't get it

until I am dead, all of you ungrateful children ...' he shouted as he disappeared down the hall.

Rosa and Arthur were left to apologise.

'HP has taken great care that Pops is well cared for. He is losing his memory and is critically ill, so a year ago when he was still cognisant, our family solicitor got him to agree to signing over the running and ownership of Flintwell Hall to HP, Arthur and me with a joint Power of Attorney. When the Hall opens to the public, we will all move into the estate houses and Pops will be cared for at Flintwell Farm with a team of specialists, if he lives that long.'

HP returned with Mrs Cribb and Howell.

'Our apologies. Pops has a knack of escaping and wandering around the Hall at night.' He took centre stage.

'That was simply wonderful Marie. Your passion for our house, given your connections, is to be applauded. You hit the mark, just what we all envisaged and on behalf of my brother and sister, we thank you, James, Randolph and Charles for such an insightful and descriptive vision of what we intend to achieve. Congratulations everyone.'

There was a knock on the door and Thomas Tilley came gingerly in.

'Sorry HP, but can you spare Inspector Passmore a few minutes.'

'Yes, be right there, Thomas.' Turning to us all,

'please excuse me.'

He returned a few minutes later looking down and thoughtful.

'What is it HP?' asked Rosa.

'Inspector Passmore has just told me that the body in the lake was one of our gardeners, and there has been a rape of one of the girls from the village. They suspect it was the boy who did it.' He was suddenly ... saddened by the news. It showed that he cared for all the people working on the estate.

Marie suddenly asked, 'can I see the Inspector with you HP? It may help, although it will take some explaining as well.'

HP had a puzzled look on his face.

'Yes, of course,' and he led her out of the room. Lisa and Rosa went with her.

The inspector was just leaving when Thomas Tilley called him back. They took him into the Orangery, and as he passed the portrait he did a double take.

'Inspector Passmore. May I introduce Marie deVille, Lisa Dashwood and my sister Rosa. Marie has family connections as you have just seen a portrait of her great great someone.'

She shook his hand and took a seat, looking very nervous.

'I don't quite know how to put this Inspector, and it

will sound daft to you I know.'

'Go on Miss deVille. In my line of work, it helps to have a very open mind.'

'Over the past few nights, I have been having very vivid dreams about my ancestors, who lived here in 1648. These dreams are unusual in the fact that, not only do I remember them in detail, but it transpires ... and totally unknown to me ... that they actually happened, here at Flintwell Hall.'

'How does this link to the unfortunate incident you found this morning?'

'Well, that's just it. Last night I dreamed that Able Jones the gardener had stolen his Lordship's beer, and I saw him and a girl on the lake edge, as she pushed him in. I think they were fighting. It transpires that he had also raped and severely beat up one of the kitchen-maids from the Hall.'

'If it helps Inspector, in 1649, we had a gamekeeper called Thomas Tilley, no relationship to our current Tilley, I believe. But the then Thomas Tilly fell into the vat of beer we brewed on the estate for the family and household, and drowned, and my ancestor the 1st Marquess of Flintwell ordered that the beer be poured away. However, Able Jones was indeed the gardener and Tilley's righthand man at the time, and instead of pouring the beer away, he stole a few barrels for himself, and overindulged that particular evening.'

Marie continued, 'I woke at 3am this morning and saw a couple around the lake in a silhouette, and thought nothing more of it. Also I could have sworn there was someone in my room as well.'

'So, you saw two people around the lake at 3am this morning? Can you describe them at all?'

'No, not really. It's so far away. There was good moonlight, but they were silhouetted against the mirror of the lake's water. I could not see that they were fighting, only that they looked like lovers.'

'Who was in your room?'

'I don't know, I just sensed that someone was looking at me. I put it down to my dreams, as in 1649, I feared my husband the Marquess.'

'Inspector,' said Rosa, 'Marie deVille Bankes was 25 and the Marquess' 4th wife. She was from a French aristocratic family ... this Marie's ancestors.'

The Inspector shook his head as if in disbelief.

'It was probably my father, the Marquess, Inspector. He is going senile and tends to sleep-walk at night. He is very disturbed by Marie's presence here as you can see she has a very close resemblance to the 1st Marquess's fourth wife.'

Marie shuddered.

'If you have any more dreams Miss deVille or any

more recollections from last night, would you please call me right away. Anything you might deem irrelevant might be important to us, so please don't hesitate in coming forward.'

They all agreed with the inspector. Just as he was about to leave he turned and asked, 'ahh ... what are you doing here exactly, if you are not a member of the immediate family?'

HP explained about the relaunch of the Hall and Marie's work with the agency.

'Oh!! Now I can see the connection. That is very coincidental, now isn't it!' ... he paused again, his head to one side as if in deep thought ... turned to HP. 'Do you by any chance, have any CCTV at the Hall, and does it extend as far as the lake. I presume it will have night vision, your Lordship?'

'Please it's HP, my father is not dead yet, so I don't go in for titles. Yes, we do have extensive CCTV given the type of hotel we are becoming and I believe it extends to the grounds as well, but I'm unsure if it covers the lake itself. I will have it checked for you Inspector.'

With that the inspector nodded at everyone and left.

HP took Marie's hand and said gently, 'come with me.'

He led her into his private study and sat her down,

pouring a large brandy in crystal goblets.

'You did very well. I am most impressed with your vision and presentation, and would like you to extend your stay here until next week. There is much I would like to go through with you and I am fascinated by your recent dreams.' He was very softly spoken with kindness in his voice.

'Oh HP, I need to check with the partners first. But I would love to stay on and help.'

'Already sorted my dear, I spoke to them today after the presentation. Now, I have a confession to make to you as well.'

She looked at him silently, waiting for him to continue. His private study was in the far corner of the Hall on the ground floor, overlooking the rear box hedge patio. He had a pair of old doors that opened to this private patio, and both were open with a gentle breeze flowing through his neatly kept office.

'It was my father who came into your room last night. I do apologise. Howell found him wandering around the hall upstairs in his PJ's, kept muttering, something Howell told me sounded like, *"where's that French whore"*. I know I shouldn't tell you this but given your dreams it may relate to you. Pops thinks he is the 1st Marquess in his deluded senility, and because of this he truly believes you are your ancestor come back to haunt him. We have got professional help for him in one of the top mental health psychiatrists, who is recommending we send him into a specialist hospital for the insane.'

Marie was quite taken aback by him confidenting in her about this private matter.

'I am telling you this because there is a direct correlation between your dreams and the recent events here at the Hall. I have been fascinated by my ancestors for a very long time and studied them in history at Oxford. I am going to employ a forensic historian to delve into the time around 1648 to 1651 as this seems to be a significant time in my family's history.'

She looked at him with surprise but still said nothing.

'I would like you to work with him when he arrives tomorrow, hence why I am asking you to stay the week with us.'

He fell silent and sat on the edge of his desk waiting for a reaction. She looked at him in a different light. He was tall, well-built but not fat, looked like he worked out. He had short, well-cut light brown hair, going on ginger, with kind, hazel-brown eyes. He was, in all, quite a handsome man … and still single! Quite a catch in aristocratic circles. She realised that she was comparing him to Charles, and … she felt attracted to him.

'I really don't know what to say HP. Of course I will help as much as I can. Those dream have made me very nervous in their vivid reality, and I am shattered from broken sleep. I would be fascinated to know the truth as well, and perhaps this will bring an end to my dreams.'

She suddenly thought about Lisa and then about her clothes. She hadn't brought enough with her for the week.

As if reading her mind, he said, 'I have asked Lisa if she would mind bringing some clothes for you from your house and she has organised this with your friend Clare, who is coming up tonight.'

'You have thought of everything, haven't you? You knew I would say yes!'

He smiled at her and took her hand, gently, again.

'It is a little self-indulgent of me as I would like to spend more time getting to know you, as well as finding out if we are related.' He said this with some sadness in his eyes.

*'OMG he fancies me!!'* Her heart gave a flutter as she suddenly realised that for the first time in her life she had two men interested in her.


She went looking for Lisa, but was told that she and her brother had left to go to Newark to collect the other guest for tonight. Mrs Pottage said that dinner would be at 8pm tonight with the additional guest.

When Clare arrived, Marie went to the front entrance to greet her. She unfurled herself out of the tight back seat space of Charles' car and looked around open mouthed.

'You'll catch flies like that,' Marie said to her and gave her a hug. 'What a way to fiddle yourself an invitation to come up here,' and laughed. 'Come on in and I'll show you around.'

Clare came up with Marie's small suitcase.

'Hey hun, hope you don't mind but Charles and I have brought Clare up to speed with things here including your dreams, which she already knew about. Don't be angry with me?'

At seven thirty, everyone met in the Orangery for pre-dinner cocktails. Clare was introduced to the family and had a tour of the house and grounds by Rosa and Charles. She noticed how there was a growing intimacy between Rosa and Charles, which shocked Clare as she knew that Marie had a crush on him. But within five minutes of meeting in the Orangery, she also picked up the vibes between HP and Marie … so that was it!

Dinner was, again, perfect. In his welcome speech to Clare, HP said it was a dress rehearsal for when they finally opened.

Towards the end of dinner, HP, Rosa and Arthur were called away to see their father. The doctor had arrived and all was not well. So, Charles, Lisa, Clare and Marie were left to enjoy coffee and liqueurs in the library. They eventually ended up in the Orangery and again, the girls took delight in reminding Marie of her dreams surrounding the activities in this glorious room.

They didn't see the family until morning.

Charles went to speak to Randolph Blake about the final construction requirements. The girls escorted Marie to her room and stayed to chat about her apparent closeness to HP and Charles' relationship with Rosa.

'You two are daft buggers. You know there will never be anything with HP, and as for your brother, Lisa, he seems to be craving for that bitch Leticia.' Marie cackled at this.

'Babes, Lettice is long gone. She wanted too much from bro and he got tired of her. He may have eyes for Rosa if you let him, though!'

'Oh God … I hate relationships. Please bugger off to bed.'

With that they left Marie alone.

She went to the huge window and looked out. There was no full moon tonight as it had become overcast and cloudy. She could just make out the lake. Had she seen the couples there at 3am? She was now doubting herself.

She ran a bath and soaked for a while, thinking about HP, what he said to her in his study and about the Marquess, who was obviously seriously ill.

She climbed into bed and snuggled under the clean white crisp sheets and comfy soft pillows … closing her eyes … drifting into sleep … now expecting to dream …

# 14
# 1651

It was pouring with rain ... had been all day. The grounds were under water in places and the kitchen servants were busy trying to stop the floor from becoming too slippery.

She heard his high pitched scream from the other end of the Long Gallery. She was sat in the Library quietly reading, biding her time before she had to go and see him. She knew the footmen and head butler were becoming concerned at their position between his Lordship and Her Ladyship and they were only too aware of the poisonous relationship between the Marquess and his fourth wife. Being French, she was feisty to say the least, but giving her her due, she was always kind and considerate towards the staff.

Look how she cared for the kitchen maid who was raped and beaten by Jones, and how she rode on horseback in all weathers to visit all the farms each week. Look at today with the rains, how her first concern was to the servants and the kitchen maids, ignoring the demands of her husband, who was getting drunker, smellier and more obese every day. He was foul to all the staff, especially Mr

Howells and his personal footmen.

He screamed and shouted all day long for his *'French whore'*. They all knew she was ignoring him, making his anger even worse, so much so that he was having problems breathing. He ate stale food left for him on wooden plates, drank four jugs of porter and six bottles of fine French wine and defaecated where he sat. His footmen did the best they could to clean him, but he hit out savagely at them every time they got near. They had to wait until his energies were spent, before they could change him and clean him. Like a baby they used a huge bed sheet as a nappy to wrap around him.

She left him to rant all day on purpose, wanting him docile and quiet, before she went to him. She knew it placed the servants in a very difficult predicament but it was for the best.

Late that evening, Marie deVille requested to see her husband alone, the footmen were to wait outside and not to come in under any circumstances.

She entered his bedchamber, a perfumed mask covering her face.

'So, you do exist then!' he shouted at her as she quietly closed the door. 'What excuses do you have wench. I have been calling for you all day, yet you disobey your husband on every occasion.'

He was sat on his huge oak chair, made for him specially by the woodman to carry his bulk. He grabbed his stick and heaved himself up onto his feet with immense effort, sweating profusely. Marie went quietly to the sideboard where his food and drink were kept and emptied half the vial into his pewter mug, refilling it with his favourite port. She approached him and with an outstretched arm, handed him the overflowing mug, then stepped back to stop him from grabbing her. Greedily he took it and downed half the contents, port dripping down the side of his mouth onto the floor, spilling onto his shirt and protruding belly.

She stood perfectly still, watching him drink and belch, unsteady on his feet.

'Answer me Frenchie. Where have you been all day? Not out in these foul rains?'

'Whilst your Lordship has been eating, drinking and shouting all day, I have been organising the household and dealing with the rains that have flooded the kitchens and cellars. If your demands were more important I would have come sooner. But you have Howell and your footmen to supply you with your needs.' Her French accent becoming more pronounced as she raised her voice to him.

He threw his pewter mug onto a side table, missing it, the contents spilling on the floor as it bounced towards the fire. He undid the front of his britches, managed to push them half down, and searched with his hand for his member.

'Come to the bed French whore. I wish to take my pleasure, so raise your skirts and bend across the bed.'

He looked ridiculous. Clearly unable to perform the act he wished to do by the sight of his limp red diseased member.

Instead, she kicked his stick away from under his colossal weight and he fell on the floor. He rolled onto his back and was then trapped as he was so overweight he did not have the energy to roll onto his side to stand up. He started to shout for Mr Howell and the footmen.

Nobody dared enter the room.

Marie bent over him and opened his mouth. She poured the rest of the vial of powders onto the back of his throat, then used the rest of his port from the bottle to fill it. He gagged on the liquid, but eventually swallowed then gasped for air.

'NEED HELP!!' he shouted.

Marie stood over his face. He looked up as she lifted her skirts and underskirt to show her intimate parts thick with black hair.

He became quiet, a smile formed on his face for the first time in many years, thinking she was going to perform some other kind of pleasure for him.

'This will be the one and only time you will see this part of me my husband.'

She squatted down and proceeded to urinate over his astonished face and into his gaping mouth.

She had purposefully drunk wine, champagne and small beer all day, and made herself hold onto it, knowing she would have a full bladder to relieve herself in this way. The steaming yellow stream went everywhere, over his ginger beard, his balding head; into his gagging mouth and over his shirt onto the floor. It was hot and smelt terribly acrid.

He cried and shouted, but the servants dare not disobey her Ladyship's strict instructions.

Outside the door, they wondered what was happening. The noises emanating from the room were horrendous. His Lordship was either giving Her Ladyship a very rough ride or she was taking her revenge on him.

They waited to see if she came out either wounded and bruised or gracefully.

There was a very long silent pause …

The door opened …

Marie deVille came gliding out looking happy and serine. She closed the door after herself, turned the key in the lock and handed it to Mr Howell.

'My husband sleeps on his bed. Please see to it that no one enters his room tonight. We shall see if his humour is better upon the morrow. But no one is to see him. Is that clear?,' the lilt of her French accent soft again.

'Yes, my Lady. I will post young Will here on the door which will be kept locked Ma-am.'

She walked slowly down the hallway to her rooms, a small smile lifting the edges of her mouth.

The next morning, she heard a female voice shouting for help. Marie was about to open her door, when Mrs Cribb came rushing in.

Out of breath she held her hands to her enormous bosoms. She was holding a handkerchief to her nose.

'Oh, my Lady … oh my Lady … it's his Lordship … the Marquess.'

'Yes Mrs Cribb, what about his Lordship? Please calm down and take your time.'

She was visibly upset and shaking.

'Well, you see … he is not moving at all … we think … he is … dead. God help us.'

Calmly, Marie took Mrs Cribb by the arm and comforted her, as she knew she had served his Lordship for many years and had seen a different side to him.

'Eh bon … let us go and see, shall we?'

They walked down the corridor, Mrs Cribb taking short running steps as Marie walked serenely, but with some haste to show concern. The door was open into the

Marquess' room and Mr Howells and a few footmen were standing over him shaking their heads.

As she entered, she exclaimed, 'Zut alhors, mon Dieu … God's truth, what is that foul acrid stench?' holding her hand held pommade to her nose.

'I regret to say that His Lordship is dead, my Lady. Seems he fell from his bed and died swallowing his tongue on his own vomit.'

Marie kept her composure, did not react and just bent over her husband to feel for a pulse in his neck. Satisfied that he was dead she turned to face the servants gathered.

'His Lordship is indeed dead. Please can you wash him, dress him in his finest clothes and take him to the chapel to await the vicar and the physician. Mrs Cribb, can you open these windows, and have his room thoroughly cleaned with salts and water. His unfortunate death is of his own doing. He must have crawled from his bedside to his chair before expiring. Out of respect we shall mourn him, although I know not why as he was not a pleasant man to anyone here at Flintwell Hall'

'Yes, My Lady,' Mr Howell responded.

'Please can you send a message to Lord Dashwood and Lord Wentworth asking if the right honourable Charles and Harry could assist me in getting my husband's affairs in order. I am unsure of your English laws to report a death of an aristocrat, and to whom we should advise. His son needs to be informed as well as he now becomes the 2nd Marquess, however he is abroad somewhere. In the meantime, I will continue running the estate.'

'Yes, My Lady.'

There was a quiet calm in the Hall, with every member of the estate silently blessing the passing away of a dreadfully cruel master.

Within half the day Charles arrived with Henry and the Sheriff of Lincoln. The Sheriff wanted to see his room and was upset that the Marquess had been moved. Marie took offence at this and squared up to the old man in his heavy robes.

'What would you have me do, pray … let his body rot further, his stench filling the Hall? It was bad enough when he was alive, but I took the decision to respect my husband in death, sire, and had him washed and dressed. He now lays at rest in the chapel if you wish to see him.' She was a formidable woman for her stature and young age. The Sheriff did not want to upset her further, as she wept a few crocodile tears into her small linen hanky.

'I am sorry for your loss, My Lady, but we have to make a report for the records of his death.'

Marie looked at the man, then to Charles, who gave her a small nod of approval as if he knew what she was asking.

'The Marquess was 69. He was grossly overweight, had many ruptured tumours, drank port from morning to night and was infested with lice. Last night I went to him, helped him into his bed and made sure he slept. Mr Howells and I believe that he rolled over, fell on the floor and was attempting to reach his bell on the table next to his chair, when he expired with the effort. Mrs Cribb found him this morning.'

He seemed to accept the explanation. She knew that none of the footmen would say anything to the Sheriff if questioned.

'Shall we pay our respects to the Marquess, my Lord Sheriff, at the chapel?' Henry sensed that they needed to move on. He knew that she and Charles were fond of each other and couldn't quite see if she was genuinely sorry for the Marquess' death. She was so cold and composed for one so young.

Henry took the Sheriff to the chapel. Once they were alone, Charles took her into his arms and held her tightly. Being quite petite, he could kiss the top of her head as it rested on his chest, his arms wrapped around her shoulders. He bent slightly to whisper into her ear, 'you did very well, my love. He is gone and now you are all mine, my Frenchie.'

She lifted her head to him, 'Charles,' she said quietly in her sweet French accent, and their lips gently brushed together, before they kissed passionately for a long time, entwined in each other's arms.

'I must show some respect and mourn his death for at least a month, before we can be seen together, mon amour.'

'Yes, I agree. But, as your legal counsel, I need to be with you to help such a young, beautiful, widower run her late husband's estate … well at least until the 2$^{nd}$ Marquess arrives back from wherever he is.'

'Je t'adore mon amour,' she said, the first time he had ever heard her speak in French.

They now needed to be very careful when in public. Servants have a habit of being indiscreet and if word got out that the French Marchioness was having dalliances with Lord Dashwood, word would spread amongst the villages on the estate, and eventually to the Sheriff's office in Lincoln.

Life at Flintwell Hall became quiet and resumed normality. Lisa Dashwood spent most of her time with Marie, and took one of their many bedchambers as hers.

Her brother was seen on most days, and would take the Marchioness out on horseback rides around the estate, visiting the farmers as she had always done, but this time with his support.

The Marquess had an official funeral in the Cathedral in Lincoln as befitted his status and was buried in the

Flintwell Estate churchyard. His popularity was measured by the poor attendance of the aristocracy as well as general society. Only a few bothered to ride the two days from London, and only a handful of local gentry turned up to pay their last respects. He was not a liked man.

It was no surprise to anyone that a closeness began to develop between the Marchioness of Flintwell and Lord Charles Dashwood of Rodewelle. All the servants in the Hall were secretly pleased and hoped that the 2$^{nd}$ Marquess of Flintwell could not be found. It was their unspoken wish that Charles Dashwood would move into the Hall. They gave them both plenty of privacy to develop their romance, which was unusual in that period.

Shortly after the Marquess' burial, Marie deVille held an early dinner to thank the local neighbours for their kindness. Lisa, Harry Wentworth and Charles all stayed over. After a delicious variety of foods cooked by Mrs Pottage, their guests left to ride back in their carriages to their own homes in the late summer light.

Lisa and Charles decided to take Harry and Marie into their confidence.

'We fear that our dear papa has only a few days left. His illness has put him into a deep sleep and we are counting the days until his last breath. Tomorrow we must return to our home and await his fate,' Lisa was very tearful as she adored her dear father.

'I too will take my leave Marie, as I wish to be of comfort to Lisa when the time comes.' Harry was besotted with Lisa and it was obvious that there would be a good marriage between the houses of Wentworth and Dashwood.

That evening, Marie had left her door unlocked with a secret squeeze of Charles' arm as she left the men in the library and took her leave.

She had changed into her light silk bed-gown and waited for the door to open. Only a single candle burned by her bedside weaving an eerie light over the room as a gentle warm breeze filtered through the partially open window.

She heard footsteps outside her door.

It opened …

Charles stood at the foot of her bed …

She watched with growing excitement as he revealed his taut, honed body … removing his breeches and slowly turning to face her …

She was sat upright in bed … her eyes on his lower torso … her pulse racing … anticipating what was about to happen … she removed her white silk bed-gown; naked underneath … her mounting arousal creating a hot, jelly like feeling in her stomach and a wetness further down …

He was a very handsome man, strong, thick black hair

covering his chest ... and as he removed the rest of his clothing she saw his erect manhood.

*Mon dieu, I want him ...* she said to herself as he climbed into her bed and took her in his arms.

*'This is the best experience I have ever had ... I want this man,'* she said quietly in French under her breath, as he took her with so much passion and love ....

'Moi aussi, je t'adore,' he whispered back in her ear.

Marie deVille was happy for the first time in her life, as she let wave after wave of glorious sensations take her to a level of pleasure she had only had once before .... with this man.

She heard a distant cry for help in the corridor ... a familiar voice ... but ...

# 15

# MONDAY EARLY JULY 2017

Marie became conscious of the noise she was making which woke her up. This dream was developing into something else, no longer was she scared of what was going to happen. Perhaps it was because the old Marquess was dead.

She heard a distant cry again … it was what had woken her up … or was it in her dream?

*'Help … someone call the doctor. Help'*

It was Rosa's voice calling down the corridor.

Marie leapt out of bed and rushed to the door, before realising she was naked. She pulled on a bath-robe and ran down the corridor.

Rosa was stood beside her father's bed trying to give him some water. Being conscious that the old Marquess thought she was a ghost, she paused at the door.

'Rosa, tell me what you need me to do. I won't come in, he may react again to seeing me.'

'Please call the doctor, he is finding it very hard to

breath and needs some help. He is slipping into unconsciousness.'

'Okay, I'll get the doctor, an ambulance and fetch your brothers,' she left and ran down to the hall telephone, dialling the number of the doctor left on the note pad.

HP appeared, hastily dressed in jeans and a T-shirt. He heard her speaking to the doctor.

'Thanks Marie, I will go up and help Rosa. Might as well call the ambulance, too. Can you find Arthur and Mrs Cribb please?' He was so calm and collected. She admired the fact that he showed concern and emotion but was not panicking.

She felt she should say something about her dream of the death of the 1$^{st}$ Marquess, but then stopped herself as she realised that it was her ancestor who had effectively murdered her husband for the love of Charles Dashwood. How ironic was that. What Marie deVille Bankes did in 1651 was still vividly real in her mind. A murderess.

She went to Arthur's room and knocked gently on the door. He opened it wide, and Marie saw Clare sat up in bed reading a paper.

*'It didn't take her long then,'* she thought.

'Arthur, it's your father, Rosa and HP are with him, and I have spoken to the doctor who is on his way. I am to fetch Mrs Cribb as well.'

'It's okay, Marie, I'll call her on my way to his room.' And he left her standing just outside his room.

'Hello stranger. Didn't take you long, eh Clare?' she said sarcastically.

Clare shrugged her shoulders and smiled, tapping the bed to bid Marie to come to her. She sat on the bed, one leg folded under the other.

'Oh god, Marie ... he is so gorgeous. Last night was ... umm ...,' she raised her eyes up with a satisfied look on her face, 'I know he is only twenty but what's six years these days ... eh? I am hardly a cougar.' She giggled at this. 'Anyway, what's happening?'

Marie was not smiling at her. She clearly had no idea how ill Arthur's father was, which was typical of Clare, only surface deep relationships.

'It's the Marquess. I think he is nearing his end. He has slipped into a coma and I have called the doctor. I think we should dress and wait in the library or Orangery until we are needed by HP, Rosa or Arthur. They will need our support, the least we can do is offer some form of help or comfort.'

'Where's Lisa?'

'In her room I would have thought.' Marie wondered if she was alone or with Henry. She didn't want to know!

Her own feelings were very mixed now. She had had a crush on Charles for as long as she could remember, and now that "horsey Leticia" was off the scene, he was making his feelings clear to her. But ... then there was HP ...!

The women gathered in the Orangery to await any news. The family doctor arrived, racing up the drive in his BMW and rushing straight to his Lordship's room. Next, they heard the siren of the ambulance, together with the two-tone blaring of a police car. There was a commotion in the main hallway. Mrs Pottage arrived in the Orangery with a fresh pot of coffee and tea. She was visibly upset with tears in her reddened eyes. She was fussing around.

Marie took her hand and asked her to sit down. Lisa poured a cup of tea out and handed it to her.

'Oh, thank you dear,' she whimpered. 'I have known the Marquess since he was a boy and I was ... um ... just a slip of a lass. My parents were in service here as were my grandparents. It's such a shock, but we've known for some time that he was failing.'

Marie said to her still holding her hand gently, 'there was a Mrs Pottage who ran the kitchens and was head cook here in the time of the 1st Marquess. It's just simply amazing that you have such a long line of heritage with Flintwell Hall. And Mrs Cribb, too. Her family were here in 1648.'

Mrs Pottage put her cup down and turned to look at Marie square on, her tone changed to one of anger.

'How on earth did you know that? It's true we have been here for many centuries. Janice at the pub told us she was shocked when she saw you arrive with Master Dashwood. She thought she had seen a ghost. And the Marquess said you were a ghost.'

'I can assure you that I am not a ghost. It transpires that I too have ancient family who were here as well, and I want to find out more about who Marie deVille Bankes really was. It appears she was only here for a few years and caused a huge division in the family by all accounts … and I have to say Mrs Pottage, that the portrait in the Long Gallery of my ancestor is very spooky.'

This seemed to calm her down. She gave a small smile and grabbed Marie's hand.

'I am sorry my dear, I don't know what's come over me recently. It's all this changing to a hotel from the family home that is upsetting, but HP knows what he has to do to save the Hall from creditors.'

Clare and Lisa just sat and watched their friend help this dear old woman with a kindness they had never seen before in her. She behaved like she was the Marchioness. Later they concurred that a union with HP would be perfect for her. Even Lisa could see that, despite the fact she had hoped and wanted her bestie to be her sister-in-law as well.

After quite a while and a lot of commotion in the Marquess' room, he was finally strapped to a gurney and wheeled out to the ambulance with Rosa and the Paramedic Nurse riding to hospital.

HP came into the Orangery with Arthur and the doctor.

'My father has taken a turn for the worse, and seems to have befallen an accident in his room which is a mystery to us all. The police will want to take statements from us all during today, so please co-operate with them.' He seemed distant and in a daze as he and Arthur left to follow the ambulance.

Inspector Helen Scott appeared at the Orangery door, and coughed to get everyone's attention.

'Mrs. Briggs has kindly offered us the Library to use as a base here. I would like to interview everyone independently and ask you to make a statement as to your whereabouts between 11pm and 8am this morning.'

We looked at her as if she had just told us some disastrous news.

'What has happened?' asked Charles.

'We are not at liberty to say now, but his Lordship's illness has been accelerated,' was all she was prepared to say.

Everyone started to speak at the same time, total bewilderment filled the room and the noise level amplified in the high ceilings of the Orangery.

Mrs Pottage had slipped out of the room and re-appeared with a fresh tray of tea and coffee for everyone.

'Well done Mrs Pottage. You read our minds,' Charles said as she placed the tray on one of the tables.

Inspector Scott asked to see Charles first. He followed her into the library and was in there for about forty minutes. One by one, the interviews continued until Marie was asked to go through.

'Ahh ... yes ... Miss deVille. Your portrait hangs in the Long Gallery,' Helen Scott greeted her. 'Please take a seat.'

Marie took a chair opposite the Inspector. She sat silently looking at this hard looking, slim, auburn-haired policewoman. She had an intelligent face, bright blue eyes and a friendly but weathered face and dressed casually in a plain dark skirt, white shirt and pink lambswool V-neck sweater. You would not think she was a police officer if she hadn't shown her badge.

After studying her papers, she looked up at Marie and smiled.

'You have a fascinating connection to the Hall I understand. Your ancestors are intrinsically linked to the Bankes family. The likeness of you in the portrait is almost a photographic copy.'

Marie shrugged her shoulders but said nothing.

'I understand you have dreams at night. Flash-backs of life in the past here at the Hall,' she paused so her words hit home ... 'The body in the lake for instance,' she paused and looked at Marie again ... her smile slowly slipping.

'What is it you want me to say, Inspector?'

'Please can you tell me everything. All about your incredible dreams,' she sounded sarcastic.

She hesitated at first, not sure how much to say. But someone must have alerted the Inspector; how else would she have known?

'Umm ... yes ... well, for the past three weeks I have been having vivid dreams of my ancestors' life here in 1648 to 1651. They are frightening, exhausting, unreal and I am taking professional help to help understand why I am having them.'

'Tell me about them.'


She recounted parts of the dreams, leaving out the emotional, erotic elements. Marie deVille's marriage to the vile Marquess, Thomas Tilley's spying and fate falling into the vat of ale; the body in the lake; and the death of the old Marquess. Helen sat listening, recording her words for a written report later.

'How did the old Marquess die?'

'I believe that Marie deVille killed her husband with help from others. Poisoned him. But he was riddled with disease and probably had a stroke or heart attack.'

'How do you know she killed him?'

'I lived through it the other night. He tried to rape her, but she tripped him up, then poured some powders into his mouth and forced him to drink wine or port … and …'

'And what … go on …'

'It sounds horrific, but as he had tried to rape her … she raised her skirts and … umm …' she tittered a little with embarrassment, 'well she pissed on his face. I remember her saying that it's the last and only time he will see her like this. It was so vivid, it was scary.'

She was shaking with sheer terror as she recalled the memory.

Helen Scott sat very still. The smile on her face had gone as she looked at Marie with an inquisitive, suspicious glare.

'And where were you between 11pm last night and 8am this morning?'

'In my room. I went to bed at the same time as the others, but alone, and tried to sleep. I woke at 3am following a violent dream and went back to sleep until I woke hearing Rosa calling for help. I went to his Lordship's room and asked Rosa what she wanted me to do. I went to get HP and Arthur as Rosa had asked.'

'You did not go into the bedroom?'

'No, I didn't. The Marquess thinks I am a ghost, so I

did not wish to cause him any further anguish by seeing me again. I kept outside the room door. Rosa thanked me for this.'

Helen Scott paused.

'The old Marquess, in 1651, was found on the floor of his bedchamber, on his back, and it was thought he fell out of bed, but was so fat and weak, that he could not move himself. His butler and footmen were ordered by Marie deVille not to disturb him. His death was recorded by the Sheriff of Lincoln as suspicious.' She paused waiting for a comment from Marie.

Marie just sat there wondering how this policewoman had gained so much information about the old Marquess, when the family didn't even know … she began to regret having told Helen Scott of her dreams.

'Did you at any time visit his Lordship's room last night?'

'No, but there was someone in my room last night. Rosa believes that her father came into my room to see his ghost.'

'So, you didn't see him in your room?'

'No, I didn't. I was so consumed by my dream that I thought it was part of the dream, not reality. The Hall's CCTV will confirm this surely?'

'Have you ever met the Bankes family before last week?'

'No … I didn't even know they existed, before my brief for this assignment at the office.'

'So, your dreams started before you were given your assignment for the relaunch of the Hall?'

'Yes, about three nights before. It's either a spooky coincidence or my subconscious telling me something.' Marie paused until the Inspector looked up at her, 'I am under some sort of suspicion, with all these questions?'

'Why do you think that?'

'What has happened to the Marquess to trigger these questions and make you delve into the past. You are very well informed about the fate of the first Marquess and my ancestor,' Marie was becoming suspicious that the Inspector had an ulterior motive.

Helen Scott was silent for a while. The other police officer sat motionless in the corner of the library.

'I'm afraid I cannot tell you. Suffice to say that we are looking into the body in the lake and what happened to his Lordship as unusual occurrences that could have criminal motives. You Miss deVille happened to be a common denominator, as your dreams seemed to have pre-empted the crimes.'

'I can assure you Inspector that I have not committed any crimes at all, and both the body in the lake and whatever has befallen His Lordship has nothing to do with me.'

Marie was forthright in her statement.

'Is there anything else you need to know, Inspector, or can I go now?'

'You can, but please remain at the Hall for the time being. I may want to ask you more questions later.'

Marie left the library and went straight back to the Orangery, where she downed a glass of wine poured from the glass carafe before sitting heavily in the seat. Lisa, Charles and Clare were there and saw that she was white as a sheet.

'You were in there for a long time,' Lisa stated looking at Marie with concern.

Charles knelt in front of Marie and took her shaking hands in his. He could see she was disturbed by her interview.

'What did the Inspector say to you?'

Marie shook her head and closed her eyes, holding back a sob as a tear seeped out of the corner of her eye and ran down her cheek. Charles put his arms around her and held her tightly, saying nothing. The others looked on.

Lisa broke the silence.

'That inspector is very suspicious of us all. She kept asking me questions about you and me, Marie; what we were doing around the lake when we found the body and asking about your dreams. Weird if you ask me!'

'Yes, she quizzed me about you as well,' said Clare, 'wanted to know how long we had all known each other, and our lives in London … nosey cow.'

Charles was still holding a shaking Marie in his arms.

'It is her job, you know. She must see everyone as a suspect and eliminate us, one at a time. Don't be angry with her, it's a tough job and very unusual circumstances.'

'Do we know what happened to His Lordship?' Lisa asked.

'No, we don't, apart from the fact that he was found on the floor next to his bed and had collapsed … either a stroke or a heart attack. I got a text from HP saying they were at Lincoln General Hospital, waiting in A&E,' Charles answered.

'They are keeping the Hall staff separate from us so we don't talk to them,' Clare pointed out.

Mrs Cribb walked into the Orangery and addressed them all.

'I have laid out a light lunch and refreshments in the dining room for everyone when you are ready.' She bowed slightly and left them.

In the dining room, the Inspector was already helping herself to some food, along with her sidekick.

'Are we all free to go now Inspector, or do you wish

us to stay for longer?' Charles asked in a formal voice.

'You are all staying in the Hall I understand?'

'Yes, we are. However, the girls have got jobs to go to in London and need to get back.'

'I would like you Lord Dashwood and Miss deVille to remain here for another day, but Miss Dashwood and Miss Hobbs are free to return to London.'

'Why do you need us to stay?' Marie asked her in a strained croaky voice.

'We may need to ask you further questions about your dreams Miss deVille. You seem to have the ability to see into the future and you may have some valuable information that will help us conclude our investigations.'

'Any news of His Lordship?' Mrs Cribb asked as Andrew Blake walked into the dining room. No one noticed Mrs Cribb standing quietly in the corner of the room, listening to the conversation with the Inspector. Mr Blake, as Managing Director, was now in charge of the Hall in HP's absence.

'Nothing to report, Mrs Cribb, unfortunately. His Lordship has suffered a severe stroke and is in a coma now. HP, Rosa and Arthur are going to remain at his bedside. If there is any change they will let me know. In the meantime, we continue our duties.' He was very efficient and showed no emotion at all as he helped himself to some cold buffet.

Lisa and Clare said their goodbyes as James Howell

offered to drive them to Newark Station.

After lunch, they heard a car racing up the long gravel drive as Rosa arrived back at the Hall looking drained and tired. Charles and Marie went to the main door to greet her.

'How is his Lordship?' Charles asked.

'He is still in a coma and on life support systems but the outlook is not good. I have come home for a bath and change, as we are now going to take turns in being with Papa. Arthur is coming home soon and then I go back tonight to relieve HP.'

'Is there anything I can do for you Rosa?' Marie asked.

'Yes please. Can you saddle up the horses and come with me for a hard ride. I need to blow away the cobwebs.'

'May I come too?' asked Charles.

'Yes please, the more the merrier. I need some company. Then I will soak in a bath for an hour before going back to the hospital.'

They met at the stables half an hour later in their riding gear. The stable grooms had the three horses saddled ready for them.

'Where shall we go?' asked Marie.

'I want to show you something. It's about an hour's ride from here, but you will be interested to see this,' Rosa answered mysteriously.

They rode out of the stable yard directly across the fields at the rear of the Hall towards one of the farms originally owned by the estate that nestled into the hillside of the Wolds. After riding up the side of the gentle hill along the bridle way onto the open land on top of the escarpment, they headed for the small village of Rothwell.

Marie loved this part of country life, which she would miss once back in the city. It was a bright sunny day with a gentle cooling breeze. As the three of them rode side by side, huge Red Kites circled overhead looking for the slightest movements on the ground before closing their wings and rapidly descending in a near vertical dive onto their unsuspecting prey.

The Wolds bridle path took them directly through a small wood, the breeze pushing branches against each other making an eerie sound; where a cacophony of birdsong erupted from the trees, the clopping of the horses' hooves raising their attention, taking them to flight in the cramped space. And then into open land again with pigeons following each other and landing on wooden fences or pieces of grassland to continue their mating ritual, heads bobbing up and down, tail feathers opening to show their interest.

The air was clear and the sweet smell of freshly harvested wheat, combined with that deep earthy aroma of newly-ploughed fields which wafted around them, together with the distant hum of diesel engines as tractors, combine harvesters and quad bikes went about their farming business. As they approached one newly raked-field a huge metal monster was crawling slowly over the raked field with wide tentacles spewing out brown sewerage that had a redolent stench that made all three riders gag, kicking their horses into a gallop to pass the menacing machine as quickly as they could.

They laughed aloud as they rode their mounts hard across the open land.

At the far end of the escarpment, they stopped to admire the breathtaking view across Lincolnshire. They could see how vast the county was, towards the North and West apart from the ridge of low hills they were riding on known as the Lincolnshire Wolds. This was the very best part of the county; in the far distance towards the south stood Lincoln Cathedral and the Castle, silhouetted against the clear blue sky, standing on top of Lincoln's Steep Hill and overlooking the city below.

'It takes my breath away every time I come up here,' Rosa said as she stared at the view.

'This is simply stunning ... Oh how I could live here all the time,' Charles said to Rosa.

His horse was standing slightly behind the girls and when Marie turned to look at him, she saw he was admiring Rosa's slim figure and tight rear seated in her saddle. He blushed slightly when he saw Marie staring at him with a look on her face which said, *"behave, you!"*

'Come on, we still have a way to go,' as Rosa nudged her horse into a trot down the bridle path at the far end of the escarpment which sloped gently towards a small village nestling in a valley surrounded by woods.

They rode on passing hikers, cyclists, other horse riders and walkers on the way.

Marie rode next to Rosa with Charles taking up the rear, she presumed so the dirty git could admire their rear assets!

'Rosa, where exactly are we going? Won't you be late getting back?'

'It will be worthwhile, believe me. We are going to a small Norman village called Rothwell; it used to be called Rodewelle in the 17$^{th}$ century. There is a cute church with a very interesting graveyard. I only discovered it two days ago when I happened to see a Facebook message about a friend who is getting married there. For some reason it rang a bell. Then I discovered what we are about to see.'

'What exactly is that, then?'

'You will see. Just be patient.'


The bridle path took them over several B-roads and through a couple of farms until they were approaching the village from the south side. On a small hillock surrounded by wooden fences and wild thorn hedging, stood a very small Norman church with its square bell tower surrounded by a graveyard, of very ancient headstones, together with progressively newer ones.

They tied their horses to a railing near the entrance gate and walked down the gravel path that led to the church. All around them were gravestones of all sizes and designs. Rosa was looking for one stone and found it at the west side of the church.

'Here we are,' she said looking smug.

Charles and Marie knelt in front of the very old head stone to read the inscription.

It said:

*In Loving Memory of*
*The Marquesas' Marie deVille Bankes*
*of Saumur France - 1625*
*Died on 23rd May 1653 – Rodewelle*
*Repose en paix*

They looked at this in silence. Marie shuddered and looked up at Charles, then Rosa with a tear welling up in her reddening eyes. She looked as white as a sheet and tried to stand unsteadily on her feet. Charles took a picture of the headstone on his mobile camera.

'She was only 28 when she died,' Rosa stated the obvious.

Marie was still silent as Charles wrapped his arms around her and held her tightly.

'Are you okay Marie?' he whispered through her soft dark hair, as her head nestled under his chin.

She nodded but still said nothing.

Rosa was wandering around the graveyard looking at all the other head-stones. She came back to where Charles and Marie stood looking at her ancestor's grave.

'It's not a pauper's grave as the stone is quite elaborate and must have cost quite a bit. So, someone must have paid for her to be buried here. It begs more questions. Who was she with after the 1st Marquess died. Where is the child she gave birth to and who was the father? How can we find out about this?' Rosa's interest was sparked. 'I can't find any other gravestone linking Marie deVille Bankes. There are no children buried here under her name.'

'Charles Dashwood,' Marie suddenly said.

'Yes, that's me my love,' Charles responded.

'No, I meant that Marie deVille Bankes went off with the Honourable Sir Charles Dashwood in 1651, just after the Marquess was murdered. She had a son, Henri by Charles.'

They stood up and stared at Marie in astonishment.

'Umm ... err ... what do you mean Marie when you

said, '*after he was murdered*'. You mean the 1st Marquess of Flintwell was murdered? By whom?' Rosa asked still astounded.

Marie stood up and brushed her jodhpurs down.

'Marie deVille murdered her husband in his room. She caused him to have a stroke and then gagged him so that he choked on his vomit and her urine. That's what my last dream was about.'

Rosa looked from Charles to Marie and back to Charles with a dumbfounded look on her face.

'What is it Rosa?' Charles asked.

She didn't respond at first. Staring at Marie in a stunned daze she said very slowly, 'that's how my father was found in his room. He had choked on his own vomit after falling out of bed with his face in his piss bowl.'

'Did you say … er … her urine?' Charles asked, his head on one side looking into Marie's eyes.

'Yes. In my dream she stood over him, raised her skirts and crouched over his face and pissed. I remember her saying to him that it would be the last time he would see her private parts. She was disgusted every time he tried to have sex with her, which he usually tried to force on her. He was basically raping her every time.'

'When was this, 1651?' Rosa asked.

'It would have been yes.'

'She died two years later … at only 28. I wonder if the

child survived and how you are related?' Charles was inquisitive.

Rosa walked quietly away towards the horses, looking at her watch.

'We need to get back to the Hall,' Charles told Marie as they followed Rosa. By the time they mounted their horses, Rosa had already headed back up the bridle path on her own, deep in thought.

Charles rode close, next to Marie.

'I now understand why the police inspector has been questioning you. The similarities to your dreams is frighteningly similar.'

'Charles ... I know ... but I had nothing to do with His Lordship's illness nor the body in the lake. I cannot explain nor stop these dreams. They are frightening and very vivid.'

They caught Rosa up across the open land.

Walking their horses three abreast again, with Rosa in the middle, she said to Marie, 'I am not sure that Inspector Scott would have wanted you to know the circumstances of my father's position. I think you can see that. I don't believe you have had anything to do with how we found Papa.'

'Has he been very ill?' Marie asked.

She nodded, 'he is going senile, and is riddled with cancer ... we have known that for a long time, which is why HP had our family lawyers draw up the legal documents for joint Power of Attorney.'

'So what happened last night Rosa?' Charles asked her.

'He did fall out of bed, having had one of his dreams, and seeing you, did not help matters ... he genuinely thought you were a ghost. He has always insisted on having that disgusting pot under his bed. It goes back to his school days and he has always used it if I can remember.' She paused gathering her thoughts, 'his mattress is quite high up and he must have rolled off it onto the floor and ended up with his face in the piss pot. Poor Papa.' She got her handkerchief out and wiped her eyes, blowing her nose at the same time.

'Come on, let's get back. It's getting late and I need to relieve HP soon at the hospital.' Rosa gently kicked her horse and went into a gallop. They both followed her.

That night after HP had returned, they were talking in the Orangery, with coffee and brandy. Rosa had briefed HP on the headstone and their conversation.

'Marie, I know a professor at Oxford who is coming up next weekend to research your family history, together with the links to the Bankes's and the Dashwoods to see if we can gather more background to who the child was and why she died so young.'

'Thank you HP. That would throw some light on our family connections.'

'Can you stay up here with us, or do you need to go back to London to your offices?'

'I think the inspector wants me close to hand as she suspects I have something to do with the death in the lake, and tenuously, your father's predicament.'

'Nonsense! I will talk to her in the morning. Anyone with a brain can see you had nothing to do with either. Just because Papa thought you were Marie deVille's ghost, it is part of his illness.'

She felt that HP was concerned for her wellbeing and she admired him for it. Yes, she was attracted to him.

Arthur walked into the Orangery.

'Ahh, Marie, just the person I wanted to see. Have you got Clare's number please? I seem to have lost it.'

'Oh, yes … I am sure she will be devastated to hear you lost her number!' Marie joked as she read out her mobile and email address to him.

'Please don't tell her I lost it. She gave me it as she was leaving and I must have forgotten to save it on my mobile.'

'So, you have a soft spot for my housemate then?'

He blushed in front of his older brother, nodded some thanks and vanished out of the door sending a text message.

'It's good to see Arthur so … engaged in someone

other than his horses, and of course Papa.' HP was closer to his younger brother than Marie thought.

'Umm ... HP, if you want me to stay for the week I would love to, if I won't be in your way. I mean you, Rosa and Arthur have a lot to contend with, and your father's illness as well. But if I can help in any way, then I would be happy to do anything.'

'I like having you around,' he smiled at Marie in such a way it changed his looks and she saw yet another side to him.

*'He likes having me around!!'* Her heart missed a beat.

'Rosa told me about the headstone and you know about how we found Papa. I am sure that it's pure coincidence. Anyway, Prof Bailey is coming on Thursday now, so we need to prepare the background for him as much as possible. Please use my study if you need the internet or need to make any private calls.'

He turned to leave then hesitated and turned around again ... 'oh and if you need me to speak to James or Randolph about your leave of absence I will happily. Now I must finish some work before I relieve Rosa. Good night everyone.' He nodded and walked back to his study.


Charles was sat nursing a large brandy bowl, swirling the golden liquid around the rim of the glass. He was observing Marie's body language with HP.

'That man fancies the pants off you,' he stated.

'Nonsense, Charles.' She blushed.

'I don't mind you know. I think Rosa has a sweet spot for me ... for what it's worth.'

'She has. I could tell that today after you spent twenty minutes ogling our arses as we rode in front of you. I saw you both holding hands!'

'What about us then?' he asked suddenly.

'Charles, I have fancied you since I was ten but we have never been on a proper date. You are more like my brother and I think that anything more romantic will never happen. Besides ... you never know if we will end up being related!'

Charles threw his head back and gave a huge belly laugh.

'Oh my God, I do love you Marie. But you are right ... our love is more familiar than intimate.'

Marie smiled at him.

'Still fancy shagging you though!!'

She threw a cushion at him and laughed. This is what she needed.

'If I am to stay here, what are your plans this week?'

'I have to go back to the office tomorrow to complete the financials for HP on this and I have a couple of client meetings, too. But I will be back on Thursday. HP wants me to be here when the Professor arrives.'

She stood up unsteadily, and Charles jumped to his feet and put his arms around her.

'You okay my love?' he asked with a frown.

'Yes. Just too much brandy and I'm bloody exhausted, that's all.'

She went onto tiptoe and kissed him on each cheek.

'Good night, brother of mine. Hope your dreams don't keep you awake,' she walked away giggling to herself. He heard her saying, 'and you fancy a shag, do you?? In your dreams!'

Marie reached her room and heard voices down-stairs; HP and Charles. She closed her door and ran a hot bath. She had to sleep tonight, she was so shattered. She closed the huge heavy curtains and lit a small incense candle that was supposed to aid sleep, then stepped into the bath, sliding down into the hot, foaming, scented water; adjusted the waterproof pillow to fit into her neck and closed her eyes. She felt all the stress and emotion seep out of her, as her muscles softened in the hot water.

She thought about what HP had said to her; *'I like having you around.'* I like being around him, too. Then she thought of Charles. *Yes, he is more of a brother than a lover even though I have fancied him since I was young.'*

Her mind turned to the headstone in the grave-yard.

*'Why didn't Rosa say where we were going. It was an hour's ride each way, she could have warned me. Why didn't she? Did she just want to spend time with Charles or is there something I am not seeing here? She obviously knew about where Marie deVille Bankes was buried, but why make it so mysterious? And how did she know about Marie deVille's baby?'*

After her bath, she climbed into bed, made the pillows just as she liked, switched off the bedside light and closed her eyes.

In the dark of the night in the far distance a dog ... or a wolf let out a series of howls.

As she fell into a deep sleep ... in the distance ... a far off melodic sound ... she could hear a string quartet and harpsichord playing chamber music she did not recognise at first ...

# 16

# 1651

They were all gathered in the Long Gallery, drinking French wine and champagne from long fluted glasses. Marie had organised a group of musicians to play violin, harpsichord and guitar music from German and Polish composers she knew from home.

The occasion was a wake for His Lordship, the 1$^{st}$ Marquess of Flintwell. She also wanted to welcome his son Henry Robert Bankes, who had inherited his father's title and becoming the 2$^{nd}$ Marquess. His family were soon to move into Flintwell Hall from their home in France.

She had gathered all the local dignitaries, the Bishop of Lincoln, the local aristocratic families as well as her set of friends to meet Lord Henry Bankes. It was interesting that the only person who had declined the invitation was the Sheriff of Lincoln.

The wake had been postponed until now, following the sad news that Lord Robert Dashwood had passed away only days after the Marquess. Lisa was devastated and Harry spent all his time comforting her. Marie had also been spending time at their home with her best friend. Charles would inherit his father's title and lands and was busy dealing with the legal and hereditary processes.

Charles was now Lord Rodewelle, and had full intentions of making Marie his bride after the appropriate period of time had elapsed.

Marie had already accepted an invitation from Charles Dashwood to live in the Manor House in the grounds of Rodewelle House with him. They agreed to be discreet for a while before she took up residence, so she planned to return to her family in France, two days' later, for six months, which they both agreed was a prudent move.

However, the Sheriff of Lincoln was still unhappy with the circumstances surrounding the Marquess' death and wanted to investigate further. Both Lord Rodewelle and Lord Wentworth pleaded with the sheriff to drop the case, but the man was a belligerent old goat who had clearly been in His Lordship's pay. No one told him that Marie was leaving for France nor did he specify any restrictions on her movements.


Her travel chests and bags were packed and loaded onto one of Charles' spare coaches. The journey to Hull would take a day as they would catch the ferry boat from Barton across the Humber River to Kingston. A merchant ship would then take her to Boulogne where her father had arranged for his coachman to meet her for the four-day ride to her family château near Tours in the Loire Valley. She was not looking forward to the long and arduous journey, but Lisa had agreed to accompany her to meet her father and mother and see her ancestral home.

As the coach left Lisa's family home in Rodewelle, she was visibly nervous as she screwed a handkerchief in her trembling hands.

'What is it Lisa? You seem to be nervous. Is it the thought of the sea crossing?'

'Yes, that and … well … you see, it's the first time I have left home on a long journey,' … *hahaha* she tittered. 'Flintwell Hall is about the furthest I have been south!' she exclaimed.

'Don't worry. It will be an adventure,' Marie exclaimed, clapping her hands.

'It's a relatively short journey to Barton through the North Lincolnshire countryside. We then take the ferry to Kingston where we will board a merchantman. Charles said the sea crossing to Boulogne will be about four to six days dependent on the winds. We will stay at my uncle's château in Boulogne to rest a while before mon pere sends us the coach to take us home.' She was excited which made her French accent more exaggerated, and it gave Lisa some confidence that the journey would be easy. But a ship!!

'Oh, mon ami Lisa, you will love our château in Tours. It's a fabulous building and the countryside is not like yours. The Loire is a deep wide river and if they are home, my brothers will take us fishing.'

It was the first time Marie had mentioned her family.

'Tell me about your family.'

'Mon dieu! Have I not told you about them?'

'No. You never talk of them, only your father the Duc.'

'I am so sorry, Lisa. I should have told you before.'

'We have a long journey ahead, so we have plenty of time to talk.'

'My family have been in the Loire Valley at Tours for over a century, and we are very much aligned with the House of Bourbon, the late King Louis XIII and the Dauphin King Louis XIV. My father is Louis Bernard deVille, the 4$^{th}$ Duc of Touraine; my mother is Marie Isabelle deVille and I have two brothers, Artemis is older by a year and Henri is only twenty-one. My father is a lawyer and attends to Queen Anne and Cardinal Mazarin, who is Regent. He is always on state business so is at Chambord, Versailles or at the Palais Royal in Paris.'

'Am I to meet these people at all. I have never met a Cardinal, let alone a Queen or King. Heavens above, I would not know what to say or how to react … you will have to teach me Marie.'

Marie took Lisa's hand in hers and looked painfully into her eyes. Marie had a troubled expression on her face.

'What is troubling you my friend?'

She cleared her throat and in a very quiet voice with her French lilt, 'Lisa, mon cher ami, I have something to tell you. Please do not be angry with me for holding this back until now, but Charles thought it best.'

'Charles? What has my brother to do with this?'

Very hesitantly she stuttered out, 'I am having his child.'

'What!? You mean ... you and Charles ...?' she couldn't finish her sentence. The coach rolled and rocked over the bumpy road as they sat in silence for a while. Lisa's expression kept changing as she digested this information.

'Do your parents know? Is this why you are going to France?' She sounded annoyed but her facial expression did not reflect it.

'Non. Charles and I thought it would be prudent to have the child in France and let things settle at Flintwell Hall, what with the Sheriff of Lincoln questioning the Marquess' death, and all. I will return to England once the baby is born and we do plan to marry, but you know how society is in England.'

She was silent.

'I am so sorry I could not tell you. I wanted to but Charles said it was best if we waited until the journey to France. He said you would understand.'

Lisa sat in silence, just staring at Marie. Then as if

someone lit a candle, her face suddenly beamed, and she hugged Marie tightly.

'I am going to be an aunt.'

'Yes ... and my sister, too. Will you be my Matron of Honour at our wedding?'

'Yes, of course I will ... wait a minute ... Charles said to me as he shut the coach door, *"don't take issue with something you will hear, it's what I want."* He was gone before I could ask him what he meant.'

'He is a very wise man, your brother, and I love him so much. He has helped me through the ordeal of being with the Marquess,' she shivered at the mention of his name. 'and we spent the night together after the masked ball.'

'So, you must be at least 10 weeks. Are you sure it's not the Marquess' baby?'

'Good grief no! He was incapable to rising to any occasion,' Marie said tittering. Lisa giggled as well.

'You could always claim the child is the Marquess' and if it's a boy he would inherit Flintwell Hall and his father's title after the 2$^{nd}$ Marquess passes away. You would still be free to marry my brother and raise the child between you.'

'Lisa. This is why you are my very closest friend. You think just like your brother does.'

'No! Is this your plan?' she was shocked as well as

pleased.

Marie just sat there and nodded.

'So, you will tell your father and mother that the baby is the Marquess' and being born in France he will have dual nationality? And, on your return to England, no one will suspect?'

Marie smiled widely as she pressed her silk dress tightly around her stomach to show the small bump, that no one had noticed before.

'Will your parents be happy for you?'

'They are relieved that the Marquess has passed on. Mon Pere only sent me to England to remove me from France during the difficult times after King Louis XIII's death. They saw the Marquess as a fitting suitor for my status, and hoped that I would still be young enough to marry again. It's coming true, and I am sure Maman and mon Pere will approve of your brother once they have met you!'

'So, my purpose is not just to accompany you on this long journey, but to be your nurse maid, too?' she laughed loudly.

The rest of the journey was spent talking about names, people, parties and who Lisa would meet in France. Marie told her much more about life at the château. It passed the time as this was going to be an arduous journey.

They arrived at the pier at Barton and saw a strange

looking boat moored. The coachman unloaded their trunks into the front of the ferry and the ladies were invited to sit on the bench seat at the back. A team of four men, wearing ragged clothes started to pull at huge oars. The ferry stank of rotten fish and the bottom was awash with water. It did not feel safe as they started to cross the wide river. Half way across, the strong current caught the boat and the captain used this to propel them across sideways until they reached an eddy in the river when he pointed the bow towards the opposite shore, towards what looked like a small port.

There were ocean going sailing boats of various sizes and designs, some French, some Spanish galleons. The port of Hull was bustling with people, animals and noise. The air was filled with a mixture of spices, rotting fish and sewerage. The ferryman pulled in next to a huge vessel with three masts. There was a name on the back 'Touraine' and Marie knew the ship. It was high tide, so the climb up the wooden ladder to the quay-side was short. The four burley oarsmen carried their trunks up on their shoulders with ease and placed them on the quay side by the gang-plank of the merchantman. Marie paid the ferryman in coins, and he introduced her to a bearded, tall man with deep set eyes and a broody, weathered face, dressed in a uniform with a corner cap.

'This is Captain Franco Verdonet, my lady. He will

take you to your quarters.'

The Captain said nothing, just looked at the two women without any expression or regard for their status. As they stood there staring at each other, some sailors in bare feet wearing funny looking clothes, coulottes trousers and smocks took their trunks onto the ship.

The Captain put his arm up and waved at them to follow him as he strode across the gang-plank onto his ship. They followed him onto the main deck and through a low door set into the middle of rear quarters into the deck above. Inside there was a small hallway with several doors off; the ceiling was low and the Captain bent low. He opened a door into a small cabin that had two hammocks slung between the outside and inside walls, either side of a small porthole.

'This is your quarters for the journey,' he said in English in a deep low voice with a heavy French accent. 'You will dine with me and my officers in the messroom across the hall. I will allow you on the upper deck twice a day. For your own security and comfort, I suggest you stay in your quarters or the main saloon. Understand, this is a merchant ship, and my men are either thieves, murderers or vagabonds pressed into my service. Only my officers are to be trusted.'

'Mai oui mon Capitan,' Marie replied in French.

'Do you know who we are?' asked Lisa, clearly put

out by his manner.

'Yes, my Lady. I work for the Duc de Touraine and he has placed me in charge of his daughter and your Ladyship. Your safety and wellbeing are my primary concern, which is why I have these rules.' Again, showing no emotion at all.

'We will be five to seven days at sea before we reach Boulogne, so make yourselves as comfortable as our bare facilities allow. We take the high tide in twelve hours.' He left them to supervise the rest of his cargo and crew.

They looked at their tiny cabin in silence. The canvass hammocks were filthy and on shaking the blankets, some insects fell on the floor and wriggled away. Two of their trunks were stacked one on top of the other, tied to a retaining ring in the wall of the cabin by rope. They left their cabin and went to look at the main saloon. It was a large room with a huge table in the middle and a desk of sorts at the end facing the wide set of windows that looked out of the back of the ship. There were wooden chairs, maps, metal equipment used for navigation, and in the corner a solitary bunk bed … the Captain's, behind a curtain. The celling was very low and the floor was on a slant upwards towards the wide windows.

'Well, we had better get used to this. It's only for the next week Lisa. It surely won't be that bad?'

By day two they were in the North Sea, either

confined to their tiny cabin or being sick over the side on the top deck. The sea swell was huge. To the women the ship inside the harbour looked massive, but now it was bobbing up and down in this vast ocean, being thrown around at will by the massive waves, being pushed along by strong southerly winds. The Captain had the full rig on, both masts carrying all the canvass he could get up. He was taking advantage of the constant winds in their favour to make as much progress as possible.

Both Lisa and Marie could not keep anything down. Wine, small beer or food simply came up straight after consumption. They felt giddy, nauseous and dirty, as there was nowhere to wash. Added to this, Marie also started to feel sick from her pregnancy. The food brought up by the cook was never very appetising, always some kind of soup, thin watery liquid with bits of fish or meat in it and soda bread. They also had salt beef or pork with peas and occasionally salted cod with biscuits made from wheat flour and water. Raisins were given to the crew to stave off scurvy, but the officers had fruit or cheese and oatmeal biscuits.

Each officer took a watch of around three hours, one fore and one aft. The captain stood by the wheel constantly studying the stars, or using the sextant, looking at the sails or watching the horizon. Nothing escaped his attention, crew, officers, unlashed decking items or his passengers.

He hardly ever slept and ate on his own. The silent, scary type.

The officers were very polite and showed them due courtesy, helping with suggestions on how to cure sea sickness. All that is, apart from one … and the surly captain.

At dusk every evening, Lisa and Marie were allowed up on the top deck where the wheelhouse was. They were able to walk … or should we say stagger, around the deck and admire the view of the sea from the rear rail. The French flag stood erect on its pole over the rear gunwale in the strong winds and the women, wrapped in shawls and headscarves, had to brace themselves against the wind and sea spray as the bow of the ship crashed into yet another wave.

It felt better to be up on the deck, as they could ride the constant rise and fall of the decking. But the captain did not like people on the rear deck. He stood straight, bold, undaunted by the ship's movement, one hand in his waist band, one on the wheel, a cheroot protruding from his lips, unlit.

This privilege was also afforded them at 10am every morning for half an hour. Otherwise they remained in their hammocks swinging around in rhythm with the ship's undulations, or in the main saloon, playing cards or canasta with the off-duty officers.

On the third day at sea, Marie noticed a young man was always stood on his own in the righthand corner of the top deck just above the rope ladder leading up from the main deck. He did not appear to be an officer as he was dressed differently and was certainly not crew. He was dressed as a gentleman and had good strong facial features, clean shaven and well built, but not fat. She was unaware of any other passengers and as this was her father's ship, she decided to investigate. On this particular morning she approached him. He turned to climb down the ladder when she addressed him.

'Pray, who may you be? 'she asked in French.

He hesitated.

She asked again in English.

He was motionless, as if thinking of an answer.

'You are not an officer, nor are you crew, so what is your business on my father's ship?'

'Lorcan Vesey, your Ladyship.' He had a curious accent, as if it were partly Irish.

'And what is your position on this ship?'

'A mere passenger, Ma'am, seeking to travel to France on business.'

'Where are you lodged, if not with us?'

'I have my hammock on the crew deck with the others, your Ladyship.'

'What is your business, if I am not being too intrusive?'

'I am a lawyer, Ma'am. I work for a firm of solicitors in Hull.'

'And, pray, what is your destination?'

'Paris my lady. I have commercial business to deal with in Paris.'

'That's very dangerous, for an Englishman to be abroad in Paris on one's own.'

'I am not English, my lady, so have free passage across the continent.'

This piqued her curiosity more.

'Would you care to join my travelling companion and I in the saloon for a small beer or some wine?'

He hesitated and looked at the captain who was observing this exchange of words. Out of the corner of her eye she saw the captain nod slowly.

'That would be very kind of you my lady.' He followed her into the saloon.

'Sorry, I didn't catch your name?'

'Vesey ... Lorcan Vesey at your service Ma'am,' he bowed then bashed his head on the low cciling.

'May I present Lady Lisa Dashwood, and I am Marie deVille Bankes.'

'I am aware of who you both are. The Marchioness of Flintwell, my lady.'

'You are well informed Mr Vesey. Pray, if you are not English, where do you come from?'

'I am an Irish citizen, but live in the North of England, Ma'am. Difficult times with Cromwell invading my country, I find it safer in France.'

'Do you know my father, Mr. Vesey?'

'I am aware he is the Duc de Touraine, Louis Bernard de Ville, and your family wines are famous in the right circles.' A small smile crept onto his face.

'Thank you.'

'May I also present my sincere condolences at the sad loss of your late husband, the Marquess of Flintwell.'

'Oh! Did you know my late husband as well?' her curiosity once again piqued.

'I was distantly acquainted with him, through Mr Tilley, your late gamekeeper, Ma'am,'

She looked at him in total surprise. She was not expecting to hear of that low bred Thomas Tilley again.

Without a tremble in her voice she asked, 'how so Mr Vesey? What was your connection with Thomas Tilley and our estate?'

'My employer bought game off Mr Tilley after a shoot or a hunt, Ma'am which he sold to his clients.'

'A professional man of the bar, trading in meat?' Her voice now was high pitched and her French accent always became very pronounced.

'Yes, Ma'am. It does sound very curious, but my master represented a number of butchers and tradesmen across Hull and Yorkshire, so he added this to his service.'

'And you paid Tilley directly, did you?'

'Yes, my lady. Always in coins or notes to Mr Tilley. I am unsure if The Marquess ever saw a farthing.' He had a curious laugh, sort of a whinny, like a horse.

'I am unaware as my late husband did not share the household expenses with me.'

'Mr Tilley had a fitting end to his life, I gather. I am told he fell into a vat of beer and drowned?'

'That is correct, Mr Vesey. He was a greedy fool, who had ideas above his station,' she said firmly.

'You were not a fan, I take it?'

'No. I did not like the man. Always spying on everyone.'

The cook came bustling in with his pots of soup and a ladle to fill our mugs with. He looked at Lorcan Vesey, not expecting him to be here.

'Oh ... you are here? Does the Captain know?' he said in a blunt Cornish accent.

'Yes, he does. May I?' he helped himself to a pewter mug, ladled some soup and gave the cook a hard stare.

Marie thought he was becoming too familiar and questioned in her own mind how true his story was. It was a huge coincidence him knowing Thomas Tilley.

'Do I take it you are moving to Paris for work Mr Vesey?' Lisa asked, seeing the distress on Marie's face.

'That is a matter of conjecture, my Lady. If my dealings fare well, I may stay in France for a while, which would be good for my wellbeing.'

'Did you say you are a lawyer? What side of law do you practice?' Lisa continued.

'I cover all areas of the law, Ma'am. Especially civil and personal law.'

'Have you ever had dealings with my late husband on matters of the law Mr Vesey?' Marie piped up.

'Not personally my lady, but my masters have in the past worked with their cousins in Lincoln on matters concerning the estate at Flintwell.'

This took Marie by surprise. What was he doing on this very ship, she was also on? Was this a pure coincidence? Was the Sheriff of Lincoln extending his reach and spying on her?

She became very uncertain of this man, and wished Charles could be with her now. She had this overwhelming feeling that there was more to this man than he portrayed. She remembered the look between him and the captain as if he was in on a conspiracy. She must ask her father how well he knew the captain.

The weather changed on day four and calmed to a

brisk breeze. It was still enough to fill all the sails still at full stretch, pulling this massive ship through the water at a fast pace. The Captain seemed pleased with their progress. On occasions, he sounded a bell which brought all the men onto the deck, and they rolled out 10 cannons to each side of the ship on the main deck. Marie heard a lot of banging as doors in the hull sides opened. The sighting of sails in the far distance alerted the Captain to a possible pirate or enemy attack and he was diligent in protecting his ship. So, these ships were man-of-war fighting ships as well as merchant ships.

After they stood down, the Captain was not pleased to see the women on the top deck, watching.

'My Lady,' he said in a gruff English accent for Lisa's benefit, 'I insist that you stay below in the saloon at all times when the bell sounds. It could be dangerous for you to be on deck.'

'No more dangerous than being blown up in the cabin Captain, and I would prefer advance notice if the ship were to sink so that I can take my place in the long boat before the men or even jump into the water,' she said defiantly.

The Captain stared at her open mouthed and said nothing, but walked off shaking his head.

Marie saw Mr Vesey several times from a distance as he now took his exercise on the upper front poop deck, clearly avoiding the women and the endless questions. *'Something to hide, me thinks!'*

Boulogne harbour was a sight to see, arriving on the fifth day. The Captain was sailing on to the Caribbean after a two-day stop in Boulogne it transpired, but Mr. Vesey was one of the first to disembark.

Marie and Lisa watched as their trunks were loaded onto a horse-drawn wagon ladened with wine casks for the Duc's estate. Her father's personal carriage was waiting on the dock-side for her to leave the ship. Her father's coachman, Joseph was there to greet Marie.

'Bonjour votre seigneurie.' He greeted her with a huge beaming smile.

'Joseph, it's been a long time since I have seen you. What a great surprise!' She greeted the old retainer in French and introduced Lisa.

'Joseph has been the Duc's personal coachman since he was a boy, taking over from his father. He has known me from birth.'

Lisa could see that Marie was clearly pleased to see a familiar face.

'Your uncle sends his apologies and suggests we travel directly to Tours. With the current unrest here it will be dangerous for you to stay in Boulogne,' Joseph relayed the message.

'Well, in that case, let's go and see if we can get a bath in this hostelry here and some decent food before we set off for the Chateau,' she explained to Joseph and marched into the hostel.

After a hot bath, which they shared and a freshly-cooked chicken, they at last took their seats in the very comfortable coach for the five-day journey to Tours in the Loire Valley.

The journey was long and arduous, the roads were not brilliant and they had to take several detours to avoid troublesome towns and villages. France was in turmoil, with an 8-year-old Dauphin King, being ruled by Cardinal Mazarin as Regent with Queen Anne, the King's mother. There were factions in the countryside who wanted a revolution to overthrow the monarchy, but this wouldn't happen for some years and was the start of the revolution. Joseph was an old man, but he was very protective and wise and kept the ladies from any harm. With him on the journey was a young apprentice from the village as Joseph had no children of his own. Every evening they would stop at an inn which Joseph had carefully selected and everyone knew him. The rooms were very basic but comfortable; straw mattresses on the floor and the food fresh and humble.

At long last, Marie shouted out, 'Le Pont de Touraine,' pointing out of the window. Look Lisa. We are nearly home, this is the bridge we go over soon that stands at the entrance to our chateau.' The excitement in her voice was evident and her whole demeanour changed as she prepared herself to meet her family after five years apart. Tears slipped out of the corners of her eyes as she started to recognise everything and she wave enthusiastically to all the farm people who stopped what they were doing, stared for a while, then jumped up and down waving and shouting out something in French.

Just over the bridge was a huge, stone gateway, ornate with a coat of arms painted with colours and inlaid with gold leaf. Joseph drove the four horses up the long, narrow roadway that led eventually, after a few kilometres to a massive chateau, so large that it dwarfed anything Lisa had ever seen in England. She was mesmerised by the sheer size.

Waiting outside were about fifty people. Most of the servants came to welcome the Marchioness home, and there, unmistakably were the Duc and Duchesse and two strapping young men in very fine clothes.

Marie jumped out of the coach and ran into her mother's outstretched arms, then to her father and brothers in turn. She wept openly with tears of joy, speaking very quickly in French. She turned as Lisa slowly exited the coach.

In English she said, 'please may I present Lady Lisa Dashwood, my best friend. Maman, mon Pere, the Duc and Duchesse. Oh, and these are my wayward brothers, Artemis and Henri.'

They all greeted her and Lisa used what little French Marie had taught her on the journey, which impressed the boys.

In a broken English accent, Marie's mother said, 'come Lisa, you must be exhausted after such a long and arduous journey. Let me take you to your chambers. We have a hot bath prepared for you and we have a light dinner tonight, just the family.'

'Thank you, your Ladyship.'

'Please, it's Isabelle. I don't use Marie. We called our daughter the same name and it gets confusing.' She gave a light laugh. Her mother was elegant with such smooth skin, and so petite, Lisa could see who Marie took after.

As they entered through the grand doors into the gigantic hall, a footman approached with a refreshing glass of white liquid. It was a sweet juice made from the fruit grown on the estate and it was so refreshing.

In the background, a myriad of servants manhandled

the huge trunks up to their rooms, as Lisa, Marie and the Duchesse walked slowly through the main gallery of the chateau. Lisa was mesmerised by its size. They had a long gallery like the one at Flintwell, but it was five times longer, higher and broader and could probably accommodate a few hundred people. It was as if the French did everything on a much larger scale to the English. She loved it.

Eventually, Marie and Isabelle showed Lisa to her bed chamber where two pretty servant girls were waiting for her next to a huge ornate metal bath pushed next to a roaring fire, despite the fact it was summer. The room was, again very large with high ceilings and tapestries mixed with portraits hanging from each wall.

'We will leave you in peace to enjoy a good soak. Marie or Artemis will come and escort you to dinner at seven. Enjoy your bath.' They left her by closing the full height double doors, ornate with gold leaf.

The two handmaidens helped her to undress and she slid into the hot, deliciously-perfumed water and closed her eyes.

She thought about the long journey here and everything she had learned from Marie. It had certainly brought them closer together. She was shocked at how the Marquess had treated her in private and of the degrading things he had asked her to do. No wonder she had detested him so much. Tonight, Marie planned to tell her parents about the baby. Her mind drifted to Artemis ... what an attractively handsome man ... and still single, too ... mmm ... what if? She could not stop thinking about the possibilities of living here in France. What a different way of life they had. Maybe, with the political state of England with Cromwell in charge, France might be a better alternative. Maybe she should stay here ... although her relationship with Henry Wentworth was probably worth progressing. They were a wealthy family, the wrong side of English politics though.

At 7pm, there was a gentle tap on her door. One of the handmaidens opened the door, curtsied and blushed, as the handsome Artemis stood with an outstretched arm.

'Mademoiselle Lisa ... I have the pleasure of escorting you to dinner,' he said in a deep French accent, but in perfect English.

'I too am honoured, my Lord, to have your hand,' she smiled at him with sparkling eyes.

At the top of the main central staircase, Lisa looked down at a sea of faces as they looked up to watch her and Artemis descend the curving stone stairs. She saw Marie talking to her parents, and the other people looked so refined in their expensive, beautiful clothes.

Artemis stopped on the second step and coughed loudly holding his other hand to his mouth.

'Mesdames et messieurs, j'ai l'honneur de vous présenter Lady Lisa Dashwood, le bon ami intime de ma soeur, Marie Celestine.'

Everyone clapped politely and Lisa whispered to Artemis as they descended into the crowd, 'do they all know I can't speak much French?'

He squeezed her hand, 'do not worry, mon chéri, I will stay close with you and translate. My honour.'

She felt a shiver of pure pleasure ripple through her inner core as she became entranced by his incredibly sexy voice and accent. She was falling for him already .... and she had only just arrived!

They circulated. Paid their respects to the Duc and Duchesse and he dutifully introduced her to the other guests. Some were family; cousins, aunts and uncles; some were neighbours and others just close friends.

A gong sounded.

'Lisa, mon chéri, it is the dinner bell. We go now to eat,' and gently took her arm on his to escort her into the dining room.

They entered the large, bright dining room, which was lit by thousands of candles. There were two huge chandeliers over the fine long dining table, and candelabra stands all around the room. She had never seen such an ostentatious table, ladened with wine glasses and very fine silver cutlery.

Lisa was seated between Marie and Artemis, and Marie squeezed her hand under the table.

'This is so wonderful, Marie,' she whispered in her ear, 'and your brother is scrumptious.'

Marie turned with a surprised look on her face.

'That was fast,' she whispered back with a mischievous smile on her face.

'Mmmm … you have a very attractive brother. You never told me he was that handsome!'

They laughed out loud, and received a reprimanding raised eyebrow from the Duc.

'Tomorrow I have to tell my parents about the child. I'm not sure how they will take it. My mother has already commented on how much weight I have put on.'

'Do you want me to be with you when you tell them, sort of moral support?'

'Please, Lisa, that would be very good of you.'

'Do they know of the Marquess' death yet?'

'Yes, they know that.'

The evening meal was substantial, all the food carried in on platters and placed in the middle for everyone to help themselves. The wine was exceptional and for both Marie and Lisa the evening passed quickly.

The next morning, after a light breakfast meal, Lisa accompanied Marie into her father's study. Both her parents were very apprehensive as they knew that bad news was about to come.

'My Father and Mother. Please can we speak in English for Lisa's sake.'

Both nodded consent but said nothing.

'I have some news to tell you. The reason I am of greater weight maman, is because I am with child.' She paused to let this sink in. Her mother's hand shot up to her mouth and her father stood stiffly.

'It is the Marquess' child?' he asked.

'Yes, mon Pere. Who else do you think it would be?' Marie had a hurt look on her face.

The Duc hesitated a while, his face had reddened … 'we were under the impression that the Marquess was … how do you say in English …ahh oui … barren?'

'Non, mon Pere,' she said firmly, tears started to run down her cheeks. Lisa went to comfort her.

'If I may, my Lord, your daughter was physically accosted by the Marquess, who forced himself on her.' Lisa was formidable in front of these two highly-respected members of the French aristocracy, but she had to support her friend in her deception.

'And you know this to be true?' asked the Duchess.

'Yes. I was there when Marie screamed out in pain.

The man was vulgar, filthy and a disgrace to his peerage.'

'You are therefore carrying an heir to the Flintwell estate,' the Duc commented.

'That is so, mon Pere. But I have a request to make of you both?'

They were silent waiting for her to answer.

'I would like to have my baby here at home, before returning to England.'

Marie's mother rushed forward and embraced her daughter, holding her tightly in her arms. Her father stood emotionless.

'If it pleases you my Lord and Lady, I am happy to remain here with Marie until the birth.' Lisa wanted their permission to stay and perhaps develop her relationship with Artemis.

Outside her father's study, Marie grabbed Lisa's hand and they both ran holding their dresses up in their other hands, out through the double doors into the formal gardens of the chateau. They found a seat and slumped down with a huge sigh of relief.

'Well that's over, thank God,' Marie said.

'We have permission to stay, my dear friend, here with your lovely family,' Lisa said.

'You mean … it gives you seven months to woo my brother?' Marie said sarcastically.

'Well … yes … there is that pleasure … but you wouldn't want your brother to end up with someone you didn't take to. But your closest friend, however …'

They both giggled and held hands.

In the distance they could hear church bells ringing … strange for a weekday …

# 17

# Tuesday

# July 2017

8am. She thought she heard pealing church bells, but it was just a notification on a new app on her mobile phone.

She sat up in bed and shook her head.

She felt exhausted … drained … hungry.

She thought it very strange how she could see through Lisa's eyes as well at times … that hadn't happened before.

She put her head in her hands as she recalled where she was and what was happening today. She had an interview with the police about the body in the lake and his Lordship's demise. She cursed these dreams she was having. She remembered that the forensic historian was coming to see HP and her on Thursday. More questions, more recounting her dreams.

How she wished that this was not happening. But deep down inside her she wanted to know about her ancestors and was she really related to these aristocratic families; the Dashwoods and the Bankes and was her own family part of the French aristocracy one hundred and forty years before the French revolution.

She felt weary and didn't want to get out of bed, but knew she had to get through today and all the police questioning.

Down at breakfast, HP was standing by the big windows talking on his mobile. Charles was sat next to Rosa. Arthur was quietly eating a cooked breakfast. As was tradition in the Hall, the kitchens placed a series of hot plates out on the side-board and everyone helped themselves. Tea, coffee and fresh juice were on the table.

'Morning everyone,' Marie greeted in a friendly but tired voice.

'Marie, that was Inspector Scott I was talking to. She wants to know if she can speak to us at ten this morning, just to tie up a few loose ends … as she puts it.' He came and took the seat next to her, opposite Charles and Rosa.

'Why does that infernal pest keep coming here? She must know that Marie could not have been involved.' Arthur suddenly blurted out in frustration.

'Come on Arthur, she is only doing her job,' Rosa intervened.

'I would like you all to be around on Thursday to meet the professor. He is researching our family backgrounds … yours too Charles, to find out what has happened over the years and how we have developed as a family. You never know … we may all be related somehow. It will be fascinating!' HP was very excited.

Marie looked glum, Rosa picked up on this.

'You don't seem excited Marie. Afraid of a few ghosts in your closet?' she said with a smirk on her face.

'Not looking forward to it, no!' she looked at Rosa, 'when did you discover the headstone Rosa?'

'What headstone?' asked HP.

'In Rothwell village church, there is a headstone for Marie deVille Banks, the 4th Marchioness of Flintwell, died in 1653. There was some inscription in French,' Charles volunteered.

Rosa looked around the breakfast table, all eyes were on her.

'I was looking for Charles' ancestral home, to see if it was still there. It's not, apparently it burned down in the middle 1600s and its now a pub. I happened to look into the local church to see if any family were buried there. I came across Marie deVille's grave by chance. There are a few Dashwoods buried there as well, but they were before 1620s.' she looked satisfied with herself. 'Oh … and I took you there as I thought it would help you … that's all.'

'Bloody hell, Marie. The professor will be interested in that,' HP said excitedly.

'My ancestors sold the remains of Rodewelle House to another land owner in the late 1600s. We have been in

Newark ever since and my namesake in your dreams Marie is buried in our family plot. He was 62 when he died.'

Charles tried to ease the building tension between Marie and Rosa, not sure why the two women were so aggressive this morning.

At 10am Inspector Scott arrived and was shown into the library. Everyone was waiting, apprehensive and tense.

'Good morning your Lordship, how is your father?' Helen Scott asked directly.

'He is still in a coma. The doctors are not sure that he will recover so it's a question of how long we prolong the coma. He is not a well man anyway, and his cancer has spread so he will have no life at all if he comes out of it.'

'I am sorry to have to hold this meeting this morning, but I just need to satisfy myself on a few questions.' She looked at Marie when she said this.

'You said in your statement that you rode your horse around the lake with Lisa Dashwood and saw the body *"floating like a log"*. Is this the first time you saw the body?'

'Yes. The body I mean. But as I told you I saw two people arguing by the lake from my bedroom window at about 3am. It was a full moon and clear sky so they were silhouetted against the lake. I couldn't see who they were though.'

'So, you were not outside when you saw them? You weren't taking a stroll in the grounds at the front of the Hall?'

'No, I was in my nightdress in my room. Why do you ask?' Marie had an angry edge to her tone.

'We have CCTV footage of the time in question and there was another person in the grounds at that time. The CCTV has picked up the couple arguing by the lakeside, but one walks off – looks like a female. The other was hit over his head by a branch and pushed into the lake by this other person.'

'And you think that was me?' Marie said petulantly.

'He was clearly murdered and we cannot get a clear view of the other person. How tall are you Miss deVille?'

'Five feet two, why?'

'That rules you out then. This person was at least six feet. This is a murder case and we want to arrest the right person.'

'Did you not say, Inspector, that the woman was raped that evening?' asked HP.

'Yes, that's right your Lordship.'

'Please, its HP. My father is still alive and he is the Marquess. So, who raped the poor girl, the guy in the lake, or the other guy you found?'

'The DNA taken from the girl matches the boy in the

lake, so the murderer could be a relative or boyfriend.'

'Or girlfriend,' added Marie sarcastically.

Helen raised her head from her writing pad and looked at her. Slowly she said, 'yes, you are right Miss deVille, it could well have been a woman, but a tall one at that!'

There was silence in the library as everyone sat pensively.

'Did anyone notice or see anything suspicious that night?' Lisa asked, in general.

'It sounds as if we were all tucked up in our beds, Inspector. So, it's a rather moot point,' HP said defensively.

It was like water off a duck's back to the seasoned policewoman.

'Turning to his Lordship. Miss deVille, you said that you never entered his Lordship's room the night he was taken ill?'

'Yes, she stood at the door to his bedroom and asked me if I needed any help,' Rosa answered.

Helen Scott turned to Rosa with a quizzical look.

'I was asking Miss deVille,' she said rather too sharply.

'Then you have your answer, Inspector. I did not enter his room as he has this belief that I am a ghost of my ancestor. But you know all this,' Marie answered sternly.

'We are trying to establish if you have any hand in his

Lordship's fall that morning. I would be obliged if you could answer my questions. The sooner I get the right answers the better for all of us.'

'Inspector, my father is very ill. He is prone to sleep walking and he did go into Marie's bedroom. He fell out of his own bed and landed in his latrine bowl. I am sure that Marie deVille had no part in his illness. We have been expecting this for some time. My father had very odd habits and one from his school days was to have a chamber under his bed. The similarities to the 1st Marquise are purely coincidental. Now can we all go please.' HP was getting fed up with the inspector's continuous repeated questions.

She sensed this and closed her notebook.

'Very well. That will be all. You are free to go. My apologies HP, but I want to be thorough with this. We have a murderer on the loose on your grounds, and we intend to find them.'

After she had gone, Marie burst into tears and sobbed heavily. HP put his arms around her and held her tightly.

Kissing her on her head, he whispered, 'it's all over now. Don't worry about anything. If you want me to cancel the professor I will, you know?'

'No, don't do that. It will be interesting to find out about Marie deVille and how she met her death. I know that I am related, but how? And her headstone puts a different perspective on her life. I wonder if I will see this in my dreams?'

'So, you dream about this every night, do you?' HP was really concerned.

'Yes. I can't have a night without living through her eyes in the 17$^{th}$ century. I can see, feel and smell everything as if I am right there. And now, I seem to be able to see through Lisa's eyes as well.'

HP sat up and had a shocked expression on his face.

'You mean Lisa Dashwood? Is she there as well?'

'Yes. Lisa also has a distant relative who was Marie deVille's best friend. Last night they arrived in France at her parent's chateau in the Loire valley, and she is pregnant with a child that is Lord Dashwood's, but she will tell everyone that it was the Marquess' child, from the last time he raped her. She killed him you know!' Marie was recounting this as if it was just a chit-chat.

'Sorry, did I hear, right? Marie killed her husband?'

'Yes. Gave him a sleeping draught and made him choke on his own vomit, then she peed on his face before he expired. And she had Thomas Tilley killed as well. Charles and Henry pushed him into a vat of beer whilst he was inspecting it during the masked ball. They climbed up the ladder after him and dislodged his feet in the rungs and he fell head first into the beer. They then held his head under with a stirring paddle until he died … oh, and she also killed the garden boy Able Jones, as well. Pushed him into the lake when he was drunk. She was quite a lady!'

HP sat quietly digesting what she had told him. Marie was now worried she had said too much.

'My dreams are horrific, and I need to seek help HP. I need psychiatric help or something to stop these dreams. I am getting very tired and can't cope much more with the disturbed nights.'

'I am utterly flabbergasted my love. You poor thing. I never realised they were so vivid.'

*"He called me, my love ... he does care for me,"* she thought to herself.

'Marie. You need to write your dreams down as it will help the professor in his investigation. You are in France now? And you say she is pregnant with Lord Dashwood's child, which she will pass off as the Marquise's child? So, she did have an affair with Charles Dashwood?'

'They were in love and what I don't know yet is if she has the child in France or back in England. But if she died in 1653 from childbirth, then she must have had another baby?'

'I suppose you will only know through the next few nights?' HP suddenly realised what he had said and put his hand to his mouth.

'I am sorry. I am suggesting you go through this hell for the next two nights to find out what happens?'

'HP. Please don't worry about that. Until I can get a shrink to penetrate my brain, I am going to have to learn to live with it. But you are right, I need to write these dreams down.'

'Please feel free to use my computer or laptop in here. This house is as much yours as mine, I believe, and I want you close to me.'

She stood up unsteadily and HP grabbed her around the waist. He pulled her into his arms and they gently kissed.

His lips were soft and warm, and he kissed her with a deep passion. She felt safe in his arms. He was slender but had a very firm, toned physique. As he held her tightly she felt his hardness push against her.

'You know that I am falling in love with you, Miss deVille,' he whispered into her ear.

'Oh HP, I feel so safe with you and I am falling in love with you too.'

He suddenly let her go.

'I am sorry ... what about Charles?' he suddenly said.

She giggled and took hold of HP looking up into his eyes.

'Charles and I are like siblings. Our love for each other is purely a sister for a brother. We have known each other since childhood and I suspect there is a family connection there, too.'

He was relieved. 'I would not want to come between you.'

'I think you need to look out for your sister Rosa. Haven't you noticed how they are always together recently?'

'Well I never!' he exclaimed. 'That explains it then!'

'What?'

'Why Rosa has been so protective of Charles and so aggressive towards you.'

'Let's go out to dinner tonight in Lincoln. Just you and me. I want to get to know all about you.'


For the first time in a long while, Marie was giddily happy. The more she thought about HP, the more she found herself falling for him. She spent all day in his study writing up each night's dreams, or as much as she could remember, putting them into chronological order.

That afternoon she went riding with Rosa and Charles and could see the little signs of romance with their touching and the way they looked at each other.

As they were riding back to the Hall up the front parkland Marie suddenly said with a smile on her face, 'HP has asked me out to dinner tonight so the two of you have the Hall to yourselves,' she winked at Charles and took Rosa's hand.

'You don't mind me dating your older brother, do you

Rosa?'

She smiled and squeezed Marie's hand, 'not at all my love, I am so happy for you both. He deserves a break and you are perfect for him.'

She showered using her most expensive gel that left her feeling fresh, washed her hair and selected her sexiest underwear, sat at her dressing table and carefully applied her makeup, not that she needed to use a lot. She looked at herself in the mirror whilst brushing her dark hair until it shone. She wondered what HP would be like when they were alone and what they would talk about. Looking at her limited wardrobe, she decided to wear her only posh dress, strawberry red, low cut, knee length, one piece that clung to her curves. She felt very … sexy and excited, ready to meet HP in the front of the Hall.

As she walked down the curving stone staircase, HP turned to look up at her … his mouth dropped open and he stared at her as if he had never seen her before. He whistled as she walked slowly down the stairs.

'Wow … you look … stunning Marie,' his face showed her a different side to him … soft, warm and loving.

'Why thank you HP. That's the nicest thing anyone has said to me in a very long time.'

He took her hand as she reached the last step and

she stopped. He raised her hand and gently kissed it. She felt an electric current surge through her body at the sensation of his lips on her hand. She leant forward to place a kiss on his cheek. The last step gave her some height to match his, as he slipped his arm around her waist and led her to his waiting car.

She slid into the soft cream leather seats of HP's Aston Martin as he gently closed her door. Driving through the gated entrance of the Hall, he headed towards Lincoln and the restaurant he had carefully chosen for its excellent food and romantic setting.

Marie was giddy with excitement. She did not know what to expect but hoped that tonight would bring them closer together.

'Where are you taking me, HP?'

'A little restaurant I know not far away. It has an excellent reputation for the fines food and wines, but it's not pretentious,' he was different somehow, more relaxed.

Dressed in cream chino's, an open necked blue pin-stripped shirt and a linen dark blue blazer, he looked striking and very handsome. God, she fancied him so much.

'So, is this where you take all your girlfriends?' she teased.

'Not at all. In fact, you are the first girlfriend I have entertained here. Come to think of it, you are my first proper date.' He was so casual and relaxed.

She turned to look at him, and smiled, excitement burning into her chest.

They arrived at a small stone-built house, covered in Virginia creeper, with a car park packed with Range Rovers and other expensive cars. HP was welcomed, obvious that he knew the proprietor well. He led them to a discreet corner table, a single red rose in the centre. HP ordered two glasses of Champagne.

'Here's to us, Marie. I hope we can see a lot more of each other, on a more … um … personal basis,' he stammered as if unsure of her reaction.

She blushed.

'I would love that,' she said with a huge grin on her face.

'Tell me more about you. I want to know everything about this Marie deVille,' he said touching her hand across the table. 'The beautiful woman sat in front of me,' he added.

She sipped her Champagne, looking at him with her head to one side.

'Not much to tell really. Born and bred in Sussex. Father is English with French ancestry, mother is from Yorkshire and very down to earth,' she stopped and giggled to herself, 'calls a spade a bloody shovel! You will love her directness, no airs or graces. Got an older brother, who's very bright and a bit of a geek. Went to University in York and got a First in English Language and Linguistics. Got my job at the agency three years ago and you know the rest.'

He was gazing at her mesmerised.

'Shall we order?' looking at the menu, 'I can recommend their meats, best chef in the world. I wish he would work for me, but he is totally loyal to Fred and Daisy who own this place.'

'Oh yes … look at this? They have ceviché as starters. I will have that and the filet – blue,' Marie was fascinated by the menu.

'What's ceviché?

'It's a Peruvian dish made by marinating raw fish in lime juice with herbs. It's delicious.'

'Okay, I will have that too.' HP said to the waitress as she came for their order and asked for a bottle of wine her clearly knew.

'So, you like raw fish and raw meat? Bit of a carnivore, are we?' He added in a teasing way.

Marie took a sip of her Champagne, looking into his eyes, with a small smile creasing her cheeks.

'What about you HP? Born into aristocracy, public school … was it Eton? Silver spoon and all that?' He said nothing but just looked at her.

She thought he had taken that comment the wrong way, as there was no expression on his face.

'I like your family, Arthur and Rosa, and I love your home. I do admire what you are doing to make your home a very special hotel, you know.'

'Being an aristocrat and inheriting old family wealth is a massive burden with death duties and so forth. My ancestors owned nearly all of Lincolnshire and over the years they have had to sell off tranches of land to pay these dues. When my father fell ill, I knew what was coming on his death, so I had to plan for it. Fortunately, my sister and brother fully support me, so we can continue our family traditions and pay this government their unfair taxes. The exclusive hotel idea was actually my sisters.' HP was suddenly very serious, and she felt in awe of his huge responsibilities.

'HP. For what it's worth, I admire what you have done to your family home and would love to be part of it.' She reached over a squeezed his hand.

The first course arrived, and she started to eat. He sat and watched her tucking in, smiling. He picked up his fork and tried a small amount of fish. His facial expression changed from surprise to a broad smile.

'Mmmm ... this is delicious,' he said as he tried another mouthful.

'You like it?' She asked.

Anyone watching the young couple in the corner would have seen the inter-action with the light touching of hands across the table, their posture and the intense focus on each other, throughout their three courses. They laughed spontaneously, held frequent eye contact and it was obvious they were in love.

As the meal came to an end, HP excused himself and spoke briefly with the owner.

He returned to the table and held out his hand to her. He held it all the way out to the car and opened her door. She turned to face him and put her arms around his neck ... and they kissed gently ... to begin with, then more intently. He held her in his arms feeling all the way down to the small of her back, totally oblivious to other guests leaving the restaurant.

'I think we are causing a hold up, so we had better go,' he whispered into her ear, his lips caressing her ear lobe and smelling her hair.

'Take me home HP … please?' she moaned with pleasure.

She couldn't remember the journey home as he drove quickly through the narrow lanes.

She couldn't remember the meal it went so quickly, but when they returned to the Hall, he took her hand and led her to his room. Taking her into his arms, she placed hers around his neck and their lips brushed together lightly … at first … before they devoured each other.

'I am sorry for not asking you first, Marie, but I think I'm in love with you. You've fascinated and enchanted me since the first time I laid eyes on you.'

'Oh, do shut up and make love to me, HP.'

He found the zipper to her dress and slid it down her back, gently pulling the front of her dress away from her curves and let it drop to the floor. He expertly unclipped her bra with a single move, one handed and slid her straps off her shoulder, cupping her small rounded breasts gently in each hand. Her nipples hardened to his touch as she unbuttoned his shirt, then pulled his belt buckle to remove his trousers which fell to the floor. She led him to the bed and laid back as he gently removed her white silk knickers.

Their love making went on until the early hours of the morning, each slowly exploring the other's body. Marie had never felt this way before. HP was a very accomplished lover, sensual, open and very intimate. She was experiencing some of the sensations she had felt in her dreams and it was amazing. She was falling deeply in love with this man.

They eventually fell asleep, HP holding her in his arms, their warm naked bodies touching, she felt safe.

A few hours later … HP was gently prodding her, smoothing her wet hair back with his hand as he held her in his arms.

'…. hush-hush. Marie, come on, wake up … shshsh … you are safe with me ….' His gentle voice penetrated her dreams and brought her out of her nightmare.

'… oh my God … HP … what was I doing?'

'Don't worry … just one of your nightmares.'

'Tell me what was I saying.'

'It wasn't what you were saying exactly … although you were shouting in French … it was more the screams, panting and holding your breath and how you were holding your tummy. I think you were living through the birth of a child.'

She was soaking wet again. Her hair was a tangled mess, her mascara had run down her cheeks as she had tears weeping from the corners of her eyes.

HP let her go as she got out of bed. She stood still for a while, gathering her thoughts, before going into the bathroom. Looking into the mirror she swore at herself.

*"How could you ruin such a romantic experience with such a sexy man ... you French whore and murderess."*

'Who were you talking to?' HP was leaning against the bathroom door, just gazing at her naked figure.

'You are so beautiful,' he said to her.

'I was talking to my inner self ... the witch who consumes my nightly dreams ... you are so sweet but I think you need to see an optician,' she gave a little titter at her own joke.

He came in and put his arms around her waist. She felt his manhood pressed against her.

'Come back to bed my love. We can sort your dream out in the morning.'

He was so gentle and led her back to his bed. He

made her get into his side of the bed and laid down on her damp side. This made her realise what a wonderful selfless man he was.

'She gave birth to a baby boy,' was all she said as she closed her eyes and went into a deep sleep.

# 18

# 1651

Her bed chamber was filled with people. Most she didn't know. She was in pain; the contractions were coming quickly. The physician had asked her to kneel on all fours for the birth. She really wanted everyone out.

'Lisa, maman … please ask everyone to leave. I don't want this to be a public spectacle for their amusement. The physician and two maids can stay to help.'

No one moved.

'GET OUT EVERYONE!' she screamed angrily. 'POUR L'AMOUR DE DIEU … VOUS ALLEZ MAINTENANT … À PRÉSENT!' Her voice was piercing from someone so small. Her face was contorted and angry … like she had some sort of a demon inside her. She was not to be contradicted … this was a side Lisa had never seen before.

The room erupted into a cacophony of grumbling voices as the crowd of people moved very quickly through the door. The Duchess asked two of the maids to stay and help the physician. It was customary for people to watch the birth in France, but Marie thought this was intrusive. She did not want all and sundry to see her semi naked, in pain, delivering her first baby.

Marie was lucky in some respects. Being petite, she didn't show much of a bump, although it was so heavy she could hardly move. She could feel the child inside her shuffling around and kicking hard. All she wanted was for this to be over. Her contractions started a day ago, with her confinement in her room. Lisa had been with her all the time, bringing her some food and water, and occasionally some port to drink.

She felt light headed. This was not going to be an easy birth, she could sense. There were two delivery position options; on her back or on all fours as if mimicking a cow. She was told it would be easier on all fours, given the size of the baby.

When the time came and her waters broke, she lifted her nightdress and assumed the position. The physician had a huge metal contraption they used on animals that looked like a pair of fire tongues. He would use this if the baby got stuck.

The past six months had been wonderful with Lisa by her side. Well … Lisa and her brother Artemis … they had become lovers. They were attentive and spent a lot of their time with her, playing cards or dice or strolling in the grounds. Before she got too big they used to go for rides through the vineyards on her favourite horse and latterly in a fine open carriage with Artemis at the reins. They had picnics on the banks of the Loire and played guitar and violin to popular music. She was very happy and felt safe in her family home.

Although France was in a period of huge unrest and the Duc seemed to spend most of his time away in Paris or where-ever Mazarin was, her mother and the rest of the family lived in ostentatious wealth, secluded in their grand chateau surrounded by vineyards, oblivious to the changing politics.

Her life in England had become a distant memory in such a short space of time. The only person she missed was her beloved Charles. Only Lisa knew that the child was his. Everyone else accepted the fact it was the late Henry Bankes, the 1st Marquess of Flintwell, who had fathered the baby.

Marie knew that after the birth, she would go back to England to start a new life with Charles Dashwood at his magnificent home in Rodewelle, and she hoped she would live happily ever after as Lady Dashwood. The thought made her happy. She did not care for Flintwell Hall but this child would be a Bankes and if it were a boy, then he would inherit the title at some point.

*"God, I hope it doesn't look like Charles. It had to be like her as the Bankes all had hereditary pale skin and either ginger or red hair,"* she thought to herself as she

spread her weight on her hands and knees in the middle of the bed.

She had been in this position for several hours now and she was becoming very uncomfortable. Her back ached in agony from carrying the weight, her hands and legs numb from all the blood running into them. They tingled with pins and needles. She longed to lie down on her back or at least sit in a chair.

Her head thumped with an acute pain in her forehead and she was very hot and sweaty.

*"Women like doing this? They have five or six children ... never again will I give birth,"* she said to herself.

'How much longer will this be?' she asked the physician.

'It's down to you, madam. This is not a precise procedure. Sometimes its quick, other times not. Being your first it normally takes a little longer. Breath regularly and when a contraction comes try to pant hard to relieve the pain and help you to push hard.'

She could feel her uterus tightening. The strong contractions were helping to push the baby into position and she felt the muscles around the uterus harden and contract. It was just like one big muscle cramp, she could feel the discomfort deep within her abdomen, along her right side and in her back.

'You might feel tightening and cramping, along with a backache,' the physician was telling her. 'It may be because of the position of the baby.'

'Agghhh … agghhh … mon dieu,' she groaned as a contraction came.

'AGGHHH … MERDE … MERDE. THIS HURTS LIKE HELL,' she screamed out, then started to pant as asked.

Lisa gave her a piece of leather to bite on and held her hair out of her eyes, mopping her brow and wiping her face with clean scented water.

Another contraction came … she pushed so hard she thought her brain would explode out of the top of her head. She screamed out, and took in a huge gulp of air, before panting like a crazed animal. Her face contorted as she tried to endure the pain, but she felt movement in the belly, as the child moved down.

'Tres bien madam … encore un fois,' said the physician.

'Go on Marie … one more push like that and it will be over … I can see it coming out,' Lisa said to encourage her.

She waited for another wave to come.

'AGGGHHH … NON … NON … IT HURTS LIKE HELL,' she cried out through gritted teeth.

The blood vessels in her neck doubled in size as she used all her strength to push as hard as she could ... a cold curdling scream, like a banshee ... and then she felt sudden release as the baby slid out of her onto the bed, together with warm liquid, some blood and the afterbirth. The baby came out so quickly, the physician couldn't catch it in time. He lifted the child up and cut the umbilical cord.

Marie collapsed onto the bed in sheer exhaustion and relief as the pain had subsided as quickly as the birth happened. She managed to turn herself around over onto her back. Her arms and legs were like jelly. The physician placed the wrapped baby into her arms.

'Madame deVille, you have a son,' he said simply.

All around everyone in the room started to talk at once, but she was oblivious to their comments. She just stared at the most beautiful baby boy she had ever seen, black hair with very distinctive features of the deVille family, with a hint of Charles. But ... no hint at all of the Bankes' complexion or ginger hair.

Her mother was sat on the edge of the bed, wiping her brow with a silk cloth, Lisa was on the other side just staring at the little boy.

'Mon cheri ... he is a handsome boy. Have you a name for him?'

Lisa looked at Marie and asked quietly in a near whisper so no one would pick it up, 'my cousin?'

Marie looked up into Lisa's eyes and gave her a very slight nod.

The last discussion she had with Charles before she left for France was to agree on names for either sex, so she knew what his name would be.

'Henri Charles Louis Bernard deVille Bankes,' she said and smiled at her little son.

Isabelle and Lisa took the little boy from Marie's arms to bathe him and dress him in his new robes. There was a wet nurse on hand to feed the little boy as Marie was washed by the maids, who also changed her bed sheets.

In a freshly made bed, she climbed in and fell into a deep sleep. They all left her to recover and went to join the family waiting downstairs in the Long Gallery to meet the newest member of their family. The Duc had just returned in time to meet his grandson. No one mentioned his lack of the famous Bankes' trademark. Lisa was dying to tell them that he was her nephew, but promised Marie she would keep the pretence going. Instead she just said, 'how he has such a strong deVille hereditary. He takes after you, my Lord,' she said to a proud looking Duc.

That night she sent a letter home to her brother via a courier, written in a code in case it fell into the wrong hands. She had decided to accompany Marie home but would return to France to marry Artemis … if he asked her!

Marie wanted to stay for another two months so the boy would gain strength and weight, but wanted to return to England before the winter's bad weather set in.

She slept for two days before she woke to a bright sunny day. Sitting up in bed, she called for her hand maiden and asked for Henri.

She immediately let her son suckle on her ladened breasts and she felt complete.

# 19
# Wednesday -Thursday July 2017

The last two days were spent in a daze. She was in love and it felt totally different to her feelings for Charles. HP was attentive and caring. It was strange knowing that she still had to work for him as the official launch of the boutique hotel was only a week away, with the planned masked ball, but it would be a pleasurable task.

Today, the professor was due and she knew she would have to spend some time with him going through her ancestral line. She desperately wanted to know if she was related to HP and what happened to Henri Charles and the other baby.

Yesterday, Inspector Scott called in person to advise Marie and HP that a local was recording her ride around the lake from a drone and picked up the body floating in the lake. On close inspection of the recording the police could see the rider's reaction to seeing the body and Marie's body language ruled her out as a suspect. This was such a relief.

She had a lot of work to do liaising with her London

office to ensure all the brochures were proofread and printed, and the exclusive mail shot and postal invitations were received by the right people. A team was due to arrive on Monday to dress the Hall for the masked ball on Friday, hailing the formal opening.

HP walked into the library, where she was working.

'We are alone, my love. Arthur has gone to London to woo your house mate, Charles is finalising the financial investment for the launch and Rosa has gone with him to the financial investors; and Lisa, I gather is spending the week with Henry Wentworth on their family yatch in the Solent.'

He took her into his arms and kissed her gently on her moist lips.

'Shall we dine at home, or do you fancy going to the pub tonight?'

'I don't fancy that pub again. The landlady gives me the creeps.'

'Okay. We dine at home. I'll cook … oh … there is one thing that is not negotiable …' he smiled.

'What's that?' she asked with her head to one side.

'I want you to move into my room. I want to tell the family about us … not my father of course.'

'How is your father, HP? Have you any hope for him?'

'It is unlikely he will come out of his coma, so we are

thinking about agreeing with the medical team to switch off his life support.' HP looked suddenly sad but resigned to the eventual reality.

'So, what are you going to cook for me?' she said to divert the subject.

'How about fillet steak with all the trimmings.'

'Accompanied by a good bottle of burgundy?'

'Mmmm ... we have some wine in the cellar ... let's go have a look to see what's there ... come along.'

He led her through the kitchens and down a stone staircase into the cellars below. It was quite a steep descent into a brick vaulted cellar, where ancient wooden racks of wine stood. Marie had a sense of 'deja vu' in the cellar, as if she had been there before. It was very spooky.

'Here we are,' said HP as he pulled a bottle from the wine rack, 'this one is twenty-five years old, from Ackermann in Saumur. Not burgundy but it should be good.'

Marie had wandered off, finding a torch near the racks. HP turned to show her the bottle, and watched her go to the end wall. He followed her, curious. She placed her hands on the wall, and pushed a couple of bricks. Nothing happened. So, she tried higher up and suddenly the wall clicked open. There was a sudden rush of cold musty air, and a smell of dank earthy mildew. HP stepped in front of her and pushed the hidden false door open, it took all his strength to push it open as it must have been closed for decades. It opened into a tunnel, the walls were covered in cobwebs and the floor was overgrown with fungi.

'How did you know about this Marie? I never knew it existed, and I grew up here, playing down here as a child.'

'It was in one of my dreams. After the death of Thomas Tilley, my namesake came through here to disguise her movements. She used this secret tunnel to return to the Orangery and the crowd of guests that evening that Thomas Tilley died, and the boy in the lake. It was used in the old days to move casks of wine into the cellar. It comes out in the beer barn.'

'Come, it's too dangerous to go inside as it has to be over three hundred years old.' HP took her hand and led her back upstairs into the kitchen.

He was an accomplished chef. The fillet steak and trimmings were delicious and they ate under candlelight in the Orangery. It was very romantic and the wine was excellent.

Over dinner HP asked her about her dreams and what sort of person Marie deVille Bankes was.

'A conniving, cold-blooded murderess ... I believe she killed three people ... Thomas Tilley, Able Jones and the Marquess. She was in love with Charles Dashwood and had his child, a boy; but passed the boy off as the son of the murdered Marquess. She was quite accomplished at manipulating people.'

'That's fascinating. You will have to tell all this to the professor when he arrives tomorrow.'

She laughed, and took HP's hand.

'I am not like my ancestor HP,' squeezing his hand. 'I want to find out how she died, so young and if we are distantly related.'

'I do too. Which is why I want the professor to find out as much as he can. Tomorrow we will get an insight into what he has discovered so far and brief him on what you know from your dreams.'

They both knew the deeper meaning of this but didn't want to say. It didn't stop them making passionate love that night, fulfilling Marie's dreams for her future.

Professor Geoff Bailey was not what Marie expected. She had visions of a bespectacled, elderly, bearded, bald man with a trilby hat and formal attire; a pipe in his mouth.

HP introduced a tall, skinny man in his mid 40s, dressed in cream chinos and a pale blue striped shirt and dark blue linen jacket. No glasses, no beard but long greying hair tied in a pony tail and hat. Quite a handsome bloke.

'Marie. May I introduce you to my old Uni friend Geoff Bailey. Geoff studied History at Oxford, then went on to do his Masters in Forensic History, becoming the youngest professor in this area.'

'So good to meet you Professor.'

'Please, I hate that title. It's just plain Geoff.'

'Come into the dining room … I think Mrs Pottage has made a light meal for us.' HP guided the way through to the dining room.

'So, what do you make of our tangled ancestors?'

'You both have a very interesting ancestral line that crosses over with Charles Dashwood's family. By the way, is he here as well?'

'You know Charles, do you?' Marie asked.

'Yes, I have known the family for a long time, through our parents. And the Wentworths as well. You know how all the old families are all related to each other somehow. Just like your's it would appear.'

'Tell us more Geoff?' Marie could hardly eat anything.

Geoff wanted to savour the delicious food that Mrs Pottage had cooked and enjoy the delicious wine HP had chosen to go with the food.

'There are a lot of gaps missing in your ancestry Marie. But essentially you and HP are not related at all, despite Marie Celestine deVille being married to HP's great great grandfather.' He chewed on some meat, savouring it in his mouth before swallowing; took a gulp of wine, wiped his mouth with the back of his hand and continued.

'You are however related to Charles, by all accounts. I found out that Marie Celestine had a baby boy in France in 1651, which everyone originally thought was the Marquess of Flintwell's ... but he was Charles Dashwood's flesh and blood. It wasn't until the boy was in his twenties that Charles Dashwood told him on his death bed that he was not his stepfather but his actual father. Marie deVille, his mother, died quite young, not sure what from ... that's where it gets hazy. She may have had another child. Charles Dashwood married into the Wentworth family and had three more children, a girl and two boys. That is where the current Charles gets his lineage from, the eldest boy Henri, Marie's son, who inherited his father's title.'

'So, I am related to Charles through the Wentworths ... but how come I am a deVille and not a Dashwood?'

Geoff laughed at this with a mouth full of more food. He swallowed hard before coughing ... his table manners were appalling, Marie thought.

'No, no, no! I see that I have confused you. This is not the link to your past Marie. Your father's great, great grandfather was Artemis deVille who married Lisa Dashwood, and that is your ancestry line through to Charles as a distant cousin.

'Of course, ... Marie went to France with Lisa Dashwood as her best friend and had her baby there at her parent's chateau in the Loire and that's where Lisa met

Artemis, who was Marie's younger brother,' Marie offered.

Geoff stopped eating and looked at Marie with his mouth open.

'How did you know that?' he asked.

'Umm ... Geoff, we need to explain something to you,' HP jumped in to help Marie, 'you see, Marie has been having nightmares or very vivid dreams every night for the last week or so. Each time she goes to bed she falls into 1648 to 1652, and relives the whole time through her great, great aunt's eyes.'

'Yes, that's right and I have written down each dream for each night so you can see the connections.' Marie passed him her note book.

He scanned each page quickly, then started to read it slowly. His facial expressions were comical as he tried to spoon some trifle custard into his mouth whilst reading. He was so intense.

Marie looked at HP and gave a small smile ... he winked at her then put his finger up to his lips to say, shhhh.

Geoff read the note book and then placed it on the table.

'That explains a lot of the blank spaces. She doesn't sound as if she was a nice lady either.'

'My impression of her is that she was a strong woman and if anyone stepped in her way, she got rid of them. She killed her husband, Thomas Tilly and that poor gardener boy.'

'So, how did she die then?' Geoff asked.

'Not sure yet. Maybe that's what I will find out tonight.'

Suddenly the door to the library opened and in strode Charles with Rosa.

'Professor, you old bastard. How the devil are you,' as he took Geoff into a bear hug.

Geoff seemed to like the closeness of his greeting with his old friend and Marie was interested to observe the interaction with Charles and Rosa. He gave Charles the same bear hug, but with Rosa he just gave her a kiss on each cheek. Was the professor gay?

The banter between Charles and HP with Geoff was interesting, clearly, they all went back a long way, although Geoff was slightly older than the other two.

Rosa came and sat next to Marie at the table and helped herself to some food.

'They are like little boys when they get together. Look at them …' she gave a little snort, 'they can't resist ribbing poor Geoff … they have done all their lives.'

'Oh? Were they at school together then?'

'Yes, they were. Although Geoff was two years ahead, he spent most of his time with HP and Charles, never mixed with his own year.'

'Is there a family connection then between you all?'

'There is a very distant one with the Wentworths, which is why we are all concerned about Lisa and Henry, but it's so far back it won't really matter.'

'I didn't know that. And Geoff?'

'Oh, honey … no worries there. He likes the boys, I'm afraid. Such a pity as he is rather dishy.'

Marie whispered in her ear, 'pity he didn't learn to eat properly.'

They both giggled which attracted the men's attention.

'What are you girls giggling at? Something amusing no doubt?' HP asked in a serious voice.

'No. HP you are always suspicious of us girls. Just filling Marie in on our connections and how we all know Geoff.'


Geoff turned to observe Marie. He was staring at her face. He suddenly turned and walked out of the dining room … a few minutes later they heard him ….

'Bloody hell … it is really you!' his voice raised and excited. He marched back into the dining room and looked again at Marie.

'That is so spooky and … and …' searching for the right word, 'incredible! You are Marie deVille Bankes in the living form,' he was so excited. He opened a notebook and read for a short while.

'This is so incredible,' he repeated, 'but what I can't reconcile, is how come you look so unbelievably like her.'

'What do you mean Geoff?' asked Rosa.

'You see, your line comes through Artemis and Lisa Dashwood. They had two sons and a daughter. Your lineage is through the male side, hence your deVille surname. By all accounts Artemis and Marie were very much alike from the portraits I have seen. But somehow you take after Marie. You are like your father, not your mother. How therefore are you the mirror image of your great, great, great aunt?'

'She is buried in the churchyard in Rothwell. It appears that she died giving birth to a baby,' Rosa offered.

'That explains her sudden death in 1653. It is likely that baby was a girl and Charles Dashwood took her as his child. She was older than his two other boys, but a year younger than Henri. By all accounts the records back then show that Lord Dashwood had four children, three boys and a girl. His marriage to Elizabeth Wentworth in 1654, a year after Marie died, was to cover up the girl's birth.'

'What was her name?' Rosa asked.

'Marie-Anne Elizabeth Dashwood.' He sat back and let the name sink in. Everyone was silent, trying to absorb this information.

'Now,' he continued, 'it appears that she married

Henri deVille, who was Artemis and Lisa's child, much later in life, when she was in her late thirties and she had one child, a boy. Henri deVille was of course two years older that her, but she would not have realised that he was in fact her uncle, as by the time she married him, Lord Dashwood had died.'

Marie sat very still, a small tear seeped out of the corner of her eye.

'So, let me get this straight. What you are suggesting, is that I could have been descended from Marie-Anne Elizabeth and Henri deVille union, and not Artemis and Lisa Dashwood?'

The room was silent.

'Er ... yes ... that's right. That would account for your biological similarities to Marie deVille in the portrait. You see Marie-Anne Elizabeth was also an identical likeness to her mother. See ...' he showed them a photograph of another portrait he found in the British Art museum.

'I don't get this,' said Rosa. 'You first state that Marie's line comes through Lisa and Artemis, which I can understand. But then you throw into the ring this other connection, of Marie-Anne marrying her uncle and producing a male line.'

'Yes, that's right. It could be possible,' agreed Geoff.

'But does that mean that Marie and I are related?' HP had a frown on his face as he asked.

'No, defiinitely not. But Marie is related to Charles and Lisa.'

'Thank God for that,' an exasperated but relieved HP said.

Mrs Cribb approached HP and whispered something in his ear. His face changed from happiness to a big frown.

'Do please excuse us. Rosa and Arthur, we are needed at the hospital now. James will drive us there.'

He got up to go, then hesitated. He approached Marie and said in a low voice.

'He is at his end. Wait for me here … please.'

'Yes, of course I will.' She gave him a sympathetic smile as the three left the room hurriedly.

♦♦♦

That night the 9th Marquise of Flintwell slipped away with his family around him. HP returned to the hall in the early hours of the morning as the 10th Marquess.

Marie tried to wait up for him, but fell asleep in his bed and once again returned to …

# 20
# 1652

Her time in France was up. She felt it was right to go home.

*"Where is home? That's a good question,"* she asked herself as she walked through the grounds of her family home pushing Henri around in his pram.

'What did you say?' asked Lisa who heard her speak in French.

'Oh! I was thinking about returning to England. But thought about where was my home now that my husband is dead?'

'Marie, you know you would be most welcome at our house at Rodewelle. I feel sure that Charles would insist on you living with us.'

'That is so kind of you. Do you think that Henry Charles will want his nephew to live at Flintwell Hall? It will be difficult explaining his dominant French looks and the lack of red in his hair or complexion.'

'If they make an issue of it, then you will have to stamp your French feet hard and insist that your genes are stronger than the Bankes given your ancestral background. They won't argue with you ... and you know that.' Lisa knew her friend well enough to know how tough she really was. But there was no denying that little Henri did resemble a combination of both Marie and Charles, so there was bound to be allegations thrown around, especially if it involved titles and money.

The journey back was just as long and arduous as the one out, but with little Henri, they needed to stop more often. Lisa confided in Marie that when she got back she was going to tell her parents and brother that Artemis had asked for her hand in marriage. Marie already knew this as she was close to her brother and he had asked her if their parents would approve of an aristocratic English rose becoming his wife. Marie was so excited for her brother and it made her think about staying in France. But she wanted Charles as a husband, and if she was entitled to it, she also wanted her rightful share of the Bankes' wealth.

The ferryboat ride back across the Humber was made in very bad weather. The rough waters and high winds tossing the little boat around the turbulent rolling waves made the women sea sick for the first time. Being an open boat, they were soaking wet when they landed on the south bank and Marie feared for little Henri.

Charles was waiting anxiously, stood on the short pier watching the six oarsmen struggling with the wind and the turning tide. His heart was pounding, partly for their safety, but more at the joy of seeing Marie for the first time in a year and his three-month-old son. He came on his faithful horse, together with his best carriage for the ladies to ride back to Rodewelle House. He had prepared a special welcome for them, and a feast that evening, although he thought that after their arduous journey their priority would be a hot bath tub and some refreshments.

He knew that Marie was returning to some turbulent times, as the Sheriff of Lincoln wanted to talk to her about several deaths, and she would need to face her stepson, who at a similar age to her, had claimed his rightful place as the 2nd Marquess of Flintwell.

As she stepped ashore, Charles took her in his arms and they kissed passionately in front of the small audience … but they didn't care. As a gentleman he helped his sister off the boat and took them to his carriage. The men put their trunks onto a separate wagon to be taken to his house.

'Let me meet my son,' he said as Marie uncovered the baby wrapped up in his blankets to protect him from the water and cold.

He looked startled at first, then a smile crossed his face as the baby wrinkled his nose and beamed at the strange tall man.

'My word, he is my boy,' Charles remarked.

Both the women looked at each other, then Charles as they realised that he was the first to see Henri, and if Charles could see the resemblance then others would as well.

'There is not a strand of hair nor a pale flaxen feature from the Bankes' gene, my brother,' said Lisa. 'Perhaps we are to face facts and brace ourselves for comments and rejection from other quarters.'

'It matters not, dear Lisa. I will gladly tell the world he is my flesh and blood, and to hell with the Bankes.' A bold statement which made Marie smile and her heart melted in greater love for this man.

'Come, let us haste to Rodewelle and get you warm and fed. I have a special treat for you all when we get home.'

♦♦♦

In Lincoln's castle, the Sheriff was sat in his office with a large glass of porter and his pipe, listening to a report from his investigator. Lorcan Vesey had returned a few days before the women, taking a faster ship to Boston and a hard ride to Lincoln. Lorcan Vesey had been in France for the whole time Marie had, watching her every move, including the day she gave birth to the boy. He had changed his appearance, growing his beard and his hair to look like a priest from one of the orders in the area. He took a billet in the local inn, giving himself the freedom to roam around the village that nestled in a small copse, not far from the gatehouse entrance to the chateau, and as most of the people worked on the land for the Duc de Touraine, he was able to have access to all the gossip and see the family occasionally. The Sheriff had known of the birth of Henri from a messenger sent by Vesey, and that there was no resemblance to the 1st Marquess.

The Sheriff had circumstantial evidence that Marie had pushed Tilley into the beer vat and drowned poor Able Jones, from so called witnesses, who believed it was her in disguise. As for the Marquess, he had learned from the staff whilst Marie was in France, that she gave instructions that no one was to enter the Marquess' room whilst she was in there with him, as well as after she left that evening. He knew she had had a hand in his death, although the doctor stated that he had died of his tumours and choked on his own bile.

He had a report from Hull docks that she was back, so he sent a summons to Lord Dashwood to bring her to Lincoln for questioning the following week. He secretly wanted to witness the first meeting between Henry Robert Bankes, the 2nd Marquess and his supposed nephew. That would be interesting, especially if the report from Vesey was accurate that there was no trace of Bankes' hereditary red hair in the boy's looks. Along with the summons, he will insist that braggard Charles Dashwood would be there as well.

The Sheriff was a close friend and supporter of the 1st Marquess and when he married the young little French aristocrat, he did not approve. He could see she was a manipulating, disloyal little whore, and his spies in the household told him that when the Marquess was away in London, she would hold parties in the Orangery for all her young suitors. Dashwood and Wentworth were also culprits, but he had to tread carefully as they were very prominent families with powerful connections.

He was determined to pin the three murders on her and wanted to see her hang in front of the castle gates upon Steep Hill. During her time in France he had successfully brought the 2nd Marquess on his side. The servants and farmers at Flintwell were harder to persuade as they all liked the way the Marchioness had treated them, and the heads of the Hall all refused to say a wrong word against her. Howell, Cribb, Pottage and even Randolph Blake the estate steward, supported the French whore. His evidence on both Thomas Tilley and Able Jones was very thin. The only way he could prove that she was guilty was to get her to confess, or drop herself in it through questioning. With the death of the Marquess he was more confident, and this is where he hoped to convict her.

When they drew up outside Charle's magnificent home at Rodewelle, the ladies were greeted warmly by Charles' servants and taken to their rooms. Little Henri was in dire need of a change and a feed, and both Marie and Lisa craved a hot bath before supper.

That evening, Charles broached the subject of the summons.

'It appears that the Sheriff of Lincoln, has summoned you to his offices next week, to answer questions on the deaths of Tilley, Jones and the Marquess.'

Marie took a sharp intake of breath and put her hand up to her mouth to stop her crying out. She suddenly started to shake. Lisa jumped to her side.

'Don't worry, Marie, Charles will have the family attorney with us when they question you, and we will insist on being there with you. There is little he has to go on, and I believe that all your servants at Flintwell are supporting you. Since we arrived back I have had a full briefing from my ladies, who have been watching what has been going on in our absence.' Lisa was so positive, it gave Marie hope.

'Yes, Sir Lawrence Boyd, who is one of the best attorneys we have and is a close family friend, will be with you in the interview. The Sheriff has reluctantly agreed to this. Sir Lawrence will want to talk to you before we go for the meeting so he is coming to see us later this week.'

The next hurdle to face was a meeting at Flintwell Hall with Henry Robert Bankes the 2$^{nd}$ Marquess to meet his nephew. Unbeknown to the Sheriff, this had been arranged directly with Marie and she would take Charles' carriage with Lisa to the Hall the following day. Young Henri Charles was wrapped up tightly in swaddling clothes and had a bonnet on his head, so that only his face would be seen.

They were shown into the Orangery by Mrs Cribb, who was pleased to see the Marchioness, but careful with her outward feelings, as the whole household was on edge.

'Mrs Cribb, how good to see you again. I trust the new Marquess is treating you well. It's been a long time.'

'My lady, it's good to see you as well … and this must be Henry Charles. His Lordship will be with you shortly.' She was unusually curt.

There was a commotion at the door, and in strode a younger version of her deceased husband. Same height, build and red hair, with glowing red cheeks. She stood to greet him.

'Your Lordship,' she bowed her head, 'may I introduce you to Lady Lisa Dashwood, and your nephew, Henri Charles Louis Bernard.' She held up the little boy so that he could see his little face.

Henry Robert Bankes paused, nodded a recognition to Lisa and peered at the young baby with his big bushy ginger eyebrows raised, creasing his pallid forehead. Up close, Marie recoiled at the memory of her late husband's stench, which she could smell off this odious man. Like father, like son, she thought.

He placed a dirty finger up to the boy's cheek and then pushed his bonnet off. He stood back and smiled, his blackened teeth grinning at Marie.

'My father said you were a whore, and this now proves it. This is not a Bankes' child. He has no features of our family. If I am not mistaken, he has a resemblance to the Dashwoods.' He seemed to relish in his own self smugness.

'I do not recognise this child as my kin. He is a bastard from your lover Charles Dashwood … it is plain to see this.'

He gave a nasty cackle, as he bent his head back and gave out a cry of sudden anger.

'How dare you bring this … thing … into my household and claim it is from my father's loins. It is a well-known fact he could not father any more children, before he married you. So, you see, you French whore, this is no kin of mine.'

He shouted for James Howell.

'Yes, your Lordship?' Howell said with a bow,

looking sideways at Marie.

'Please remove these ... people from my house and never let them back inside.'

He turned to Marie and stepped up close to her, bent down so that his face was inches from hers, with spittle spraying her face he said,

'Go now woman ... but be assured you will be hearing from my attorney and I suspect the Sheriff as well. You killed my father, didn't you?' His face was bright red and his breath stank like a sewer.

Quite composed, Marie stood her ground with no emotion on her face, still holding her baby boy.

'I will gladly leave the Hall, your Lordship. But know this,' she hesitated so that she knew every servant in the room heard her, 'your father was a bully, a braggard and took pleasure in abusing me throughout our short marriage. He killed himself with his excesses. He was riddled with disease he got from his whores in London, and his drinking. He was fat and unhealthy. What he attempted to do to me the night he died was disgusting and all will soon know, if the Sheriff does question me.' She paused again holding his stare.

'Know this, and know this well ... I did not kill your father ... I had no need to. He fell and choked on his own bile. You look as if you are heading the same way.'

She looked at him up and down from her diminutive

height, pulled herself up to her full five feet two inches and turned on her heels to follow Howell out to her waiting coach.

Lord Flintwell just stood open mouthed as she marched head held high, followed by Lisa Dashwood and Mrs Cribb.

'Mrs Cribb, if you value your position here, you will attend me,' he shouted at her.

Mrs Cribb turned slowly to face him.

'No need your Lordship. I have a position at Rodewelle House with the Dashwoods.' Turned, head up and marched after Marie.

As they reached the carriage, door held open by James Howell, Marie turned to Mrs Cribb and said, 'ride with us Mrs Cribb, we will send someone to collect your belongings tomorrow.'

'Ma'am, if you please, I will bring Mrs Cribb's belongings along with my own and Mrs Pottage tomorrow.' James Howell had a smile on his face.

'How come Howell?' she asked, surprised.

'Lord Dashwood has offered us all positions at Rodewell House, my Lady, and we have accepted,' he bowed and closed the carriage door, still smiling.

Marie leaned out of the carriage window, 'does the Marquess know this?'

'He will by tomorrow morning, Ma'am, when his

morning food does not appear,' he was giggling by now. This made Marie's heart raise up and she laughed as well.

'Did you know about this Lisa?'

'I have to admit that I did. My brother had approached several of the servants at Flintwell before we arrived back from France, and they have all agreed to come.'

Mrs Cribb was holding young Henri in her arms, 'well Ma'am, you will need help with this little one, now won't you?'

The journey back to Rodewell House was filled with laughter as they recounted the 2$^{nd}$ Marquess' words.

Charles was waiting for them to return, and was curious towards their levity. Over refreshments in the main salon, they recounted the whole meeting with the 2$^{nd}$ Marquess and how he had rejected Henri as his nephew.

'Well, that's it then. We shall officially confirm that he is my son, and announce our engagement Marie,' he announced to everyone's surprise.

'This is what you want, Charles?' asked Lisa.

'Of course. Wouldn't have it any other way. He is my son, both Marie and I know this, so I will give Henri my name and he will be my son and heir, and dammed all those that disapprove!'

Over dinner that evening, after the main course was served, Lisa coughed loudly and banged her spoon against her glass. Everyone fell silent and looked at her as she pushed her chair back and stood up.

'As we are all here, I have an announcement to make.' She paused to make sure she had everyone's attention. 'Artemis deVille, who as you know is Marie's brother, has asked for my hand in marriage, and I have accepted, if my dear brother gives me his blessing.' She looked over at Charles, who was holding Marie's hand and smiling as if he was expecting this.

Everyone talked at the same time. Marie looked pleased taking Lisa's hand as she resumed her seat.

'You have known about this Marie?' asked Charles.

'Of course. I encouraged my brother and Lisa to spend time together whilst we were at home, and both my parents approve of their union as well. It will unite our families if we were to wed as well, Charles,' she added with a smile on her face.

He looked into her eyes and smiled at the thought, saying nothing, but squeezed her hand.

News of this spread around the community like wildfire. Although most of the key servants had joined the Dashwood family, there were still some connections with Flintwell Hall and information soon reached the Bankes family ... and of course the Sheriff.

Marie had been summoned to a court hearing with the

Sheriff in front of a judge to hear a case of murder against her. This meant she needed a legal team and her English would not stand the scrutiny of clever questioning in an English court of law. She needed somehow to derail his evidence.

One night in the light of a full moon, after Charles had fallen asleep under a heavy draught of powders, Marie dressed in a dark cape and hood and riding boots and slipped out of the house through the secret door in the wine cellar. Without being seen she headed towards the stables and her horse … she took with her a rope and her stiletto knife. There was one person she knew had evidence against her before her time in France, during that year. He could be a serious problem to her in court.

# 21
# Friday-Saturday
# July 2017

Marie was woken up by the click of the door as HP entered the bedroom. It was just past midnight. He tiptoed towards the bathroom to change into his nightwear, a T-shirt and jogging shorts. He came out of the bathroom and switched the light off, tiptoeing towards the bed. Marie was awake and switched on the bedside table light.

'Sorry, did I wake you up?' he asked.

'No ... I was awake waiting for you. Has he gone HP?' she asked in a soft voice.

He came over to her side of the bed and sat down. She knelt up and put her arms around his shoulders and held him tightly. He turned towards her and nestled his head into her bosom. He was quietly sobbing. She stroked his head whispering softly to him in French.

'Tout va bien mon amour, tu es avec moi maintenant. Je t'aime.'

His French was good, and he understood every word,

as he looked up at her, with a tear running down his cheek.

'Moi aussi, Marie de Ville. Je t'adore … have done for some time now,' he finished in English.

She held him in her arms as they hugged, then laid back on the bed. Her silk nightdress was held together by a flimsy silk cord, which he pulled to undo the bow, and opened the gown to expose her naked body. He knelt on the bed to remove his T-shirt and joggers, as she watched him.

He pushed her back onto the pillows and kissed her lips with so much tenderness that she felt a wave of sheer pleasure wash over her.

They made passionate love … for most of that early morning. He had just lost his father and here he was making love to this beautiful French woman … now his girlfriend.

He knew now that he wanted her to be an important part of the rest of his life.

Marie had not closed the drapes over the huge sash windows, and dawn was breaking.

HP was lying on top of Marie, stroking her hair and gently kissing her lips, cheek and neck.

'I love you, Frenchie. I want you to share my life from now on … will you?' he whispered.

She looked into his eyes. Her arms were around his neck. The bed sheets half covered their naked bodies as he lay between her legs. She felt his arousal as he waited for her response.

'Qu'est-ce que c'est ça?' Are you asking me to marry you HP?'

'I don't want to ruin what we have together, and there is absolutely no pressure. But I do want you to live with me … um … and then, let's see what happens … um … I mean let it happen naturally?'

'You mean like this,' she giggled as she wriggled herself into position so he could take her once again.

    She wanted time to think.
    Yes, she loved him.
    Yes, she wanted to live with him.
    Yes, her life would change dramatically.
    Would she marry him?
    That would be utterly bizzare! The second Marie deVille to marry a Bankes in 365 years. But she wanted to make sure they were not related in anyway. They were waiting for the professor to finish his investigation into her blood line. It all looked like it led through the Dashwoods they thought.
    What about her job in London?
    She thought that she could work here in the boutique hotel running their marketing department.
    She smiled.
    She didn't need to convince herself that her future was

here with HP at Flintwell Hall, as a hotelier.

HP was studying her changing facial expressions with interest as these thoughts went through her mind.

'I am intrigued,' he said to her. They were now lying on their sides facing each other, his head propped up by his hand as he gently stroked her face with his other hand.

'Oh?' she said.

He looked at the shape of her mouth, her soft lips and clear hazel eyes, framed by her wild dark black hair, messed up by their lovemaking.

'You are beautiful,' he said. 'I fell in love with you the first time I saw you. Before any of our family history was discovered. It was love at first sight.'

She leaned up and kissed him gently.

'I don't expect an answer now, you know. I respect that you need to think about a lot of things, but we do need a marketing guru to run the Hall, and perhaps this would be your role if you were at my side, and part of the family.'

She stroked his chin.

'You are so considerate, mon amour. It is as if you can read my mind.' She looked into his eyes.

'Oui,' she said simply.

'What does that mean?' he asked her.

'It means, yes ... I will live with you in sin ... for the time being.' She hesitated, then with a cheeky smile added, 'until of course a proper proposal is made.' He kissed her and jumped out of the bed. He was so happy.

'HP,' she said to him in a stern voice.

'Yes, what is it?'

'In light of your father's passing we need to be respectful until after his funeral, so I would suggest we keep this to ourselves and pick the right time to tell the family. So please promise me you will say nothing to Rosa or Arthur, or Charles and Lisa until the time is right.'

He stood still, naked, the morning sun lighting him up like a statue.

'You are right my wise Frenchie. We can announce our engagement after the funeral,' he said deep in thought.

'But … you have not proposed to me properly yet,' she teased.


As they were getting dressed after taking a shower together, Marie asked, 'HP. When will professor Bailey have his findings on my blood line?'

'I will call him later today … why?'

'I just want him to confirm that I am related to Charles and his family, not to you,' it came out as a very blunt statement in her French accent.

HP laughed. 'Yes, of course we will get his assurance.'

He kissed her.

'Today and the rest of this week will be arduous as we

organise Papa's funeral. Do you need to go back to London to organise things there? It's a good time as I will be running around like a blue arsed fly. Better to be out of the way … but promise me you will return for the funeral?'

'Good idea, and yes of course I want to be by your side at the funeral.'

She knew she had a lot to do as well. Talk to Lisa and Clare; they would need to find a new housemate. The dreaded meeting with her bosses as she resigned from her job. Packing up her belongings.

'Marie, my love,' HP broke her thoughts.

'Please don't say anything in London just yet. Don't go resigning or letting your house go. Act as normal.'

'You read my mind again, mon cheri. I was just thinking about everything I had to do.'

'It's good to make a list, but let's get through the next week first, besides, we still haven't finished the launch of the Hall yet, so James and Randolph will need you to help with the masked ball and the formal opening of the Hall. Then you can move in!'

'The masked ball. Yes … we need to postpone that don't we, until after the funeral,' she said out loud.

'That's my Frenchie,' he said as they left the room to go for breakfast, holding hands.

♦♦♦

She left quietly as Howell drove her to the station. HP was locked in his study with Arthur and Rosa talking about the funeral and the estate. They had a meeting with the family solicitor to understand the will.

In London, Marie went into work early having travelled down the afternoon before.

She was at her desk before anyone else arrived, so a very surprised James, perched on her desk and looked at her without saying a word.

'Hello James.'

'I got the news yesterday about his Lordship. Very sad.'

'The family were expecting it so it's not a shock as such, but still sad when it happened. We should postpone the launch and the ball so I'm working on new dates now so we can email the guest list. I am hoping that everyone will still be able to attend. It was hard work getting them all to commit to the original date.'

'You are a pastmaster at this Marie. We have every confidence in you.' He hesitated ... 'so what's news with you then. You were at Flintwell Hall for a long time. Is there anything Randi and I need to know?' he was fishing.

'I had to stay on and help Charles with the finishing touches. It will all be part of the marketing brochure, plus we got a lot of shots taken. I have Heidi finishing the launch brochure for you to approve now. The masked ball will be a hoot, too. Loads of ideas.'

He had his inquisitive face on, she knew him well enough that her flannel didn't appease him.

'What's Geoff Bailey doing at the Hall?' he asked directly.

'You know the professor?'

'Yes, went to Oxford with him and Charles.'

*'Time to be straight'* thought Marie.

'He is looking into the hereditary history of Flintwell Hall and the connections with my ancestors and those of Charles as well. There is definitely a connection.'

'So, you are related to the Bankes then?'

'No,' she laughed, 'there is a tenuous link through the Dashwoods. Apparently, Marie deVille, however she is related to me, had a child with Charles Dashwood in 1652 who kept the deVille surname, although he was brought up at Rodewelle House with the Dashwoods. That's as far as Geoff has got.'

'Well, well, well. Now that is interesting,' he said smiling.

'What do you know that I don't, James?'

'Only certain questions about you from HP in recent weeks. He seems besotted … hint, hint?'

She blushed and kept her head down concentrating on her computer screen so he couldn't read her expressions.

'His Lordship will not be interested in a lowly advertising exec like me, I can assure you,' was all she said.

Just in the nick of time other members of staff walked in and James was called in to see Randolph.

Tonight, she was meeting up with Lisa and Clare, and expected to be bombarded with questions about her relationship with HP. It was going to be a tall order, keeping their relationship quiet.

She got a text from HP at midday.

*Funeral on Tuesday 12pm at the chapel. Huge crowd coming. I want you there with me. Going to tell Arthur and Rosa about us tonight. Finding it difficult to focus. Missing you already. HP xxx*

So much for keeping it quiet for a week, she thought.

*Missing you too. I will be there. Can I tell Lisa and Clare tonight but swear them to secrecy? We ought to let Charles know as well. Why the change of plan ... about us?' Hugs xxx*

*Can't keep it to myself. Should be sad for losing father, but you make me feel happy. He would have approved if he had got to know you. Yes, go ahead. Xxx*

*OK. Will you tell Charles? Not work though. Love you. Xxx*

That was that. She would not tell anyone at the agency until the time was right, although James had a bloodhound's nose for these things.

Now that she had the funeral date she could press ahead with the opening launch and the masked ball, a week later.

That night she got to her house at 7pm. Lisa and Clare were expecting her.

'No food in so we have a table reserved at the pub. You okay with that hun?' Lisa asked as she hugged Marie.

She had a long soak in the bath, her mind racing with a thousand thoughts. Her dreams at night were becoming normal, so she was no longer scared ... still wary of them ... but she was slowly concluding that her great great great whatever she was, was a cold-blooded French murderess. She knew that she had killed young Able Jones, pushing him in the lake, and her husband the Marquess as well. Thomas Tilley was helped on his way into the beer vat by Charles and Henry at the masked ball. Who else was there? Would Geoff Bailey find out more?

'So young lady ... spill!'

Lisa was on the edge of her seat in their usual corner unit at their local ... drinks on the table and food ordered.

Both Clare and Lisa were leaning forward.

'You know, don't you?' she asked.

'We don't know anything. But the time you've spent with HP makes us jump to either right or wrong conclusions,' clever Clare quipped.

Marie sighed and took a sip of her vodka and tonic looking from Lisa to Clare and back.

'Okay. HP has asked me to move in with him ... you know ... as his partner. And ... yes, before you ask ... we have.'

'I knew it!' exclaimed Lisa, 'I bloody knew it!'

'Has he asked you to marry him? ... are you engaged? When's the announcement and the party?' Clare said all at once.

'I am going to move up to Flintwell Hall after his father's funeral and will oversee the official launch of the Hall. So, in a couple of weeks' time. No ... he has not proposed, although I think he wants to. We have decided to take it one step at a time,' she beamed.

'Oh My God,' they both screamed out together. The pub went quiet and everyone turned to stare at them.

They resumed their seats, giggling and Marie proceeded to tell them all about her relationship with HP, the police and her dreams. She left out Geoff Bailey and his investigations into her ancestors and her link to Lisa's family.

Later that night her mobile pinged with a text from HP and another from Charles.

*Congratulations cousin! Great news from HP about you both. My full approval. Hugs. Charlie xxx*

That meant a lot to her … cousin? *Yes, I suppose I am,* she thought as she settled under her duvet to sleep …

# 22
# 1652

They arrived in Lincoln by coach. Marie, Lisa and Charles stepped into the George Inn where they had booked rooms for the night. They were due to meet with the High Sheriff and his team of wardens, including Lorcan Vesey. Charles had his attorney, Sir Lawrence Boyd there, together with a Sergeant-at-law to represent them in the Court of Common Pleas the following day. They met at the Inn for a briefing before they went to Lincoln Castle. He wanted Marie to say nothing at all as it was incumbent on the Sheriff to produce any evidence he had against Marie deVille Bankes. They were aware that in such troubled times Oliver Cromwell had given sheriffs additional powers to help them keep law and order across the land.

Sir Lawrence summed up their case.

'In the cases of Tilley and Jones, we know that Her Ladyship was at the Hall, as there are so many witnesses to prove that. Tilley fell off the ladder in a drunken state and Jones drowned himself also, consumed by beer. His Lordship is a different situation. You were in His

Lordship's chamber and gave orders to his footmen to remain outside and not to enter under any circumstances. This is where it becomes your word against theirs. The information I have gathered from the servants was that his Lordship seemed to be enjoying himself and you exited his chamber smiling. They assumed you had performed ... aghh ... how do I put this delicately ... ahh yes, your wifely duties. You asked that he was not to be disturbed until the morning as he was sleeping. However, we understand that the Sheriff has evidence that he was already dead soon after you left the room. He had one of his men working on the staff in the Hall.'

They all looked at each other, astounded that their attorney should know this but not themselves.

Marie said to Lisa, 'I thought I recognised that man on the ship.'

'What man?' asked Charles.

'His name is Lorcan Vesey and he claimed to be a lawyer on business to France. We spotted him at my father's chateau in the Loire later that year disguised as a priest. He worked on His Lordship's personal staff as a first footman but he had changed his appearance which is why I didn't recognise him. Howell disliked him.'

'Oh? And how do you know that?' Lisa asked.

'He came to me concerned at the freedom Vesey had around the Hall and asked if I had approved this. It was the first time I knew about it ... but then he disappeared soon after His Lordship died.'

'If I may my Lord, the best course tomorrow will be to prove the Sheriff incompetent. He is an arrogant self-obsessed man and it will be possible to turn the court around. My Lady, you should say nothing at all. We will ask them for the proof.'

Marie was happy with that with her knowledge of Vesey ... he would not be in court.

♦♦♦

As they entered the court the following day, Marie looked calm and composed but did not look at anyone. Lisa was looking for that odious man who had been following them through France, Lorcan Vesey, but he was nowhere to be seen. The Bankes family were there as were people she did not recognise.

The Sheriff entered the court and all stood, except for Marie, who just stared at him.

This was noticed. The Sheriff seemed nervous and not his usual belligerent self.

'All rise for His Lordship,' an announcement was made.

Marie heard Charles whisper under his breath, 'thank God for that.'

Marie looked up at the side door to the judge's chair and in walked a tall, thin man dressed in a black gown with white fur collar, looking very serious. His gaze held on Charles for a few seconds before he nodded to everyone and sat down.

'Who is he?' Marie asked quietly behind her hand.

'Sir Richard Barington, Baronet and my father's best friend,' he smiled.

A clerk stood and read out from a scroll.

'Marie deVille Bankes. You are summoned here to court to answer charges of murder against Thomas Tilley, Able Jones and Henry Bankes, the 1$^{st}$ Marquess of Flintwell. How do you plead?'

The attorney stood up.

'My Lord, my client is not guilty. If it pleases your Lordship, may we ask the Sheriff to present his evidence against her Ladyship, as she is innocent of all alleged charges.'

There was a general murmur in the court as the Sheriff and his attorneys all looked at Sir Richard to make a comment.

He remained silent and nodded at the Sheriff.

The Sheriff stood and pointed at Marie. His face was reddened by his anger and his rotund figure seemed to shake.

'That French …' he hesitated to choose his words,

'woman cold bloodedly killed His Lordship and Master Tilley and …. we have evidence of her deception. She is guilty.'

'This "woman" as you disrespectfully called her is a member of the French aristocracy and until his death was the fourth Marchioness of Flintwell. I would caution you to respect her position in society and remind you that she is innocent until you prove her guilt, which it appears you are unable to apart from rhetoric and innuendo.' Sir Richard got into his stride. 'Please present your case, Sheriff and those persons who you say have witnessed her alleged crimes.'

'My Lord, our key witness has … aghh … failed to attend today. Until he shows, we call upon mistress Bedlow, who witnessed her Ladyship returning from the beer barn shortly after Thomas Tilley fell into the vat.'

A very timid looking servant maid from the Hall was marched in by the Sheriff's men. She stood in the witness box, nervous and eyes down.

'Mistress Bedlow, you have worked in Flintwell Hall for five years in her Ladyship's quarters?' asked the Sheriff.

'Aye, sire, that I do.'

'Did you see her Ladyship sneaking back into her chambers wearing a black hooded gown on the night of the masked ball soon after the hour of eight pm?'

'Um … not exactly sire.'

'What?' he screamed at her.

She jumped with fright.

'I did not see her enter her chamber sire, as I was serving wine in the Orangery, where she was dressed in a white gown with a mask of feathers.' She stood defiantly, but shaking like a leaf.

'You have changed your tune mistress Bedlow. May I remind you of the consequences of lying in court.'

The sergeant-at-law for the Dashwoods intervened. He stood and waited for Sir Richard to acknowledge him.

'Mistress Bedlow, may I ask how you know you were in the Orangery at that time?'

'Yes, sire. Thomas Tilley was exposed by her Ladyship for dressing up as a gentleman at the masked ball. He was spying for His Lordship. He was ejected from the Orangery by Lord Dashwood and Lord Wentworth and appeared to be very drunk. I was with her Ladyship all of this time and she never ventured outside.'

'Why, pray are you here as a witness for the prosecution?'

She hesitated, her eyes darting from the Sheriff to the Marquess and back down to the floor.

'Mistress Bedlow?' prompted the sergeant.

'Cause, I was told to say things that are not true against her Ladyship,' she broke down crying.

'Oh ... by whom?' the sergeant-at-law asked.

She was silent, shaking her head and in floods of tears.

'Please say, who it was who coerced you here?'

'I will lose my position sire if I do and my family as well.'

Marie looked at her and smiled, nodding her head.

Janice Bedlow looked at her then to Charles who also nodded.

'It was the Sheriff here and His Lordship,' she said reluctantly.

'His Lordship? You mean Lord Dashwood?'

'No, sire. It were The Marquess' son,' she pointed at the 2nd Marquess, 'Im over there.'

Sir Richard looked up.

'Is this correct Sheriff?' he demanded.

The Sheriff's face went a bright red. He was fuming. The Marquess stood to leave the court.

'Sheriff, have you any evidence that is not invented or can be proven without doubt in this court?'

'My Lord, my key witness Mr Vesey, who has evidence and has followed that woman for over a year, has disappeared. No doubt he has been abducted by them,' pointing at Charles Dashwood and Henry Wentworth.

'I despair of you Sheriff. You are accusing two Lords of distinguished families of abduction without proof. I have no option but to rule this case as unsubstantiated, you are free to go your Ladyship with our sincere apologies.' He nodded to Marie, then looked up at the Sheriff. 'I will be reporting you to the High Justice in London, no doubt Commander Cromwell will look upon you with despair.'

He stood, bowed at Marie and Charles and walked out.

Everyone was amazed and the tension in the court rose along with the voices. The Sheriff scowled at Marie and Charles, turned and marched out.

Charles walked over to Janice Bedlow.

'Mistress Bedlow, collect your family and report to my overseer at Rodewelle House. You will be joining my staff. Thank you for your honesty.'

♦♦♦

Two days later, Lorcan Vesey was found hanging by his neck from the branch of an old oak tree at the entrance to Flintwell Hall with a small wound in his side made by a steel blade of sorts.

# 23
# Sunday-Tuesday
# July 2017

At 6am, there was a loud crack and her bedroom filled with sudden light. A few minutes later the distant sound of thunder echoed through the open window as a strong breeze flapped the curtains. Marie woke up from a deep sleep, sat up in bed and shook her head. She was once again soaked in sweat. She was getting used to this and wondered if one day the dreams would stop. Then hard driving rain hit her window and splashed through the opening onto her bedside table.

She got out of bed … stretched and yawned at the same time, opened the curtains and shut the sash window … stood there looking out at the start of a very dreary day.

Wow … that was a vivid dream! Now she knew that Marie deVille Bankes was a cold-blooded murderess, as she clearly had stabbed and hung Lorcan Vesey from that branch. She had no idea how she achieved that. She must have been a very strong woman.

It occurred to her that it was strange that none of her dreams reflected the acts of murder committed by Marie, except for the Marquess … and she remembered that in detail!

Then, why not the others. She couldn't remember being around the lake pushing young Able Jones in, nor killing Lorcan Vesey. Marie deVille was her spitting image in every detail; height, build and looks … but her ancestor must have had the strength of a man. She was an accomplished rider and swordswoman, she knew this, but could someone else have killed Jones and Vesey?

Her mobile pinged, distracting her from her thoughts. It was HP.

*Good morning my love. No more dreams I hope … well only of us? All going well here. Lots of help with the funeral plans, which is on Tuesday. I am coming to London tomorrow to see the family solicitor about Dad's last will. Can I stay with you tomorrow night? Then we can go to Dad's funeral together? Chance to catch up. Dinner? Invite Lisa and Clare too if you want. Love you. HP xxx*

Her heart soared and beat faster. God, she loved him and she would see him tomorrow as well. Bonus!!

*Morning hon. Thunder and lightning disturbed yet another dream. I know more now! We need to see Geoff asap. I can't wait to see you and welcome you to our humble little house. Will ask the girls later. Still in bed ... naked!! There's a thought for you! So pleased it's all arranged. Hope the legal side is not too troublesome. Love you too. What's your ETA tomorrow? Hugs xxx M.*

It was Sunday morning and usually the girls had a long lie in, so Marie decided to go for a walk to clear her head. It was pissing down, that type of rain that came down in a 30° slant with the wind blowing so hard an umbrella was useless. She buttoned her wax riding coat up to her neck, put a deerstalker hat on that was an ornament in the hall, and left the house quietly. She had nowhere in particular to go, and soon she found herself in a small park under a shelter. She sat down out of the rain and pondered.

Her mind raced from the final plans for the launch of Flintwell Hall as a boutique hotel and the masked ball, to HP and her future life with him.

Did she want to marry him? She would become the Marchioness of Flintwell, as HP was now be the 10$^{th}$ in line of succession of this hereditary title. Gosh, life would be so different, especially if she was involved in running the hotel with HP, Arthur and Rosa. That would be fun!

Arthur had been seeing Clare quite a lot, although she didn't say much about him.

Come to think of it Rosa and Charles were also dating!

A triple wedding? She laughed out aloud and shook her head at the thought of a massive Bankes wedding day!

She chuckled to herself. Then a serious frown appeared on her forehead as another bad thought came into her head.

The disturbing past of her ancestors. The thought of her being in the same position as her ancestor … but HP was younger and a totally different man than the horrendous 1$^{st}$ Marquess … she also recalled the horrified look on the landlady's face as she looked at the portrait hanging in the pub. Would that attract unwanted publicity? She needed Geoff Bailey to confirm that she was not in any way related to HP. Being a cousin of Charles and Lisa would be fantastic though.

She heard a bell chiming in the distance, looked at her watch and realised she had been gone for an hour. There was a text message and a missed call from Lisa wondering where she was. She texted back, stood and braced herself for a damp walk back to the house.

Life was certainly going to be interesting this year!

'I am here in your street, but which house are you?' he was outside her front door … teasing her … and she knew it.

She raced down the stairs two at a time, opened the

front door and jumped into his arms, nearly knocking him backwards. He had a small duffle bag on his back, an attaché briefcase in one hand and a bunch of roses in the other.

'Wow! ... now that was a greeting!' as he held her tightly in his arms, her legs dangling in mid-air.

'You know you are very beautiful, my Frenchie, and I can't tell you how terribly in love with you I am.' He had put on his very best posh, upper class British accent.

She planted her wet lips on his and gave him a French snog. She was so happy right at that moment.

'Where are we going tonight and are the girls coming too?'

'I booked a table at the 3 Keys Inn and both Clare and Lisa said they would meet us there at 7pm.'

'It's now 5, so what are we going to do for the next two hours,' he said with a grin that lit up his face.

Over dinner they discussed the funeral tomorrow, which everyone was going to; then the launch and masked ball at the Hall at the weekend.

'It's not too soon after your father's funeral, is it HP? I mean, to be respectful of the Marquess?' Lisa asked.

'No, not at all. That's the way Papa would have wanted it. Besides, it's about time we opened our doors for business and got some revenue coming in.'

'Marie, are you going to stay up in Lincolnshire after the launch?' asked Clare, although she had already been told by Arthur that she would be joining the management team of the hotel.

She blushed and looked at HP. He answered for her.

'I suppose it won't be surprising to you both to know that I have kind of asked this lovely lady to be my partner, and to join the management team at Flintwell Hall.'

'You mean you are going to get engaged?' asked Lisa, her eyes wide open.

'Well, yes. If she accepts my proposal, which she hasn't yet.'

'What's wrong with you girl? You need your head examined. Gotta say yes and put the poor sod out of his misery!' said Clare, and they all laughed.

Marie blushed and said nothing but had a smile on her face as she took a sip of her wine and squeezed HP's hand under the table.

The next day they were all ready for the train journey up to Lincoln and on to the church in the grounds of the Hall for the funeral at 3pm.

♦♦♦

The church, or should we say chapel, was small and the turnout for his Lordship was huge. Thomas Tilley and

James Howell had installed a loudspeaker system and a huge 60" house screen outside for those who couldn't sit in the chapel. The pews inside were reserved for the array of titled and wealthy friends, and of course the family. The guest list was like a who's who of the aristocracy, the Hall would host them all in the Orangery and main dining room, a sort of preview to the grand opening as a boutique hotel.

As they arrived at the hall, HP took Marie to his study and closed the door.

'I want you at my side in the chapel, my love. I want everyone to see that we are a couple. It may not be etiquette, but I have discussed this with Arthur and Rosa and they agree that Clare, Lisa and Charles should also be in the front pews as the family. It will cause an outcry from the older ones but ... sod them,' he was quite emotional, the first time she had seen this side of him.

'I am more than happy with that, HP,' she came up to him and squeezed his hand. 'Come, let's go to the chapel and wait there for the hearse to arrive.'

As they left the Hall to walk down the path to the chapel, they saw Clare and Arthur holding hands outside the door talking to a number of people with Rosa and Charles talking to Lisa and Henry Wentworth. All the Hall staff were there, plus the tenant farmers in their best suits. In fact, there was quite a crowd gathered outside, most of whom HP vaguely recognised ... but he was head down heading for the front pews and didn't want to talk to anyone just yet.

Rosa and Charles were already in the second row, with the Earl of Ashwood sat next to his son. HP stood in front of the Earl, bowed his head and shook his hand without saying a word, turned and lead Marie into the Marquess' seat in the chapel, his new rightful place. Marie held his hand tightly as they could feel a thousand eyes on the backs of their necks.

The organist started to play, Arthur and Clare came in with Lisa and Henry Wentworth and they all squeezed into the front pews, next to Marie, Clare taking her other hand. They sat in silence … waiting.

The Very Reverend Cannon Ainsley walked down the aisle and bowed to HP as a signal that the cortege had arrived. He stood at the altar.

The music changed to the funeral march, which was very droll and sad.

There was a loud squeak as the double doors of the chapel opened and the six pall bearers walked very slowly and solemnly down the aisle; His Lordship in an oak coffin draped with the House of Flintwell flag and a plain coronet of flowers. It was what his Lordship had requested in his lucid days.

HP stood to address everyone. He spoke fondly of his father and mother and of the work his father had done during his lifetime. His speech was short and to the point and finished by an open invitation to everyone to come to the Hall for refreshments.

The burial in the churchyard was attended by the family only as the Hall staff escorted everyone else to the Orangery entrance. Marie stood by his side. He held her hand tightly and although quiet, she felt his grief and emotion.

Arthur and Clare, Rosa and Charles stood next to them in silence looking into the grave, with Lisa and Henry opposite.

A very tall, distinguished looking elderly gentleman, leaning on a walking stick, stood on the opposite side of the grave to the family looking at them all through his glasses, his bushy eyebrows raised.

'Henry Percival,' he broke the silence around the grave with his deep baratone voice, 'you are now the 10$^{th}$ Marquess of Flintwell. I see you have done well with the Hall and your father asked me to help you wherever I can. Is this your fiancée?' He had an authoritative voice that commanded respect.

'This is our uncle Thaddeus Bankes, The Earl of Fallowdale, our late father's brother.' Arthur introduced them.

'Uncle Thaddeus, may I present Marie deVille … umm … my …'

'Fiancée, my Lord. HP meant to say that we are engaged to be married, although Lord Flintwell was sadly too ill to know,' Marie interjected seeing HP stutter.

'Marie deVille? That name rings a bell.' He raised his bushy eyebrows in sudden recognition. 'Ah, yes, there was a Marie deVille back when our titles were first given to us, if my memory serves me, she was the fourth wife of the first Marquess.'

'Yes, that's right my Lord. She was related to me but we are not sure how. It's thought through the Dashwood line we think,' Marie answered.

HP stood silent, just looking at Marie.

'We shall get to know you better over a nice glass of something pleasant. Shall we all go to the Hall and leave my brother in peace.' He took his walking stick and marched off with Arthur, Rosa and Lisa following.

HP held Marie's hand and stood still waiting for them to be alone.

'Did I hear right, my love? Are we now engaged to be married?'

'Yes, Henry Percival Bankes. Yes, I will marry you,' she said in a firm but happy voice. 'I know it's a very strange place to accept your proposal of marriage, by your father's grave. I know he didn't take to me, but I'd like to think if he had have been of sound mind, he would have had a different opinion of me.'

They embraced and kissed.

'Tut, tut. Disgraceful behaviour, and your father only just in the ground, God bless him.' It was a sharp voice with a slight Irish accent.

They turned and stood looking at a woman in her late sixties with a scowl on her wrinkled face. She was dressed all in black with a black hat and a walking stick.

'Aunt Grace. We did not see you there. Marie, may I introduce you to my father's sister, Lady Grace Barton.'

She did not extend her black gloved hand and seemed to be very stiff.

'Aunt Grace, I proposed to Marie a few days ago and Uncle Thaddeus asked if she was my fiancée. She had not given me an answer until just now. Father I think would have approved.'

Grace Barton shrugged her shoulders. 'Welcome to the family ... Marie ...?'

'deVille your Ladyship. Marie deVille.'

There was a sharp intake of breath, as the name hit his aunt between the eyes. Before she could respond HP took her hand and said, 'Aunt Grace. Yes, Marie's ancestors go back to the 1640's when the first Marquess married her namesake as his fourth wife, and you will see a portrait in the Long Gallery that resembles Marie. But we have researched her line and she falls from the Dashwoods, so not a distant relative of ours.'

'That may well be, Henry Percival, but it remains that she will become Marie deVille Bankes, the Marchioness of Flintwell when you marry. A lot of people will have something to say about that.'

'Let them. They are all small minded and sunk into the past. I love her and we are to be wed. That's all there is to it.'

He turned from his aunt and took Marie's hand and led her back to the Hall.

Back at the Hall, everyone was tucking into the array of sandwiches, canapes and mini pies that Mrs Pottage had prepared. James Howell and the ground staff served drinks and tea.

HP excused himself from Marie and took Rosa and Arthur into his study, closing the door. They came out twenty minutes later, and Rosa came straight up to Marie and hugged her, as did Arthur.

'HP has just told us. What fab news honey and welcome to madness!' Rosa was brimming.

'HP wants to announce your engagement today, I suggest you go and see him. He is in the study with Uncle Thaddeus and Aunt Grace. But put your steel pants on!' Arthur warned.

Marie walked into the study.

'You wanted to see me HP?'

'Yes. With your permission, I would like to announce

our engagement to our friends and family today. Uncle Thaddeus and Aunt Grace now understand and approve, and they are the closest I have to parents now.' He took both her hands and looked into her eyes with a deep loving affection, 'Do you agree?'

She was surprised and worried at the speed of this. She stood silently thinking, both Aunt Grace and Uncle Thaddeus were looking at her expecting an answer.

'HP, it all feels so rushed. I have not even told my parents. You've not even met them yet. What if it gets in the papers and my parents read about this tomorrow in the Mail?'

She was silent.

'I only said yes just now as it was such a significant place, especially after your Uncle the Earl asked if we were engaged. It felt the right time to say yes. But now to tell all and sundry ... do we have to today?'

'I like this girl Henry Percival. Knows her mind. You will do well in this family. You have my fullest support my dear,' Aunt Grace said to Marie taking her hand from HP's grasp.

'I also think Marie has a point, young man. Don't you think you should ask her father for her hand in marriage first, old boy ... eh, eh?' Uncle Thaddeus said.

HP looked sad and dejected.

Marie took him in her arms, although she was so short

it was more like around his waist. After a while, he said.

'Uncle, you are right. I have not followed protocol. I will ask your father for your hand in marriage next weekend; can you invite them to the opening or the night before?'

'That's a deal. They would love to come,' she said happily.

'But how do you know … you haven't asked them yet?'

Then the penny dropped.

He laughed aloud, 'you little minx, you have already spoken to them, haven't you?'

She smiled and walked out of the study holding onto Aunt Grace's arm, chatting to her in French.

As they passed the portrait, they all stopped.

Uncle Thaddeus and Aunt Grace looked up, then at Marie and back again.

'Strewth … it is the spitting image of you my dear. How very strange that must be for you to see yourself hanging on the wall looking down,' he said.

They joined the other guests and started to mingle.

Rosa pulled Marie to one side with Lisa and Clare.

'Shall we have a giant wedding day and all get married together … sort of a quadruple wedding?' she giggled and passed around glasses of champagne.

'A toast. To us all. Without meeting you Marie, Arthur would not have met Clare, nor would I have realised that Charles was free from that bitch Leticia and you Lisa would not have met Henry Wentworth.'

'Aren't we all very lucky girls,' Lisa said.

'Cheers. Here's to the Flintwell Girl's Club,'

'Mmmm … that sounds good,' said Marie, 'the Flintwell Girl's Club,' repeating the name again to see how it sounded.

That night Marie's dreams took on a very different form … more like a story …

# 24

# 1653

A year later, life in the Lincolnshire Wolds had been peaceful. The country was still in great turmoil with no royal crown on the throne and run by Parliament in the hands of Oliver Cromwell and his elected Barons. But London was so far away, none of this affected the families in Lincolnshire.

The Sheriff of Lincoln had been summoned to London to account for his actions, and was never heard from again.

Lisa Dashwood returned to France in the summer and married Artemis deVille in a quiet ceremony, attended by Marie, Charles and young Henri. She now lived in the chateau with this old French aristocratic family, and was of course, Marie's sister-in-law. The journey to the wedding was still as arduous as before but with Charles at her side and baby Henri in his travel crib, she felt safe. They stayed for a month at the chateau before returning to Rodewelle House.

Marie hoped that she would marry Charles soon. She believed she should let a year go by after the death of the

Marquess, before she remarried. So, she lived in a manor house in the grounds of Rodewelle House, which was a magnificent building, too large for one person to live in it. To keep respectability in these times, both she and Charles agreed it would be better for her to live apart as living together unwed was disgraceful. She knew it would not be for very long and besides Charles was a very regular visitor to the manor house, which had a small and very loyal staff … Janice Bedlow and her family.

♦♦♦

For several weeks now every morning, she felt violently sick. Hot sweats and shivers kept her confined to her bedchamber until the physician arrived. He conducted some tests and asked her quite a lot of questions.

'What is wrong with me, pray tell me?'

'My Lady, I believe that you are with child again, it looks as if you have been carrying the child for quite a while. I would say that you were a good seven months.'

She looked silently at him, the expression on her face and her intense stare was so forecefull, he stood back.

'How could I be pregnant and not know it?' she asked sternly.

The doctor paused a short while, disturbed by her manner.

'It has been known that some women have carried a child to full term without the knowledge of being pregnant. It is rare I must say, and we don't fully know why or how. Have you been experiencing a gradual weight increase, ma'am.?'

'Don't be impertinent. Those are questions you should not be asking a lady!'

She was quiet for a while standing perfectly still with her hands on her small belly.

'I feel no child within me, so how can this be so?'

'My Lady, all I can say is that it has happened before. The baby sits differently in the womb and seems to be a smaller child than normal.'

She was silent again, just looking at the doctor.

Her deep penetrating stare made him very nervous.

In a low menacing voice, she hissed, 'this news must be kept discreet. In fact, so discreet you will tell no one. Is this understood, Doctor Melder?' her French accent accentuating the chilling message.

He nodded, bowed and left the room quickly. Outside the door he leaned against the wall of the main hall and breathed out, shuddering. He had met her several times before under the Marquess' roof and she was always a sweet, pleasant little woman with so much grace at such a young age, but this time he was intimidated by her whole composure and the venom in her voice.

What was he to do about this? His oath to his profession did not allow him to talk about his patients, but she was a dangerous woman. He would leave notes of their conversation in case anything happened to him.

♦♦♦

She had to think ...

Damn ... this was not what she needed right now ...

Another child by Charles out of wedlock.

She would now be seen as a harlot.

She could not trust that physician. He needed to be silenced somehow.

The bigger question was how she could get Charles to marry her now? Her garments were always larger than her frame, so she could carry it off for a while. Then she could become a recluse in Rodewelle House until the child was born and everyone would think they had it within wedlock.

This had to be handled with great care. Could she dupe Charles into marriage before she delivered this baby, then how would she account for being pregnant and not telling him?

Yes, that would work. Both Henri and this child would be theirs for all the world to see. They could live happily ever after. Lord and Lady Dashwood ... had a nice ring to it.

She began working on her big plan to make this happen.

First, she had to silence Dr. Melder.

She had her horse saddled and rode as fast as she could to the village outside Flintwell Hall where Dr Melder lived on his own. There was no one around at the far end of the small sleepy hollow, as all the villagers were out working on the farms or at the Hall.

She knocked on his door, and after a short delay the door was yanked open. He stood there with a surprised look on his face.

'My Lady ... is there something wrong?' he asked.

'I need to see you privately, Doctor ... may I come in?'

He opened the door wide for her to glide in. He looked outside for her carriage, but saw her horse tied to a ring on the wall of his house.

'Was this wise riding all the way from Rodewelle to see me in your condition, ma'am.' He showed her into his surgery situated in the front room of his house.

'It is about my condition that I have come to see you Dr Melder. You believe that I am around seven months pregnant by your estimation?'

'Yes, that would be correct. What is the problem?'

'I am uncertain of your discretion Doctor. I am to marry Charles Dashwood and would like to know how it is possible to carry a child for seven months without knowing it?'

He was silent for a while, looking at Marie, then responded in a deep grave voice.

'You mean, Lord Dashwood is unaware of your pregnancy and you wish him to believe that the child was consummated within your marriage.'

'Exactement, Docteur!' she exclaimed, her French exaggerating her nervousness.

He stood by his desk observing this diminutive but powerful woman. He knew of her growing reputation for one so young and the accusations made by his good friend the Sheriff, now incarcerated in London. He had a dilemma. His Hippocratic Oath forbade him to discuss patient details with anyone, but he had recorded his visit to Rodewelle House and his examination of Marie deVille Bankes in his private notes.

'Well Doctor Melder, what is your opinion?'

'It could be prossible to carry an infant without knowledge, as I said to you before, it's been known, but it would most likely be a small child and its health questionable. I certainly would counsel you to discuss your current state with Lord Dashwood, before your nuptials, as this would be seen as a miracle, and, if asked, I could not lie to his Lordship.'

She stood very still, thinking of what to do next. She had to silence this man. Under her bodice, she carried her stiletto short blade knife.

One of her father's guards had taught her how to end a man's life by sliding the very thin blade between his ribs straight into the heart, or through the neck into the main carotid artery.

Doctor Melder was an elderly man and it would be a simple task, but he had to be seated at his desk, so that when found it would appear as if he were asleep, and she would be back at her house in the grounds of Rodewelle, by this time.

# 25

# The Launch & Masked Ball JULY 2017

She woke in a complete daze, not quite understanding what had happened. She was exhausted with the disturbed sleep. She had a lot on her mind.

Everyone at Flintwell Hall was working overtime to finish the preparations for the big launch on Friday, followed by the Masked Ball on Saturday. Sunday was to be when the first official paying guests arrived.

Marie and the marketing team had done extremely well in advertising the launch of the Hall as a boutique hotel, and had been able to get time on the breakfast shows on all TV channels with the help of Charles Dashwood and Henry Wentworth. A world-famous magazine wanted exclusive rights to attend the masked ball in return for a huge spread in the next month's issue, published in every country in the world. They had approaches from every corner of the industry, from the web marketing hotel groups to the established media. The fact that a standard double room was priced at £500 per night amd up to £2000 for a suite per night, put them in a unique position of appealing to the super rich.

The most amazing fact was that they had advance bookings for up to a year ahead, and that was just on hearsay!

HP and the family board members were astounded by the reaction they had to the marketing plan that Marie had pulled together with her team.

After the funeral, the family busied themselves with all the finer details for the launch to cover their emotions at the loss of their father.

Marie was at HP's side during the funeral and after the funeral never return to London. They planned to marry quietly in the chapel six months after the launch of the hotel.


The day of the actual launch started out with a clear blue sky and bright sunshine. It was perfect. There were around 60 people invited from around the world and only the most exclusive travel operators would attend. It was the most sought after invitation of the year. People were coming out of the woodwork to receive the embossed cream linen invitation card. Those travel and hotel writers who were not invited started to put out negative reviews, having not seen the hotel. There were huge debates going on in the industry about the exclusivity of this boutique hotel. The interviews on the major TV channels were made on Marie, HP, Rosa and Arthur, and they were successful in answering some very difficult questions about the affordability of the hotel and why they were banning the masses.

'What we have is a unique experience that few other hotels can offer. If you can't afford it then it's not for you,' said HP in an interview with an American TV host.

Most of the guests travelling from abroad were being offered accommodation at the Hall for the Friday night and would attend the masked ball.

They arrived for 12 noon and after a light lunch of champagne and canapes were given an escorted tour of the Hall and its facilities. There were 10 in a group accompanied by a family member or one of the senior staff. This was followed by tea over a presentation, given by HP and Marie.

Everyone, including the family, Randolph and James could see the magic relationship between HP and Marie. They glowed in each other's presence and made it seem as if she were already a family member.

That evening they dined on estate-caught game and home-grown vegetables, cooked by the new celebrity chef.

It was a total success. That evening, all the social media was brimming with accolade and positive statements.

Saturday was the masked ball.

They were still in bed, although it was 7am.

'Marie, my love. I have invited Geoff Bailey to the ball tonight, He wants to see us on Sunday ... privately. Apparently, he has all the answers to your questions. So, brace yourself!!'

Perching on her arm, lying sideways, she looked at HP.

'What does that mean?'

'He has found out a lot about your ancestor.'

'And now you expect me to go through the whole day and night, waiting until Sunday to find out?!'

'Ha, ha, ha,' he laughed, 'yes ... and no cheating either. He is under strict instructions to say nothing until Sunday.'

♦♦♦

People started to arrive at 6.30pm. The hotel guests drifted down from their rooms as others arrived by private car. Several helicopters landed on the front lawn to deposit their wealthy patrons.

All the hotel staff were in 17th-century servants' costumes, and Rosa had recruited additional waitresses and waiters to circulate with drinks. Champagne flutes, soft drinks and wine were on offer from the meandering staff, whilst other drinks were available at the main bar as well as the three mobile bars set up outside and in the Orangery.

Everyone arriving was given a platinum disc with a number on it. This would be their entry to a draw to win the star prize of a week at the Hall & SPA.

The theme for the masked ball was $17^{th}$-century gentry and all the guests went well beyond what would traditionally be expected … just a mask to hide your face. The gowns and clothes that they all wore were magnificent.

Food stations were set up around the Hall inside and out with freshly cooked canapes and other unusual finger food available to their grazing guests.

A seventeen strong string orchestra would play in the Long Gallery for dancing; $17^{th}$-century baroque music, that would eventually be replaced by a rock band in the garden at 11pm. Fireworks would finish the evening off at 1am with carriages called at 2am, although the Hall would be open to anyone wanting to party long into the early morning.


Mingling amongst their guests, the Bankes family and Marie sought first impressions and answered all their questions. The aim was to see everyone before they got hammered.

Feedback was excellent and the very high standard of the party certainly impressed the right people.

The Hotel was going to be a success, and once the band started playing, HP took Marie's hand and they quietly vanished into the far end of the formal gardens.

Alone, he took her into his arms and gently kissed her wanting lips.

'I love you Marie deVille, and whatever happens tomorrow will not change the way I feel about you. We are going to live long and happy … I promise you.'

♦♦♦

They sneaked off at 2am, up to their private quarters. They were so shattered they both fell into a deep sleep …

… when it all started again … for Marie.

# 26
# 1653

She was pushing her horse hard. Galloping as fast as her horse could go, across the unploughed fields behind Flintwell Hall, through the woods that led to the bridleway, which was the most direct route over the Lincolnshire Wolds to Rodewelle. Her dark hair was encased in the hood of her riding cloak, which fluttered in the wind as she rode at speed. Her skirts were raised to allow her to sit facing forward, hooking her right leg around the pommel of the saddle with a horn added to the near side of the saddle to secure her right knee. Her left foot was placed in a "slipper stirrup", a leather-covered stirrup iron. This saddle allowed her both to stay on and to control her horse, at least at slower speeds.

As she had mounted her horse at the doctor's house she felt a sharp pain in her abdomen, it was similar to those pains she had before Henri was born … contractions.

*'Damné et merde,'* she said to herself, *'it's the last thing I need right now. Please … hold tight until I get back to Rodewelle.'* Thinking that the contractions were the start of the birth.

She had to be back before sundown, as she was expecting Charles tonight. Her servants would not divulge the fact that she had been gone most of the day.

In her bodice she carried the stiletto knife she had wiped quickly on his shirt before hiding it in her corset without its protective sheath, which she could not find in her rush to leave the doctor's house.

It was gradually growing darker; the sun setting in the west over the far end of the Wolds. She knew the upper Wolds bridleway quite well, and although it had a few fields with grazing sheep and cows, it was mainly open moorland. She spurred her horse onwards, holding onto her reins and the back of his mane to keep centred riding side-saddle. Her contractions were becoming more frequent now, making it difficult to ride her horse. Still she had to get home.

Rodewelle village sat in a small valley, surrounded by gradual hills ... the only way in was down into the bowl of the valley ... some parts were steep. She was in a hurry to reach her house at the far end of the Rodewelle estate to the north. She had to navigate a steep ravine carved out by a stream. The ground was loose and rocky, and her horse started to slip and slide as she drove it recklessly on. She nearly fell off twice as her horse lost its footing, saved by her tight grip on his mane.

Her contractions started again, the pain was excruciating, the baby wanted to come out ... she took a deep breath, exhaling hard to try and quell them.

The ground levelled off. She just had the rolling parkland to cross before arriving at her small country manor house. So, just a short while ... she was nearly home.

Deer and stags looked up from their grazing to see the brown thoroughbred galloping by, his head stretched forward pulling on his bridle as his stride widened; his rider was also head down as if to streamline herself with the horse.

That afternoon, the estate woodmen had cut down several trees to open the parkland to more light, but had not had the chance to clear the smaller trunks out of the long grass. There were also clumps of loose bales of hay around for feeding the deer and sheep.

With the end of her ride in sight, and in time to beat the sunset, Marie dug her left foot into his sides to spur him on faster across this flat parkland.

The wind in her face had dislodged her hair and it was loose outside the hood getting into her eyes.

She didn't see it.

Her horse jumped over the first set of felled tree

trunks.

She was not expecting this, and it dislodged her seat. She regained her grip on his mane and gripped the saddle side horn with her bent knee.

Then her horse caught its leading front hoof on one of the next set of logs and lost its balance, its front legs caved in.

This time, Marie was catapulted into the air as if ejected from a giant sling.

It felt like slow motion as her foot left the stirrup, and riding side saddle gave her nothing else to hold onto. She sailed through the air, her mind racing. She thought about everything she had to do in those split seconds … and the baby within her.

She somersaulted through the air ...

She hit the ground hard …

… and sat there in a slight daze …. with a sharp pain in her right side just underneath her bodice.

She was conscience of a huge contraction and a warm wet feeling between her legs. She instinctively knew the baby was imminent and she would have to deliver it here … alone, sat on the grass ...

She remembered what the wet nurse had told her in France about the best position to deliver Henri, so, she got on her hands and knees. At the next contraction, she pushed as hard as she could, her face bright red from the strain …

she felt some movement. She waited again. The next wave came over her and again she pushed with all her might, screaming out to the startled deer, stag and sheep.

More movement as she felt the baby inside her progress towards its birth.

Conscious of the pain in her right side, and that she was feeling very weak and tired, she knew she had to deliver this baby. The light was fading, and she could see startled eyes all around looking at her.


'Agghhh, mon dieu …merde … s'il te plait, sors mon petit bébé.' She screamed aloud at her four-legged audience.

Another fierce contraction came, and she braced herself … panting hard, then pushing with all her remaining strength as her hands slipped on the dewy grass.

She felt a sudden relief and looked down to see a little pink body lying on the grass between her legs. She rolled onto her side and saw it was a little girl. She took off her shawl and swaddled it into the soft wool and covered it in her coat.

As she lay down on the grass she felt her right side again, and there was sticky blood seeping over her clothes. She felt weak and tired, conscious of her horse nearby making loud blowing sounds out of its nostrils … she couldn't see where it lay.

How was she to get home now? She pulled the small infant closer into her warm body, tucking her legs up in the foetal position … and felt herself losing consciousness …

She slipped into another world …in her eyes she saw a bright light … she saw Henri and a little girl stood next to the love of her life … Lord Charles Dashwood …

She never felt the stiletto knife puncture her heart through her corset …

… the slow loss of blood ended her short life.

♦♦♦

At dusk, several hours later, two of Charles Dashwood's gamekeepers first heard the frantic "neighing" sound of a distressed horse, then saw the horse rolling on the ground, clearly in agony. The horse had broken its front legs. The side saddle was covered in blood. They had no option but to put a bullet through its head. They looked around to find the rider. They recognised the horse as her Ladyship Marie deVille's regular mount.

Laying on her side on the grass several yards away from the struggling horse, they found her limp body holding a bundle of something close to her in her arms, blood seeping from under her corset.

They also noticed a lot of blood from under her skirts.

They were just about to check if there was any life in the woman when the bundle she was holding moved and they heard a tiny little cry of a baby.

Marie had died of her wounds and given birth to a baby girl ... the umbilical chord was still attached.

One of the lads leapt onto his horse and rode at speed back to the house to find his Lordship.

# 27

# SUNDAY

# JULY 2017

She heard his voice … it was distant or whispered … she also hear the muted cry of a baby …

She was being shaken gently … but it wasn't Charles' voice … he was holding her in his arms sat on the grass brushing her hair away from her face and kissing her gently. She felt his warm tears against her cheek … and his sobbing broken heart beating inside his chest.

'Marie … wake up. Marie, my love … please wake up. You are having another of your dreadful dreams.'
His voice was different, more cut and crisp, like Henry Bankes.
She opened her eyes and tried to focus.
She was in a bed, not in a field.
She looked around the room … then up into HP's worried face.

She knew she was not dead ... nor did she fall from her horse ... in fact she was very much alive and in HP's arms.

She was soaked in sweat again ... her hair a mess, last night's mascara painting streaks down her cheeks. What on earth did she look like?

HP was kneeling on the pillows against the bedhead, holding her in his arms and rocking her gently.

'There now ... it's over ... you are awake and safe my love.'

'She's dead,' Marie blurted out suddenly.

'Sorry, who's dead?'

'Marie deVille Bankes. She was thrown off her horse and bled to death from a knife wound. She was pregnant as well.'

To HP this did not make any sense and the look of surprise on his face said as much.

'She was a murderess. She killed Doctor Melder in his home because he knew she was pregnant with Charles Dashwood's child.'

Now HP was confused. Who was Doctor Melder?

Marie sat on the bed, her arms wrapped around her knees rocking backwards and forwards.

'She was a horrible woman. She wanted to conceal her pregnancy to marry Charles Dashwood. Then she planned to reveal that she was with child soon after the wedding, lying about how far gone she was.'

HP looked at her bewildered.

'So that's the end of Marie deVille?' He was thinking how to put this next ... 'Ugh ... will your dreams end now?'

'I never thought about that,' she said smiling for the first time.

'We are meeting Geoff today. Let's see what he has to say first, then offer your dream last night to him. Let's see if we can bottom this, so that we can get on with our lives. I want us to be so happy Marie, without your ancestor haunting us every night.' HP was exasperated, she could see.

♦♦♦

They met in the Orangery. HP sat next to Marie holding her hand as Geoff paced up and down in front of them.

He was excited and animated ... his hands moving as if conducting an orchestra.

'You have a fascinating past Marie. This has been a real challenge to work back through your blood lines to find out who your ancestors were.'

He paused, stopped pacing and stood in front of her, his hands together as if in prayer in front of his face.

'I can categorically say that you are NOT related to HP or his side of the family.'

You could see the tension in Marie's face ease and a smile crossed her face. HP squeezed her hand.

'As far as my investigations go, you are related through the male blood line to Henri deVille, the son of Artemis deVille and Lisa Dashwood, who married his niece, Marie-Ann Elizabeth Dashwood. She was the daughter of Charles Dashwood. Marie deVille was in fact your … let me get this right … great, great, great aunt. She was Artemis's elder sister.'

He let this sink in first, although he suspected she knew this. HP looked relieved.

'So why has Marie been having these awful dreams?' he asked Geoff.

'That I don't know. Psychiatrics – you need to see a medical professional for that … or a psychic.'

'What did you find out about Marie deVille Bankes?' Marie asked.

'She came from an old aristocratic French family. The deVilles go back to the 14th century. Her father Louis Bernard was the 4th Duc de Touraine and had a vast estate in the Loire Valley. Wine was his main business but he also was close to the Royal Family, especially the Dauphin King and his mother. Due to the political unrest in France, he wanted to protect his daughter. So, he arranged a marriage to Henry Fortescue Bankes, who had been made 1st Marquess of Flintwell by King Charles 1st five years before his arrest and execution. Henry was in his late 60s and had three wives who all died at an early age, leaving only a son. Marie was only 25 and already very accomplished in most things. She spoke good English, she was an accomplished horsewoman, swordswoman, and very literate. Rare in those days.'

'I gather she was not a happy woman though?' Marie prompted.

'Funny you should say that. When researching Flintwell Hall for the launch, I discovered that it was Marie who had this magnificent Orangery built, by a Dutchman when they were a novelty. She had it designed in such a way that the marble seating, discreetly positioned around the room, was in fact love seats. She had a lot of affairs from what I can establish, but one in particular was Lord Charles Dashwood of Rodewell, now Rothwell. She had a son by him. Henri deVille Dashwood, who was brought up and ostensibly adopted by the Dashwoods after her death.'

'How did she die?'

'That is a mystery. She is buried in Rothwell church and died at 28 in 1653, but how she died is unrecorded.'

'She fell off her horse and bled to death from a knife wound. She was carrying Charles Dashwood's second child when she murdered Doctor Melder.' Marie's statement made Geoff stand still and stare at her.

'How do you know this?' he asked.

'Marie has been having very vivid dreams about that time …1648 to 1653. All about her family and this house.' HP said.

'Yes. Last night I lived through her death.'

'It's strange that researching the archives in Lincoln, I discovered that there were several deaths during her short life at Flintwell. There was a gamekeeper, and stable boy, the Marquess himself and a Doctor Melder.'

'Charles Dashwood is recorded to have had a daughter in 1653 who was named Marie-Ann Elizabeth. So, she could have been the baby born when Marie deVille fell off her horse. That would make Marie Celestine deVille your great, great, great grandmother. In other words, you are related through the Dashwoods for certain,' Geoff said.

'Thomas Tilley was the gamekeeper and he fell into a vat of beer, pushed in by Charles Dashwood and Henry Wentworth on the night of the masked ball, Able Jones drowned in the lake down there … she pushed him in and he could not swim. She killed the Marquess by using poison and Doctor Melder was stabbed through the heart.' Marie said this without any emotion as if she were reading from a book.

Geoff was astounded, his mouth opened and lost for

speech.

'Um ... aagh ... how did you know all that? It's true they all died in those ways, but the killer was never found. The Sheriff at the time tried to accuse Marie deVille but she had powerful friends who got rid of him. He was hung at the London gallows for disloyalty to Cromwell.'

HP sat quietly looking from Marie to Geoff.

'Marie ... you seem to know an awful lot about this!'

'Yes, I do. I hope now that my dreams will disappear.'

'Why don't we write these down and perhaps eventually turn this story into a book. I would love to work on it with you ... call it therapy?'

♦♦♦

Six months later, the local community was buzzing with the news that there would be three weddings at the tiny chapel in the grounds of Flintwell Hall.

Rosabella Bankes married Charles Dashwood

Arthur Bankes married Clare Hobbs

And ...

Marie deVille married Henry Percival Bankes – 10th Marquess of Flintwell and she would become Marchioness Flintwell or Lady Flintwell.

Marie's maid of honour was Lady Lisa Wentworth,

who had married Henry the month before.

Marie and HP went on to have four children and the boutique hotel became a worldwide 'must go' destination hotel with a unique history … but only if you could afford to stay!

A book was published eventually … and sold worldwide, but given as a gift to guests of Flintwell Hall Hotel.

# The End

# Thank You!

Thanks for reading my book.

If you loved this book and have a moment to spare, I would really appreciate a short review on Amazon.com/Kindle or my Facebook page: www.facebook.com/chrisdaleauthor.

Your help in spreading the word is gratefully received.

You can also stay up to date with my other books or new books I am writing by subscribing to my mailing list on: www.chrisdale.info/contact/

or e-mail me at: chris@chrisdale.info.

**All of photos of CD by**
**Chris Lynn Photography**
www.chris-lynn.co.uk

# ABOUT THE AUTHOR

Chris Dale was born in 1954 in Lima, Peru. He came to the UK in 1964 for a private school education, spent five years in Cheltenham, and finished his education in France. He built his life skill experience's through a varied career in aviation, the travel business, and then in brand management in the food and brewery markets through the retail food industry. In 2004, he set up his own Management Consultancy business working in these markets specialising in launching and managing several different brand products. At the same time, as an aviation nut and a private pilot himself, he set up The POM Flying Club at Humberside Airport, which he still owns and runs today.

In July 2014, Chris suffered a major stroke which forced an early semi-retirement from the business world, and a total change of direction. The upside of the stroke has created his joy of writing his books, with many more to come.

He now spends his time writing and managing his books as an indie author; managing his beloved flying school as a hobby, and does some voluntary work locally.

The writing continues …

**Also by Chris Dale**

**My Stroke …. "just get on with it …."**

**The Boy from Peru**

**The Magic Christmas Table**

**The 14:52**

His four romantic thriller novels:

**Crimson Love**

**The 42 Million.**

**The Bentley Regatta.**

**The Chameleon Pilot**

Look out for the sequel:

# The Ghosts of Rodewelle Hall

# By

# Chris Dale

Printed in Poland
by Amazon Fulfillment
Poland Sp. z o.o., Wrocław